**"Stay with me." Ashley didn't even care about all the ways those words could be interpreted.**

Ty's eyes fluttered open. His right hand moved and lightly grasped her wrist. Her gaze shot to his face. He held her gaze. "I trust you."

The words echoed in her head. *I trust you.* Even after this morning, when she'd been so furious with him, when just an hour ago she'd been yelling at him, he trusted her. Trusted her to do what was necessary, even if the task was ghastly.

Which told her he knew her better than she thought he did.

Then his fingers tightened a little. "Last night...still should never... But I'm not sorry."

He said it with more energy than she would have thought he had. And apparently it was the last he had, because the moment the words were out, his eyes rolled up a little and he passed out.

\* \* \*

**Don't miss each thrilling book in
The Coltons of Kansas miniseries!**

\* \* \*

**If you're on Twitter, tell us what you
think of Harlequin Romantic Suspense!
#harlequinromsuspense**

Dear Reader,

Every book I write is special to me in one way or another. But this one I felt a particular affinity for, because of the setting. I was born about three hundred miles from the fictional town of Braxville, Kansas, albeit in Iowa. True, we had moved before I was a year old, but we went back to visit family every year (by car, mind you, an endless trip when you're a kid), and it frequently involved a stop in Kansas. And I remember those trips vividly, the vast distances, the real, true amber waves of grain and the flat of it all. Sometimes I think that's why I'm not truly happy now unless I can see mountains. Probably why I now live where I can see them every day. But I digress.

What I remember most about those trips through the Heartland are the people. When we got a flat tire, a man driving down the road in a tractor stopped and helped my dad change it. When we encountered some major road construction and ended up having to ask for directions to the interstate (yes, there was a time before Google Maps), we didn't just get directions, the gentleman actually drove out of his way to lead us to it. And I remember we once had an overheating problem, and the owner of the gas station we stopped at let me watch TV in his home behind the station while he and my dad fixed it. Because that's who they are, these people of the Heartland.

It was a pleasure to revisit them in this story. Happy reading!

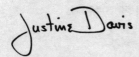

# COLTON STORM WARNING

**Justine Davis**

HARLEQUIN

ROMANTIC
SUSPENSE

Special thanks and acknowledgment are given to Justine Davis for her contribution to The Coltons of Kansas miniseries.

ROMANTIC SUSPENSE™

Recycling programs
for this product may
not exist in your area.

ISBN-13: 978-1-335-62673-8

Colton Storm Warning

This edition published by arrangement with Harlequin Books S.A.

For questions and comments about the quality of this book, please contact us at CustomerService@Harlequin.com.

Harlequin Enterprises ULC
22 Adelaide St. West, 40th Floor
Toronto, Ontario M5H 4E3, Canada
www.Harlequin.com

Printed in U.S.A.

**Justine Davis** lives on Puget Sound in Washington State, watching big ships and the occasional submarine go by and sharing the neighborhood with assorted wildlife, including a pair of bald eagles, deer, a bear or two, and a tailless raccoon. In the few hours when she's not planning, plotting or writing her next book, her favorite things are photography, knitting her way through a huge yarn stash and driving her restored 1967 Corvette roadster—top down, of course.

Connect with Justine on her website, justinedavis.com, at Twitter.com/justine_d_davis or on Facebook at Facebook.com/justinedaredavis.

## Books by Justine Davis

### Harlequin Romantic Suspense

### *The Coltons of Kansas*

*Colton Storm Warning*

### *The Coltons of Roaring Springs*

*Colton's Secret Investigation*

### *Cutter's Code*

*Operation Midnight*
*Operation Reunion*
*Operation Blind Date*
*Operation Unleashed*
*Operation Power Play*
*Operation Homecoming*
*Operation Soldier Next Door*
*Operation Alpha*
*Operation Notorious*
*Operation Hero's Watch*
*Operation Second Chance*

Visit the Author Profile page at Harlequin.com, or justinedavis.com, for more titles.

# Chapter 1

"It's your own fault."

Ty Colton gave his colleague a sour look. Mitch was a good friend, but he was also a sarcastic son of a gun. At least to his colleagues he was. He managed to rein it in with clients. Or maybe he was sarcastic to them because he had to rein it in with clients.

"How did getting stuck babysitting get to be my fault?" Ty asked, letting some of his irritation into his voice.

"If you hadn't gone all heroic and saved that Sawyer kid last year, you'd still be flying under the radar, dude."

"If I was heroic," he pointed out, "I should be getting rewarded, not punished."

"Would that life were that way," a deep yet quiet voice came from behind them. They both turned to see Eric King, the founder of Elite Security, the man who was technically Ty's partner but whom he most times deferred to as his boss, walking toward them with his ever-present tablet in his hand. "But then again," Eric went on, "a true hero doesn't ask for any reward."

Ty studied the older man for a moment, judged he wasn't really angry and said deferentially, "You would know."

He meant it. He admired Eric King more than any man he knew. Including—perhaps especially—his own father. Fitz Colton was many things, but a loving, involved parent was not one of them. From the first day he'd met him, Eric seemed to care more about the path Ty was on than his father ever had. Once he'd decided the family business wasn't for him, that seemed to be the end of his father's interest in his eldest son.

And unlike his father, Eric didn't bark out orders gruffly. He didn't have to. Ty's sister Jordana, a police detective, had once told him his boss reeked of command presence, and he supposed that was a good description. He reminded Ty more of his Uncle Shep—newly returned to their hometown of Braxville—than anyone. Not surprising since Shepherd Colton had spent even longer in the Navy than Eric had in the Marines. Not, Eric pointed out, that anyone ever really left the Marines.

"Buttering me up won't get you out of this, Colton," the man said, although his eyes warmed enough that Ty knew the compliment had registered. "They asked for you specifically, so you're locked in. Mitch, you'll be his backup."

"Damned social media," Ty muttered, knowing that was probably how this family had discovered him, in that photo that had gone viral of him carrying little Samantha Sawyer from the warehouse where she'd been held for ransom. The rescue operation had been kept under the radar, but these days everyone with a phone fancied themselves a journalist, and one of them had caught that moment. When he'd first seen it, he'd simply been glad the terrified little girl's face had been hidden as she sobbed into his shirt. By the fiftieth time he'd seen it, he'd been well and truly annoyed.

Jordana had teased him, pointing out every time the shot turned up somewhere, and telling him to enjoy his fame. His brother Brooks, on the other hand, understood. "I wouldn't want it," he'd said. "It'd be hard to stay a *private* investigator when your face is all over every public domain in the country."

Of course, Brooks had been a lot more understanding about many things lately. Especially since he and Gwen Harrison had gotten engaged.

Ty barely stopped a grimace. He was happy for them. He was happy for Jordana, too, whose growing happiness with businessman Clint Broderick was obvious. Even Bridgette, the girl of the Colton triplets, had settled into a happy reunion with her high school sweetheart.

*So the Colton kids are three for six on the happy-ever-after front. Too bad the oldest can't get it in gear.*

He shook off the fruitless thoughts—he'd about decided that kind of happy wasn't in the cards for him—and focused on the matter at hand. He didn't like the idea of being pulled off the case his family had been sucked into after the grim discovery of two bodies sealed in the walls of an old Colton Construction building. He was getting close, really close, to unraveling that decades-old case.

But Elite Security had first call on his time, and the police—including his sister the detective—had warned him about jurisdiction issues, and not contaminating the case. Not that that had stopped him from doing a little digging of his own. But that was going to have to go on hold, at least for now.

"So what's the deal?" he asked.

"Parents worried about their daughter, who's been threatened. They've got a lot of clout, and this could be a good thing for the company." Eric grinned at him. "Almost as good as your heroics."

Ty grimaced. Dealing with bigwigs was never his favorite thing. "Is it a credible threat, or are we just keeping them happy?"

"Research is working on that."

"Who threatened the kid, and why?"

"Some guy named Sanderson, out of Kansas City. Another reason they came to us."

Ty frowned. "Name sounds familiar, but I can't place it."

"Research is working up a profile now."

"Research is busy," Mitch put in with a lazy smile. "What do they have on the parents?"

For the first time in this discussion—perhaps the first time since he'd known him—Eric looked...not uneasy, Ty didn't think he even could, but wary. And that alone made the hair on the back of Ty's neck stand up. "Research didn't need to find out who they are. I'm guessing we all know."

*Uh-oh.* "Drop the bomb," Ty suggested, already not liking it.

"Her name's Ashley Hart."

Ty frowned as he discarded the first thought that had come to him. Mitch let out a low whistle, indicating he hadn't discarded the seemingly impossible idea. And another look at Eric's face told Ty he shouldn't have been so hasty.

"Not…Andrew Hart? The Westport Harts?" In wealth and prominence, the Connecticut family ranked right up there with the likes of the Rockefellers. Although by Hart standards, the Rockefellers might still be considered new upstarts; the Harts had been American aristocracy as long as, say, the DuPonts.

"The very same," Eric said.

Ty groaned. "Great. So I get to not just babysit, but babysit some spoiled rich kid?"

Mitch snorted. Ty looked at him. "Like you weren't one, *Colton*?" his friend said, but he was grinning.

"Yeah, yeah," he retorted, his own grin a bit wry. "Hardly on that level."

"Speaking of babysitting," Eric said rather pointedly, "if you two are through?"

"Sorry," Ty muttered. "So where do I connect with the little darling? Westport?" *Hartford airport*, he thought. It was about twenty miles farther than La Guardia or JFK in New York, but a lot less hassle. He'd make up the time just getting out of the airport. Then he—

"No," Eric said. "She's in McPherson."

Ty blinked. "Our McPherson? McPherson, Kansas?" The town of some thirteen thousand just east of his hometown of Braxville hardly seemed like a place someone from Westport would likely be visiting, let alone a Hart.

"Yes, our McPherson."

"Why?"

"She was there for some meeting about the Lake Inman wetlands expansion."

Ty drew back. "Wait, I thought you said she was a kid."

"She is." Eric grinned at him. "But I'm old. To me, you're a kid."

Ty scowled at Eric. The man might be pushing sixty, but he looked a decade younger and was fit enough to put both him and Mitch on the floor. Probably at the same time. But before he could say anything, Eric's tablet chimed, and he waited as the man scanned the message. Then Eric tapped the screen a few times as he spoke. "Details on where you're meeting up and the threat report. I'll send it to your phone. Mitch, liaison with Research and send whatever they turn up on to Ty when it's ready."

"You mean I don't get to help wrangle?" Mitch's disappointment was clearly mock.

Eric finished sending the details before looking up at them. "Ty can handle it. McPherson's close enough you can get there in a hurry if need be. I'll be tied up with the loose ends of the Rivera case, but I'll be on our comms."

Ty nodded. The high-end private communication system was one of the things that made Elite work so well. They didn't have to rely on easily hackable cell networks or internet to connect with each other while on a job. Mitch, meanwhile, just looked relieved at escaping. "Anything else?"

"Nothing that's not in the report. Obviously, handle with care."

Ty sighed. He was not looking forward to dealing with some East Coast high-society type. But he said only, "Yes, sir."

He looked at Mitch, who was grinning at him, his relief obvious now. Eric turned to go, then turned back. "Mitch, make sure you look at the file now, too. You'll need to know who he's watching, in case you have to back him up. There's a photo up front."

Ty's brow furrowed as Eric walked away. There had been something a little too pointed in that look he'd given Mitch, who was pulling out his phone to follow the order.

"Damn," Mitch said. And it was heartfelt.

"What?" he asked.

"You have all the luck."

"Luck? Aren't you the guy who was just—"

He stopped dead when Mitch held out his phone. And Ty found himself looking at one of the loveliest women he'd ever seen. The picture had clearly been taken at some formal occasion. She was wearing an off-the-shoulder dress, white trimmed in black, but he barely noticed. Not with those lovely slender shoulders and delicate throat on display. Her face was...refined, his mother would call it. Delicate features. Dark bottomless brown eyes. Her dark brown hair was pulled back into some loose sort of knot, and small gold earrings her only jewelry. Not that she needed any adornment with all that luscious skin showing.

He sucked in some air, only then aware he'd stopped breathing for a moment.

Damn, indeed.

# Chapter 2

Ashley Hart paced her small suite, focusing on the patterned carpet rather intensely so she didn't look up and glare at her innocent phone again. She'd barely stopped herself from blasting her irritation to the skies via a social media post, but she'd vowed long ago to keep her family, especially her parents, out of all her timelines. She didn't want to be listened to because she was a Hart of the Westport Harts, but because she was right.

Because she was telling the truth.

She stopped at the window that looked out toward the small town. She knew it was half the size of Westport, but that was probably the smallest difference between it and the oceanfront community she'd grown up in. Yet, in a way, looking out over the vast flat of the Kansas prairie was sort of like looking out over the vastness of the Atlantic. It was an interesting comparison, in any case.

She turned and paced back, this time waving her hand over the silent phone to light the lock screen and check the time.

Ten minutes. This guy had ten minutes to show up or she was leaving. She was already fuming over this whole thing, anyway. Her parents were overreacting. This was hardly the first time she'd made someone angry with her. When she'd been overseas, in an especially rural area, she'd had an entire community angry with her for helping their long-time enemies set up a medical clinic. And back home, she'd had other communities—for that's how she sometimes thought of them—here in the US calling her names she hadn't even known the meaning of. Sometimes her social media feeds held as much anger and threats as accolades and appreciation, almost always hidden behind the cutesy names and the general anonymity of the internet.

Why this threat was so different, she didn't know. Except that it had been sent to her parents instead of her. She loved them, adored them in fact, but she was twenty-seven now, and while she always listened to them, they did not tell her what to do.

Except when they did.

What they'd told her this morning was to stay in her hotel room until the security they'd arranged arrived. A top-ranked firm, they'd said, as if the Harts would settle for anything less. She wondered, somewhat idly as she paced, what need there was for something called Elite Security here in Kansas, in the middle of—

She caught herself. She hated when she fell into the trap so many in her circle did, dismissing everything between the coasts as flyover country. It was called the heartland for a reason, she reminded herself. And hadn't the size of the group that had shown up to meet with her and discuss their concerns told her they cared as much as she did about what happened here?

And yet, even with the awareness she worked so hard at, she still had almost slipped into that dismissive mind-set. No wonder many people here disliked people like her.

Enough to make threats to her parents? Apparently.

But if she'd been going to let threats stop her, she would have given up her various causes long ago. Because whether she was trying to preserve something or change something, it seemed there was always someone who was against it. Sometimes they came around. Sometimes they did not. The times she liked best were when she and the opposing interest were able to reach a compromise that both found acceptable, if not perfect. Then she felt as if she'd truly accomplished something.

*Unlike now, stuck here in this room.*

That was it. She was done with this. She needed to get moving. She wanted to spend some time researching. One of the people at the meeting had worked at the local library and mentioned there were extensive references there about the very thing she was here for. The library wasn't that far away, according to her map app. She could easily walk it. And she'd like a nice walk outside, some fresh air.

She liked doing that in different places, seeing how different the air smelled. From the salt-tinged air of her home turf to the cool, exotic scent of a rain forest to the air here that seemed impossibly tinged with both dust and damp at the same time, she loved it all. She thought that maybe she would come back here in the spring, when the vast fields were green and growing. She wanted to see where so much of the food the nation ate was actually produced. And perhaps one day, she might write a paper on the subject of how each region of the world, probably each microclimate, had its own distinct scent. It would be interesting to visit places scientists said had the same climate and see if they smelled the same.

She laughed at herself, but also promised her curious mind that someday she would take time for such esoteric projects.

Decided now, she glanced in the mirror over the large dresser. The black jeans and mock turtleneck sweater would do, she decided, and her hair still had a little wave at the ends that brushed her shoulders, from having been in a bun to keep it out of her way while she traveled. She picked up the black hoop earrings from the top of the dresser and slipped them back in place, then grabbed up her jacket and the rather oversized bag she carried while traveling. She liked having her tablet at hand to make notes with as various ideas came to her. And she would need it at the library, anyway.

She would stop at the desk and leave a message for this security person, saying where she'd gone and to meet her at the library. *Or not,* she added to herself with an inward smile.

It was a pleasant ride down, and as the elevator doors opened at the bottom, she stood back to let the older couple she'd been chatting with on the way exit first. As she waited, she glanced around the lobby, her gaze snagging on a man coming in through the glass front doors. *Nice,* she thought. *No, better than nice,* she amended, as she watched him stride across the lobby. Dark hair, short and a little tousled looking, tall—very tall, a couple of inches over six feet, she guessed, and…well, built. Or well-built. Lord, she was grinning at her own silly mental jokes now.

"Don't blame you, honey," the woman who had introduced herself as Ella Roth whispered, looking back over her shoulder. "That's a fine hunk of man."

Ashley felt herself flush slightly. She wasn't in the habit of being so obvious. But that was indeed a fine hunk of man. She wondered where he was visiting from. He didn't have the air of a big city guy, but of someone used to the wide-open spaces. She couldn't quite picture him walking between towering skyscrapers.

They matched, she realized suddenly. Beneath a lightweight jacket, he was also in black jeans and a black-knit shirt, although his was a crew style. Which was nice, because it would be a shame to hide that very muscled male neck. And the way he moved, making her all too aware of what was obviously a powerful body beneath the clothes...

There she was, flushing again. She needed to get outside in cooler air. Her weather app said it was about fifty-six outside, not much warmer than it likely would be at home. That would do it.

Maybe she should wait until he was gone before approaching the desk to leave her message. She didn't want to be caught blushing at the sight of a total stranger. But the idea of dodging said stranger didn't sit well with her. And he was headed toward her.

*Toward the elevators, idiot. Not you.*

But then his gaze locked on her. There was no other word for it. And he did, in fact, head directly toward her. As if he'd recognized her. Knew her.

Belatedly it hit her. Oh, surely not. This couldn't be the guy, could it?

*Of course it could. Look at him. Isn't he the living image of what every woman would want as a...protector? A bodyguard?*

She sighed inwardly. Kansas might not be the first place people thought of for top-notch security firms, but if this guy was any example, they obviously could grow them right.

"Ms. Hart," he said, as he came to a halt before her, holding out a photo ID. He had a voice that sent a ripple through her. Deep, and the tiniest bit rough. "I'm with Elite Security."

*Of course you are.*

She saw Mrs. Roth, walking toward the lobby, look back at her and smile, giving her a thumbs-up gesture. She resisted rolling her eyes.

"You going to check my ID?" he asked, and her gaze snapped back to his face. He looked just as good up close. Better, in fact, with those dark blue eyes and annoyingly thick eyelashes. And that jaw.

"Don't need to," she said with a barely suppressed sigh.

"You always need to," he said, rather sternly.

It didn't seem wise to explain that she didn't have to because all of this was just her luck. Not only having to worry about her parents' fears, and tolerate the only thing that would ease them, but end up with a guy who looked like he'd walked off the cover of a men's fitness magazine. She would have said some Hollywood tabloid, except he looked too tough for that make-believe world.

But then she laughed silently at herself, knowing anyone and everyone would laugh in turn at the idea of Ashley Hart moaning about her luck. She'd won life's lottery when she was born not only into the Hart family but to two people who adored her as much as they adored each other, which was saying something.

"Yes, you're quite right," she said. "I was...thinking of something else."

She looked at the ID card with the logo of an encircled globe in the upper left corner. Were they that big that they covered the world? Then she hit the photo, a typical ID card picture with no expression, just that chiseled face and those eyes, looking...annoyed. At having to stay still long enough to have his picture taken? At having it taken at all? Or was annoyance just his default mode? She imagined he could get away with a lot of it, with those looks.

She looked back at the living man before her, not that she really needed to compare him to the image; there was no mistaking him. Something in the way he was looking at her made her want to look away again. And in fact she did, ashamed of herself even as she did so.

This was going to be a definite pain.

"And," he added, "you're forgetting to ask for your code word."

Her gaze shot back to his face. Now she was thoroughly annoyed. Not at him, but at herself. How often had her parents lectured her never to trust anyone who came to her claiming to be from them who didn't have the code word? It had been part of her life since she'd been old enough to understand, but somehow this man had blown it right out of her mind.

She stiffened her spine. "You're quite right. What is it?" The moment she asked, she knew this would be amusing.

"Fluffy." She'd been right. Even the look on his face as he said it was amusing.

"My childhood pet," she said, unable to resist grinning at him. "I was seven."

"I've got no room to talk. My dog was Ripper."

"How very male of you."

"Says the girl who named her...cat? Dog? Fluffy."

"Actually, she was a turtle."

He blinked. "You named a turtle Fluffy?"

She nodded, still grinning. "Because she wasn't."

She saw his lips start to curve, actually saw him fight it. "At seven, how did you even know it was a she?"

"My dad and I worked it out. He made me look everything up and go through it step by step, length of shell, shape of plastron, length of front claws, that kind of thing."

"Don't they live a very long time?"

"They can, yes. Fluffy's still going strong, although she's teaching at my old elementary school now."

He didn't fight the smile this time, and she felt like she'd been given an award, which sent up a red flag in the back of her mind. But before she really recognized the warning for what it was, the name printed on the card, with the bold signature above it, very belatedly registered. Tyler Colton.

Jolted, she looked back at him.

"Colton?"

"That's what it says," he said flatly, his amusement and his smile vanishing.

Her first thought was the former president, and without much thought—a rarity for her—the question poured out. "Any relation to the—"

"Yes." He said it bluntly, and with obvious irritation. "But I'm not in the family business."

She gave yet another inward sigh. No wonder her parents had decided upon this company. Nothing like having someone connected to a former president looking out for your, as her father put it, strong-willed daughter.

# Chapter 3

Ty was having a little trouble. One of his strengths, one that Eric had helped him hone and believe in, was reading people. He was good at telling when they were diverting, avoiding or downright lying. But at the moment, he couldn't seem to focus on those aspects of the exquisite woman before him.

He estimated she was about five-seven, and slender. Not skinny but lanky, like a spring foal who'd figured out her legs at last. Unlike in the photo, her hair was down, and it gleamed as if catching what light there was in the elevator alcove. And her eyes were the kind of deep rich brown that seemed so mysterious, and yet they held a sharp, observing intelligence only a fool would overlook. Her features were delicate—except for that luscious mouth.

The mouth he was staring at. He slammed back to

reality and cursed at himself silently. *Some security expert you are.*

"—good friend of my father," she was saying.

He'd entirely missed the first part of that. "Your father," he said, trying to cover.

She nodded. "They met when he was considering running and going around the country, assessing support. My father was the one who urged him to do so. They've stayed good friends, even now that he's out of office." She smiled. "He was a good president, I think."

Joe Colton. She was talking about Joe Colton. That was why she'd reacted to the name. He'd thought she'd heard about the lawsuit and all the problems Colton Construction was having these days. Problems he would much prefer to be digging into, despite being warned off by Jordana and her partner, Reese Carpenter. He should have known better. Why would their little—relative to her life, anyway—problems matter to the likes of her?

"He's a pretty distant connection," he said, his voice rather gruff as he tried to cover his discomfiture at having so completely blown this initial contact. "I don't have anything to do with that branch, really." *It's enough dealing with my own.*

"Yet you felt defensive about it?" she asked with one elegant brow arched at him.

Okay, now she had him thoroughly embarrassed. Because he had kind of snapped at her. "No. I mean…I was referring to my family, not him. My father's company is…in kind of a mess at the moment."

Her brow furrowed. "I saw some reports about… Colton Construction, right?"

He grimaced. "Yes. It's kind of the main topic around here lately."

"I'm sorry." She sounded like she meant it.

"No need." He tried to get a grip. "But where were you going? You were supposed to stay in your hotel room until I got there."

"I felt trapped in that room."

"You'd have really felt trapped if that guy who threatened you had been on that elevator."

Her chin came up. "But he wasn't. And Mr. and Mrs. Roth were delightful. Besides, I was only headed to the library."

"Without protection."

"It's not that far. I wanted the walk."

"It's not that close. Two, two and a half miles. And you were going to walk. Alone." She shrugged. He studied her for a moment. "You're not taking this at all seriously, are you." It wasn't really a question, because he knew she wasn't, he could feel it.

"My parents are…protective."

"You'd make quite a target under normal circumstances. Doing what you do just raises your profile. It's understandable they feel protective."

"Too protective."

"From what I gathered, I doubt they believe there is such a thing."

She gave him a look that seemed nothing more than curious. "Is that how your parents are?"

"No."

She let out a short breath that verged on disgusted. "Why? Because you're a big strong man?"

He couldn't help it, the corners of his mouth twitched. "I am. But it's more because we don't hold a huge chunk of the world's wealth, tempting slimeballs who want to get rich the easy way."

"That has nothing to do with this," she said, sounding rather offended. "This is strictly me."

"You can attract your own threats, is that what you're saying?"

She blinked. Looked as if she were winding up for a fierce retort. But then suddenly, unexpectedly, she smiled. Widely. And it was devastating.

"Touché, Mr. Colton. It's been known to happen," she said. "I seem to have a tendency to anger certain kinds of people."

"The kind who would like you to mind your own business?"

"But what I get involved in is my own business. Mine and everyone who gives a damn." A crusader. Dear God, Eric had stuck him with a crusader. "Now, if you don't mind, I'd like to get to the library. I have some research to do."

"Research?"

"Yes." She gave him a sideways look. "I don't rush into these things blind, Mr. Colton, nor jump on any passing bandwagon. My name bears weight, so I make sure I do my homework."

"A responsible do-gooder, huh?"

She drew up sharply. "You say that as if you think those two terms are mutually exclusive."

"Sometimes they are. And I know that from personal experience."

She looked about to say something else, then stopped. "I need to be on my way," she said, and he knew that wasn't what she'd been going to say. He wondered what had made her change her mind.

"My car's out front."

"I told you, I want the walk."

"You'll be safer in the car."

She smiled at him sweetly. Too sweetly. "Isn't that your job, to keep me safe wherever I am?"

The expression, and that syrupy tone that matched it, grated on him. But he kept his voice level. "And your job is not to make that impossible by being stubborn about it."

"Not the most diplomatic approach I've ever seen."

"You want a diplomat, you'd better head back home." *And someone else can take over this job I didn't want in the first place.* "I understand your family hangs out with that bunch."

She looked, finally, perturbed. "I see why you avoid the presidential branch," she said coolly. "They'd likely throw you out."

"Likely," he agreed. "I don't have the Machiavellian instinct needed for that crowd. The question is, is that a point for or against me?"

She studied him for a moment. He saw…something in those dark brown eyes change, as if she'd reached some sort of conclusion. "Well," she said, her tone quite different now, lighter, "since that's something I lack as well, I suppose I'll have to say it's in your favor."

He couldn't help it, her words made him smile. He hadn't expected that. "I have trouble believing you couldn't swim in that world, if you wanted to."

Her eyes widened, and he wondered why. He hadn't meant it as a criticism, except maybe of that world of politics, which he loathed. It was part of the reason he'd walked away from the family business; there was too much of that involved for his taste.

Then, quickly, she recovered. "I could swim with sharks, too, but I'd expect consequences."

And this time he laughed, almost unwillingly. And apparently surprised her, since she nearly gaped at him. But he pointed out, "In one sense, that's what you do, anyway. And right now there's one circling, so to ignore it would be foolhardy."

She looked strangely pleased, then thoughtful. And finally she sighed audibly. "All right. The car it is."

So she could see reason. He felt suddenly better about this whole thing. "Good. I'm out front."

She only nodded and started walking that way. He instinctively scanned the lobby, but there was no sign of anyone suspicious. Of anyone watching her, other than the desk clerk who was simply looking with obvious male appreciation. And he couldn't blame the guy for that. She was as beautiful as that photograph showed, in a big city sort of way.

But for an uber-rich East Coast sort, he found it interesting that her clothing was so simple. Even her jeans weren't some fancy designer-label type, but instead the classic brand that he himself wore.

To determine this, he realized he'd been looking at what was admittedly a nice trim but curved backside, which was not someplace he wanted to go. This was a job, she was a client—or rather her parents who owned half the world were clients—and so unattainable to an average guy like him, it was incalculable.

But, he thought as he followed, that didn't mean he couldn't appreciate.

# Chapter 4

Ashley was glad he was a half step behind her. She was having trouble keeping her expression even as she analyzed two very unsettling facts. No, three. One, he was entirely too attractive for her to maintain her usual buffer with men she was forced by circumstance to be around. Two, her heart had nearly stopped when he'd smiled. And three, when she'd made him laugh, she'd felt a rush of pleasure that had completely startled and disconcerted her.

Maybe it was just because he had a great laugh. It had the same rough edge as his voice did, which somehow made it even more special. And he'd looked surprised, as if it had been a long time since he'd laughed.

*My father's company is...in kind of a mess at the moment. It's kind of the main topic around here lately.*

It seemed there was reason for him not to laugh easily

just now. She made a mental note to do a little research on that, too. Only in the interest of knowing whom she was dealing with, of course. And because she felt a bit foolish in assuming that since he was a Colton, and related, even distantly, to *that* branch of the family, that the presidential connection would be front and center.

His vehicle was a black SUV of the sort her parents—and probably that presidential branch of his family—often used when attending official functions. He stopped to talk with the valet, and Ashley thought she heard the words, "No one went anywhere near it, Ty." She knew she hadn't mistaken the admiring look the young woman gave him. Understandable.

When he gave her the option of front seat or back, she gave him a sideways look, wondering if he expected her to assume she'd be driven around as if he were a glorified chauffeur.

"Back windows are tinted dark enough that you wouldn't be seen."

She raised a brow at him. "Are you saying a threat is imminent and I should hide myself?"

"Not yet, although that may change. And if it does, you'll need to follow orders without question."

She gave him a slightly sour look. "I've never done that very well."

"So your father said."

"Did he?" She'd have a word with Dad when she got back home. The last thing she wanted or needed was him spreading the idea she was hard to deal with, which was how that would be interpreted by many. Her goals depended on cooperation, which was hard enough to get. Starting with a distorted perception of herself made it that much harder.

Without addressing his follow-orders comment, she merely said, "I'll sit in front, then." She smiled at him, again too sweetly. "Until I'm ordered otherwise, that is."

"Up to you," was all he said. He opened the door for her, but since it was his vehicle and he was standing there anyway, she didn't quibble.

"What if I wanted to drive?" she asked once they were inside the car, as much out of curiosity as out of an uncharacteristic need to prod this man.

"Sure. Just show me your defensive and tactical driving certificates and it's all yours. Seat belt," he added.

She frowned as she reached for the belt and fastened it. "Tactical driving? Is that like offensive driving?" She knew what that meant. Her parents' actual chauffeur, Charlie Drake, had explained it to her a decade ago. She'd just passed her first defensive driving test, at the behest of her father, and joked that she was now ready to learn offensive driving, being completely unaware there really was such a thing until Charlie explained it.

"It's more specific."

"Like?"

"Threat assessment. Motorcade tactics. Attack recognition and avoidance. Escape and evasion. High speed in reverse. PIT and counter PIT maneuvers. TVI, if you prefer. Want me to go on?"

Her brow furrowed as she dug for a memory. "PIT… pursuit intervention technique. I've read that. But not TVI."

He'd been reaching to start the vehicle, but now drew back slightly and turned to look at her. "Tactical vehicle intervention. Almost the same thing, with a little more flourish and some different approaches."

She nodded. "I'll remember."

"Why?" He looked genuinely curious at her interest.

"Because I always do," she said simply.

She could almost feel his interest sharpen. "Always?"

"Pretty much. Sometimes it takes longer to call it up, but it's almost always there."

"Just verbal or images, too?"

*Definitely interest*, Ashley thought, as she studied him in turn. "Both. And to a certain extent, video."

"So if you've seen someone before, you'll remember them later?"

*If you mean you, then yes, I'll remember you. Probably a lot longer and more clearly than I'd like to. Then again...*

"Ms. Hart?"

She snapped out of the uncharacteristic meandering of her mind into odd places. Belatedly remembered who—or rather, what—this man was. A bodyguard. Of course, he'd be interested in her ability to remember people she'd seen or met. And no doubt would care less if she remembered him. This was a job to him, and if she were guessing right—and she was fairly sure she was, from a couple of his comments—one he wasn't really happy about.

"Yes, I remember people. Places I've seen. Things I've seen done."

"Accurately?"

"Quite."

He gave her a slow nod. "Good to know."

Watching as he finally started the car, she could almost see him filing that bit of knowledge away, as if it were something he might need to reference later. Or in the manner of a man who wanted to know all the tools at hand.

She was seized with an uncharacteristic attack of

nerves as the silence spun out in the car. He drove, as she'd expected, with a quiet competence. And smoothness. She had a tendency toward motion sickness when not driving herself, another reason she'd chosen the front seat. But she had the feeling she could probably read a book with him at the wheel, he was that smooth.

"You'd be a great chauffeur," she said before she thought. She wondered if he'd take offense.

"A connoisseur of chauffeurs, are you?"

"Not by choice." She now felt compelled to explain. "I tend to get queasy as a passenger." He gave her a slightly alarmed look, as if he were wondering if she was about to demonstrate here in his car. "I'm fine," she added hastily, wondering how on earth he was able to rattle her when she was usually *the queen of keeping her cool*, as her best friend Kate said. "You're very smooth."

"So I've been told."

She nearly gaped at him. But then she caught the slightest twitch at the corner of his mouth she could see. And suddenly she was laughing. And relaxed.

"I love this library," she said, feeling better now. "I had my meeting there yesterday. It's just beautiful. They remodeled it a few years back. There are stained glass windows that are a wonderful touch. I want to get a closer look at them. I didn't have time yesterday."

He didn't answer until they were pulling into the parking area of the long, low white building. He parked, shut off the motor and turned to look at her.

"So this is a…personal visit? We're not walking into some kind of protest rally?"

She laughed, gestured at the nearly empty lot. "Does this look like a rally to you? Let alone a protest?"

"Just checking. I saw video of that group out in Inman."

"I actually had nothing to do with that."

"Except to stir them up."

Her laughing mood vanished. "If you followed my media feeds, you'd know I repudiated what they did. It was far too early for that kind of response."

"Seems like they went off the moment your name was attached to the wetlands issue."

"I can't help that."

"Like I said, you stir them up. That's what activists do."

"I'm not an activist, I'm an advocate."

"Po-tay-to, po-tah-to."

She was frowning now, feeling a bit beleaguered. "Is that all you think I do?"

"Isn't it?"

"If any of the causes I espouse devolve into screaming protests, it's only after I have spent considerable time and effort under the radar to avoid it. I meet, negotiate, offer solutions, work toward compromise long before I ever turn to garnering public support and protest. That is my utter last resort. And I consider it a failure on my part."

She'd had to explain herself and her approach often before, but she usually managed it without the irritation even she could hear snapping in her voice. Something about this particular man truly set her off. With an effort, she got control of emotions she didn't usually have to rein in, and set herself to what she called her pleasant chat mode. She was not going to let this man divert her. He was doing a job and to keep her father from ordering her straight back home, which would mean she would have to defy him to get her goals accomplished, thereby causing more tension at home, she had to let him do it. So she would, and otherwise she would ignore the guy.

Too bad he was also the sexiest guy she'd come across in a very long time.

# Chapter 5

"This library has some very forward thinking ideas," she was saying as they reached the entrance, which was shaded by a large awning-style overhang. "I especially like their Automatic Advance Reserve program, where you can sign up for your favorite authors and they'll notify you when they release a new book and hold it for you to check out."

"Not bad for flyover country, huh?" he said, irked at her apparent surprise that small-town Kansas could actually be, if not ahead of the curve, at least even with it.

She gave him a sideways look. "Not bad for anywhere. I'm going to suggest it to several places."

"Don't you just buy a book if you want it?" He was genuinely curious, not for the first time.

"Yes," she admitted easily. "But not everyone is as fortunate as I am."

*Well, that's the understatement of the century...* But he supposed he had to give her credit for even being aware of that. Many in her position weren't.

Once inside, he looked around with interest. It had been a while since he'd been in a library, and he was a little surprised she was so enthusiastic about it. But he had to admit this was nice. The equipment was modern, and it ran from communal areas with comfortable chairs that could fit in a living room to computer stations to a magazine section, with more print magazines than he'd seen in quite a while in a space with windows that showed the outside.

But it was the stained glass windows she'd mentioned that really caught his attention. The train in the window to the children's area was fun. A pair of windows farther on represented the sunrise and moonrise. Then there was one that was almost a mural and, according to the title, showed the progress of knowledge. That was a bit esoteric for him, but he did like the one with the big tree, appropriately named Under the Reading Tree.

"That's my favorite," she whispered. He glanced at her, expecting her to be pointing at the mural one. But instead, she was smiling in delight at the unexpected image of a dragon, no fire-breathing in sight, as he sat happily reading.

"Why?" he asked, a little surprised.

"Because that's what it's all about, isn't it? Flights of the imagination?"

He was totally disarmed by that smile. That this woman of all people, the daughter of a family who could buy this whole town, took such joy in a simple thing amazed him. He'd like to meet her parents someday, because obviously they hadn't lost sight of what was important if they'd been able to raise a daughter who could still react like this.

Then he nearly laughed at himself. Yeah, that was likely, him hanging around with the likes of the Harts of Westport, Connecticut. That he was with one of them now didn't count; this was business, and he'd better stick to it.

"You mentioned you wanted to do some research?"

"Yes. One of the staff told me before the meeting yesterday that they have thousands of historic photographs, a history archive, including newspapers from the 1870s forward, and historical local and state plat maps covering the county. I want to see those, track the changes to the McPherson Valley Wetlands, and how and when they happened."

"Too bad they don't show the real cost." He thought he'd kept his voice fairly neutral, but she gave him a narrow glance, anyway.

"What's that supposed to mean?"

"There was a man who'd been farming around here for sixty years, on land his family had owned for well over a century, when someone decided half of it should be protected. That *willing surrender of property* to the state you…advocates talk about? Not so willing. He just couldn't fight the government anymore and took his own life the day after they took it over."

"That's horrible. But hardly my fault." She turned then, facing him head-on. She might be more than half a foot shorter than him, but there was a gleam in her eye that warned him he'd gone a step too far. "You make a lot of assumptions, Mr. Colton. Including, obviously, that I don't care about people."

"Maybe you do. Maybe it's just the fallout after your mission is accomplished that you don't care about."

"Are you always so rude to clients?"

In fact, he wasn't. Ever. And he wasn't sure what it was about her that prodded him so. Other than her looks, of course. But he'd worked with beautiful women before and never had a problem keeping a leash on his words.

He'd never had one send him into overdrive just from a photograph, though. Because those beautiful women he'd worked with before had, for the most part, proved to him that there wasn't all that much behind the beauty. But Ashley Hart, a woman he'd half expected to be the worst of that sort, had turned out to be a different kettle of fish entirely.

And he'd better keep himself in line or he was going to blow this job, a job that could catapult Elite Security to an entirely new level.

"My apologies, Ms. Hart. I was out of line." He gave her a contrite nod. "Please, proceed with your research. I will stay out of your way unless there's a need for me to interfere."

She looked, oddly, almost disappointed—and as if she had some further retort on the tip of her tongue and he'd spiked her guns. But in the end, she said nothing, just turned and headed for the separate room where a sign indicated all the historic documents were stored in a controlled environment. A woman from the library staff greeted her, they chatted a moment—Ashley was quite cordial and warm, he noticed—then went into the room. Ty took a look to be sure they were the only ones inside, and that there was no other way in, then settled down to wait.

He took out his phone and texted their location to the

office via the encrypted connection. They could find him easily enough with the tracker on the car, but this was protocol. Eric himself responded—a good reminder of how important this case was, and Ty gave himself another silent lecture on behaving himself.

He grabbed one of the desk chairs a couple of rows of bookshelves down and brought it back to sit just outside the door to the room. Anybody after her would have to go through him, and that wasn't going to happen.

Except for a group of school kids, apparently arriving for a story hour, the place was as quiet as a library traditionally was. He got up now and then to stretch and move around, although he was constantly scanning the area that had access to the door to the document vault.

He was starting to wonder just how long she planned on being in there when his phone signaled an incoming text. Thinking maybe he should have muted it—library, after all—he pulled it out. The incoming was from Mitch, so he opened the app. When he saw what it was about, he stared for a moment, sure he was gaping at the screen.

Then he was on his feet and moving fast. He burst into the archive room, startling the women who were standing by a table that held what looked like a very old map. But he was focused only on one, the woman who stood there with her phone in her hands.

"Are you crazy or just stupid?" he snapped, grabbing the phone out of her hands.

For an instant, she looked actually frightened, which made him wish he'd toned it down a little. He didn't like scaring people—unless they were the bad guys—but especially women. Not that that made the question any less valid.

But she recovered quickly, and drew herself up with a haughtiness that he suspected Harts learned from the cradle. "Give me back my phone."

"No," he said bluntly. He slid the phone—a very high-end one, of course—into a pocket.

"No?" She looked stunned.

*Nobody ever say no to you?* He nearly laughed at the thought, because he guessed it was quite possibly true. And he could almost feel her anger growing. It practically vibrated the air around her. Ms. Ashley Hart of the Westport Harts was rapidly building toward an eruption.

He decided a change in tactics was called for. He shifted his focus to the still-startled librarian and said with an almost courtly politeness, "My apologies, Mrs. Washington. Ms. Hart may have failed to mention to you that her life has been threatened, and now she has broadcast to the world *exactly* where she is by posting the photograph she just took of your map."

The woman's eyes widened, and she paled slightly. She turned to stare at Ashley, who was gaping at him. "That's absurd!" she almost yelped. "How dare you barge in here and—"

Ty cut her off and continued speaking to the older woman. "I'm sure Mr. Washington would appreciate it if you made it home this evening, so we'll ensure your safety by leaving immediately."

Ashley opened her mouth, he even heard her intake of breath, as if she were readying a barrage of angry retorts. He imagined she was quite capable of that. It seemed to be intrinsic among those who ruled the world—or fancied they did. But suddenly she stopped. She looked at the librarian's horrified expression and shut her mouth again.

*Well, well...maybe she's not quite as self-absorbed as I thought.*

"My own apologies, Mrs. Washington," she said with exquisite grace and warmth. "It's not a true threat, you're not really in any danger, but perhaps caution is wisest. I'll come back at a better time for all concerned," she added with a sideways glare at Ty.

She waited until they were back in his car before she held out her hand. "My phone," she said icily.

"No," he said again.

"I don't know what authority you think you have over me, Mr. Colton, but I assure you it does not include stealing my personal property."

"My authority includes doing whatever is necessary to keep you safe. Including saving you from yourself. What were you thinking?"

"That your fellow Kansans needed to know what they risk losing."

"And to do that, your parents have to risk losing you?"

She gave a dismissive wave of one slender hand. "It's just talk. People bluster when they're able to hide behind the anonymity of the internet. I get threats all the time. They're not real."

"So you've said. But your family's own security staff's analysis deemed this one more valid. Elite agrees."

She blinked. "My family's security staff? They have nothing to do with me. I told my parents long ago I didn't want them trailing after me." Her chin came up. "And I don't want you."

He couldn't help it, he grinned at her. "I've been told that before."

"I'm sure you have," she said tartly.

"Not usually by a beautiful woman, though."

She ignored the compliment and stared at him a moment before saying, as if she were merely pondering the question, "At what point, do you suppose, does self-confidence become arrogance?"

He smothered another grin. He was starting to like the way she talked. But he answered her with dead seriousness, "At about the same point someone decides that just because she says so, her loving parents will stop worrying and looking after her."

Her eyes widened slightly, and something flickered in the dark brown. They really were amazing, those eyes. Deep. Endless.

She let out a long audible sigh. "Point taken, Mr. Colton."

She'd surprised him now. Apparently, the loving in the Hart family went both ways. He filed away the knowledge that he was already certain would be a key weapon in the battle to keep her safe.

That the battle would mostly be with Ashley herself, he already knew.

# Chapter 6

"I should have known they wouldn't leave it alone," Ashley said rather glumly, staring out the windshield as they pulled away from the library. "What exactly constitutes a threat analysis, beyond looking at the person making the threat?" *And going over this vehicle with a fine-tooth comb and a couple of electronic devices I don't even recognize, even though it was parked in a nearly empty lot at a library, of all places?*

"Do you mean generally or in this case specifically?"

She gave the man in the driver's seat—in more ways than one, since he still had her phone—a sideways look.

"Yes?" she suggested.

He smiled at that. It wasn't quite as heart-stopping as that unexpected grin had been, but it was a close thing.

*And you need to stay focused or he really is going to end up running your life the entire time you're here.*

"In a case like this, where we're not certain of the identity of the person behind the threat, it involves analyzing the reason for the threat, the specificity of it, studying the language used, the method of conveyance, what history we have of possible prior threats. And in cases like this, we work on tracking location through ISP or carrier identification, although that's not particularly reliable without further data."

"My parents are certain," she said. "They're convinced it's William Sanderson, that man who wants to build his tract of luxury homes, and thinks I stopped him from getting his permit."

"Didn't you?"

"I hope so," she said proudly.

"So you're proud of stopping someone from pursuing their livelihood?"

"I'm proud of stopping him from destroying an important wetland for migratory birds."

"So birds take precedence over humans?"

She'd heard variations of this often since she'd found her calling a few years ago. Although she had to admit, he was calmer about it than most. "They can coexist, with some care. That's all I ask for."

"What you're asking for," he said quietly, "is control over what someone does with their own legally purchased private property."

"No, I'm asking him to understand and control what he does with it." They'd reached a stoplight and he looked at her, so she turned in the passenger seat to meet his gaze. She spoke earnestly now, warmed to her beloved subject. "People just need to understand, to know what effect their choices will have. Then they almost always do the right thing."

"The over-optimism of that assumption is boggling," he said, as he glanced back at the traffic light. His words were laced with a cynicism that surprised her. "But even if that were true, there's still the biggest question."

"What question?" she demanded, stung a little by his optimism comment, given she'd often heard it, especially from her parents.

He looked back at her and said flatly, "The *right* thing according to who?"

She blinked. "Well it's obvious what the right thing is, isn't it?"

"Not to me. The right thing according to who? You? What gives you the right to decide that?"

He was surprising her. She hadn't expected to have to defend her beliefs with the man hired to protect her.

*Then why are you?*

Speaking of obvious questions… "I don't have to explain myself to you."

"No, you don't. I'm just the hired help, after all. And worse, from flyover country. So I couldn't possibly be as smart as you. We hicks need elites around to tell us what we're doing wrong."

She wanted to retort sharply, but had so many things tumbling through her mind she couldn't pick one to start with. This conversation was sliding downhill rapidly, which bothered her. She thought about that for a moment. Wondered if it was because she'd gotten out of the habit of actually arguing her case. So often now she went places, gave a speech and left. If there were questions, they were generally from people who already agreed with her. And more recently, the discussions took place on social media, where she had time to think and lay out her best and most persuasive arguments. She actually hadn't engaged in this kind of rapid give-and-take in a while, and it showed. She was rusty. And how odd that it was this man of all people who made her realize that.

Or maybe it was just him. This man, who had quite literally stopped her breath the first moment she'd seen him.

*We hicks...*

She grimaced inwardly. She didn't think that way, truly she didn't, but she also couldn't deny that many of those she associated with did. She'd warned them time and again that not only were they wrong, that kind of attitude only antagonized people they were trying to persuade, but it seemed innate in so many. No wonder he assumed she was the same.

It was a moment before she responded, with every stereotype she could think of. "Yes, you hicks, in your bib overalls, chewing tobacco and spitting, smoking corncob pipes, speaking with a drawl and dropping g's all over the place." He was gaping at her now. "Yes, you seem just like that. And by the way, you've got the green."

As she said it, the faintest of polite honks sounded behind them. Unlike the blare you got in a big city when you missed the instant response to the signal changing, she acknowledged.

His head snapped back forward, and they started moving again. And, she noticed, he gave a wave of apology to the driver behind them. As opposed to the rude gesture she was more used to in the city.

When they were clear of the intersection, he said, in a musing sort of tone, "Just like you coastal elites are all arrogant, presumptuous, look down your nose at everyone not from there unless they're from an acceptable place on the opposite coast, and carry your Ivy League college degrees around with you to show off?"

"Exactly," she said pointedly.

He smiled. It looked somewhat rueful. "Point taken, Ms. Hart," he said, echoing her earlier words.

"So can we agree to drop the assumptions?"

"And just get along? A city girl from the upper crust and a guy from farm country?" He lifted one hand and rubbed at his chin as if deep in thought about her question. It was so perfect, so exaggerated. She knew he was being as mocking as she had been. And a smile played around the corners of her mouth.

"Sounds like the tagline for a fish out of water movie," she said. *Or a romantic comedy.*

That thought rattled her completely, as did the realization that for all the mockery, even that chin he was rubbing was attractive. And his hands, hands that were strong, capable…

He laughed, and it sent that little ripple through her that she'd felt at the first sound of his deep rough voice. She again had to yank her mind off a path she had no intention of traveling.

When she finally spoke again, she did it quietly. "You may have that backward, Mr. Colton. In 1648, one of my ancestors, along with four others, settled on land purchased from the Pequot people. They had to get permission from the town of Fairfield to do so. They were all farmers, Mr. Colton. I'm descended from farmers who worked as hard as the farmers of Kansas. Harder, most likely, given the advances in modern equipment and methods."

"And I live in Wichita, about fifteen times the size of your Westport," he admitted.

She wasn't surprised he knew that. Her parents wouldn't hire a firm who didn't do their homework. "So in truth, I'm the small-town girl, and you're the city boy."

"Consider the assumptions overturned," he said.

"Agreed," she said, smiling. But then what she'd just thought about them doing their homework went through her mind again. "What about this threat made you—your company decide that this one among all the threats I get is serious?"

"The specificity in part," he said. "And timing. The responses to your posts are always quick enough that we can surmise he follows you on several platforms." He gave her a sideways look. "And the posts he made about your talk at the library last night were almost simultaneous with your remarks."

It took her a moment to realize the implication. "You...You're saying you think he was there?"

"It's a definite possibility. And why your parents are so adamant you lie low until the threat is identified and eliminated."

She lapsed into silence. She had to admit the thought of someone who wished her ill—even dead—sitting in that room within feet of her was unnerving. Perhaps she did need to take this a little more seriously.

They were pulling up to her hotel before he spoke again. "Let's get you packed and checked out of here."

She blinked. "What?"

"You should do it in person at the desk, and mention that you're heading home."

"What?" she said again. She was not used to feeling behind, but this man was annoyingly short on explanations for his rather dictatorial orders.

"Just in case. Since we don't know for certain who

this person is, or where he might have contacts, it can't hurt to plant a false trail."

That did make sense, but she still felt a step behind. It was not a sensation she liked; she was usually the one in the lead. "But why am I checking out? I still have—"

"You're checking out because you announced to the world that you're staying at this location," he said. Then, with that sideways look again, he added, "You know, that post about your *surprisingly well-appointed* room?"

She felt herself flush. She wasn't easily flustered, but somehow this man catching her expressing something that fairly reeked of those assumptions they'd agreed to discard did it. Her mind raced as they crossed the lobby, trying to remember if she'd posted anything else that could be interpreted that way. Looking at her timeline through that lens, she was afraid she had. She needed to look, assess and determine if she needed to make a post explaining and apologizing. She needed to—

She'd been digging into the outside pocket of her leather bag, where her phone lived, without even thinking about it. Without remembering it was no longer there. And why.

"May I have my phone back, please?" she asked, very politely to contrast with her earlier imperious demand.

"When we get to the safe house."

She drew back sharply. "The what?"

"You're not familiar with the term *safe house*?"

"Of course I am. That's ridiculous."

"It will only be until the threat is neutralized."

"I have a hearing in front of the county planning commission in three weeks about this, and I have organizing to do. Supporters I need to mobilize. I will not stay locked away—"

"You will if I say so."

*Talk about imperious demands!* "I will not."

She heard him let out a long sigh. "Your parents told me you were exceptionally bright, with a killer memory, but a bit naive. They failed to mention the stubborn."

"A bit naive?" she repeated, taken aback.

"They take the blame for that themselves, by the way. Said they probably sheltered you too much."

She was gaping at him now. "They…actually said that?"

"They did."

She was going to have to have a word with them. She was not naive. She just chose to think the best of people. And that if given the choice, they would do the right thing. Most of the time.

She consciously unclenched her jaw. "Because I love my parents, I will go," she conceded, but added firmly, "for now. But don't expect me to be happy about it."

"Not my job to keep you happy. Just alive."

For some reason that set her off even more. A reason she didn't care to analyze just now. "Two weeks," she said warningly, as they reached the elevator alcove. "I'll tolerate it for two weeks."

He hit the up-arrow button. "We'll start with that," he said mildly.

She bit back a retort that it wasn't a negotiation. They stepped into the elevator and she turned to face the front. And as the doors slid shut, she couldn't help thinking about the moment just this morning when it had been reversed, when those same doors had slid open and she'd seen a tall, built, gorgeous man coming into the hotel.

She hadn't realized that moment would end up being something that would disrupt her entire life.

# Chapter 7

She packed with much less care than Ty would have expected of a Hart. She simply tossed everything from the small closet onto the bed and then loosely rolled each thing up. But the carry-on-sized bag had a designer label, and he was guessing the clothes did, too.

"Want some help?" he asked, more out of reflex than anything.

She paused with a sweater nearly the same color as her eyes in her hands. And those eyes were fastened on him in a rather intent way. Then she gestured toward the dresser near where he was standing and very sweetly asked, "Want to get my underwear out of the drawer?"

For an instant, he was taken aback. But only an instant. She was testing him, of that he was sure. He just wasn't sure what she was testing for. So he merely reached out and tugged open the top drawer. He was met with a froth of lace and silky-looking fabric, in about three different colors. He gathered the whole lot and walked the two steps to set it all on the foot of the bed. And if he noticed the size and shape of the lacy bras in the process, well, what did she expect?

She was looking at him as if waiting for…something.

"Was I supposed to recoil? Or maybe start drooling?"

"No. I just expected you to tell me to do it myself."

He shrugged and said easily, "I've got three sisters. I've done their laundry. Doesn't faze me."

Now she was staring at him in an entirely different way. "You've done your sisters' laundry?"

"And they've done mine. My mom's kind of equal opportunity that way."

Suddenly she smiled, and it hit him like a runaway freight train all over again just how beautiful Ashley Hart was. "I like the way she thinks."

"She's the best," he said succinctly.

"What does she do?"

"She's a nurse, at the hospital in Braxville." Ashley looked surprised. "What? You expected a socialite who dabbles because she's a Colton?"

She gave him that too-sweet smile he was already learning to be wary of. "As you expected of me? No, I try to be more open than that."

"Sorry," he muttered. "I didn't mean to break the truce."

"I'll forgive it, since it was in defense of your mother. And by the way, the reason I reacted was that my mother was a nurse when she and my father met."

He blinked. "Oh." He hadn't expected that. Realized he should have read the family background part of the file Eric had sent him a little more closely instead of focusing mainly on the subject of this operation.

"It's one reason medical causes are so important to us," Ashley added. "She's seen firsthand the difference donations in certain areas and fields can make."

He tried to think of something to say that would make up for him blowing their agreement to drop the assumptions. "That's admirable. She must be happy to be in a position to do that."

"It's a calling, for her."

He studied her for a moment. Tried not to notice how lovely she was, and focused on those eyes, and the intelligence gleaming there so obviously once you knew what to look for. "And for you?"

"Absolutely. There are many things I support, but spreading good medical care and practices is chief among them."

So she wasn't solely some environmental crusader, what some would likely call a tree hugger. He was always wary of people so sucked up into a single cause that they were incapable of seeing anything else and put everything into that basket, as his mother said.

They were passing the city limits when she asked with a frown, "Where is this safe house?"

She said it with a bit too much emphasis on the last two words, and he knew she was still none too pleased about this. He was glad he'd cleared this with the family earlier. It was easier to present it as a done deal than having to explain he was spiriting her off to a place he, in part, owned.

"It's actually a fishing cabin." He gave her a sideways look as he got on I-135 and headed north. They'd actually be within spitting distance of Braxville when they got off and headed west. "And the exact location you'll keep to yourself. Please." He only added the last because he'd seen her stiffen at the order.

She didn't speak again, but her jaw was set. Ashley Hart clearly wasn't used to being ordered around. And why would she be? She'd inherited billions upon millions from her grandparents and was the only child of her equally wealthy parents. Nobody told that kind of money what to do, unless she let them.

He thought about trying a softer sell, convincing her to just let him do his job, since the goal was to keep her safe. But at the moment, he didn't think she was in any mood to listen. At the same time, he didn't want her sitting there stewing, maybe thinking of ways to make this more difficult than it was already going to be. Because he had a feeling when she discovered one particular aspect of the Colton family fishing cabin, she was very much not going to be happy.

They were off the interstate, almost halfway there, and it had been done in silence. He glanced at her again. "Tell me something. If Sanderson had been going to build, say, affordable housing instead of luxury homes, would your reaction be different?"

"Making assumptions yet again?"

"No. Asking an honest question."

She didn't speak for a moment, but he'd swear he could feel her eyes on him as he drove. Then she said, "In the same place? No. The type of housing doesn't matter, the destruction of habitat does." His peripheral vision caught her tapping a slender finger on her knee. "Looking for hypocrisy, are you?"

"Just trying to understand."

"What's hard to understand?"

He shrugged. "Since most of your efforts in this kind of situation seems to be toward making people stop doing things, I can't help wondering…who, exactly, are you saving the world for?"

"Everyone," she said, sounding puzzled.

He could risk a glance on this smaller road and looked at her. "But you don't want them to do anything with it? Kind of like having a beautiful piece of jewelry and never wearing it, isn't it?"

Her brow furrowed. It seemed she was considering it, at least. "I gather you're not an environmentalist," she said, her mouth quirking.

He looked back at the road, traffic lessening the farther they got from the interstate. "Not an answer to my question, but I'll bite. I think we should protect what we have on this planet, but not worship it."

He'd probably really ticked her off now. But at least she wasn't stewing about the safe house.

To his surprise, after a moment she said, "I understand that. There are many who cross that line into thinking humans should be removed altogether."

"Excluding themselves, of course," he said dryly.

"I'm not sure some I know wouldn't include themselves."

"Now that's scary."

"On that, we agree."

"Hey, miracles happen," he quipped. And when he heard her laugh, it was much more gratifying than it should have been. And he couldn't help smiling.

Mr. Tyler Colton was… Ashley wasn't sure what he was. All she was sure of was that, aside from being armed—she'd caught a glimpse of a handgun on his belt beneath the jacket—he wasn't what she had expected. She'd seen flashes of the kind of authoritative demeanor she'd never liked in her family's personal security people, although there she had long ago resigned herself to the necessity. Her family was prominent and wealthy enough to be targets for all kinds of unsavory people.

She'd had to accept it there, so she supposed she might as well accept it here. Besides, this man was a lot more intriguing than brusque and rather crusty Mr. Patrick who led the home team, as it were.

*Not to mention gorgeous.*

Yeah, that, too.

But he'd surprised her with the jewelry comment. In one sentence, he'd presented his viewpoint in a way that made more sense than most of the arguments she heard. And she couldn't deny there was validity to it. She wasn't one of those rabid sorts who placed people at the bottom of the hierarchy of things to care about. She just happened to believe people should be more careful, that they could be more careful and do a lot less damage.

She studied him while he was focused on driving. She told herself it was because she needed the distraction from being a passenger, and almost believed it. But he really was very smooth, as smooth as their driver back home. And from what he'd said, he'd obviously been well trained.

He was also the first man in a very long time to spark this kind—or almost any kind—of interest in her. She was all too aware that in her position, as the only child of very wealthy parents, and the heiress to her grandparents' vast fortune, she was an obvious target for fortune-hunting males. Because of this, she very rarely let anyone past the gates, as it were. So rarely that it startled her that the thought had even formed. Then again, looking at that profile—those chiseled features, that jaw, the slightly tousled hair that somehow made her fingers itch—it was no surprise. Obviously, they would be spending some time in close proximity, so she supposed she'd be better off admitting his appeal so she could steal herself against it.

"Is this what you usually do?" she asked in a very impersonal tone.

He didn't look at her, but he did answer. "Personal protection? It's a lot of what we do. But not all."

*We*, she thought. She didn't guess he was short on ego—how could he be, all six feet two of him, broad shouldered and solid muscle, with that hair and those amazing dark blue eyes?—so he clearly felt a part of a team, not a solo act. That was telling. "What else?"

"Risk assessment. Corporate security. Event security. On occasion, we work a support role for a bigger operation, coordinating with government agents for an official visit."

"You sound like a sales brochure." She made sure it didn't sound like a dig.

"We're good at what we do. My boss has built a good thing. We're not as big as Pinkerton, but we're as good."

She shouldn't, she supposed, be surprised he knew who handled their security at home. Her father had gone with the storied company not solely because of their long and famous history, but because he knew several of their people and trusted them.

"Speaking of that, Pinkerton's got offices in Omaha, St. Louis and Oklahoma City. So why us?"

"If you're laboring under the misapprehension that my

parents discussed this with me, I'm sorry. They didn't bother."

He gave her a sideways glance. "They probably didn't want the fight."

She drew up straight. "Are you saying I'm stubborn again?"

"Are you saying you're not?"

"No. I happen to think stubborn is just a facet of persistence, which is a very useful quality."

One corner of his mouth—he really did have a rather lovely mouth—twitched. "Well, that's a nice way to pretty it up. Doesn't make it any easier to deal with, though." She started to say something about that being his job but before she could, he added, very quietly, "Especially when it's someone you love and you're afraid for them."

Her parents. He'd been talking about—and apparently thinking about—her parents. The instant he put it that way, the moment he planted the image of her parents afraid for her, her retort died unspoken. And the stubborn faded away.

"I'll try to remember that."

"I thought you said you always remember."

"I do." *It only gets foggy when emotion gets in the way.*

She was feeling emotions—and other things—around this man that she would do well to ignore.

## Chapter 8

Ty saw her looking around the inside of the SUV as if she were only now noticing some things that were out of the ordinary. The extra mirrors that gave him a wide visual range. The two fire extinguishers, one on each side. She reached up and rapped a knuckle lightly against the window beside her. Then she looked at him.

"Bulletproof?" she asked.

He didn't bother to deny it. He already knew she was too smart to fool. Besides, maybe it would stir her to taking this more seriously.

"We prefer the term ballistic glass," he said easily. "This is level five. Will stop handgun fire and many rifle rounds. My boss had to pull some strings to get it, military has first call." She barely winced. Points for cool.

"What else?" she asked.

"Body is lightly armored. Special gas tank. Run flat tires."

She looked over her shoulder toward the back of the big SUV. "Do I even want to know what you've no doubt got stored back there?"

He gave her a sideways glance. Thought of running down the list of weaponry in the equipment lockers that took up about half the wayback of the vehicle. Decided that would be both unwise and unprofessional—something he was not used to feeling but had been poking at him ever since he'd spotted her across the hotel lobby. Instead, he just lifted a brow at her. "I don't know. Do you?"

She sighed audibly. "No. Probably not."

"Just let me do what I'm trained to do, Ms. Hart."

"Two weeks suddenly seems like a very long time," she muttered.

He wondered what she thought would happen if the threat hadn't been rounded up by her self-selected two-week deadline. Did she really think her parents would simply go along, let her go back to her regular life and pretend there was no danger? From what he'd picked up in his brief video call with them, that wasn't just unlikely, it was guaranteed not to happen.

But he'd deal with that if and when it happened. Right now, he just wanted as little hassle as possible. *Sure. You're only dealing with one of the three richest heiresses in the country, if not the world. No hassle at all.*

He kept his eyes on the road, but one of his assets was excellent peripheral vision so he saw more than she probably realized. And he saw her tugging at her bag, the big brown leather satchel-type thing he'd noticed before if only for the lack of some blatant designer label.

She wasn't looking at it, just reaching with long slender fingers into a side pocket. Then in rapid succession, she stopped, frowned, then let out an exasperated breath.

"I'd like my phone back now."

*So you can post exactly where you are?* "When we get there."

Just by the way she moved her head, he sensed her irritation. And he knew he was right. She was going to explode when they arrived and she saw all the facets of the Colton family fishing cabin.

*Tough. Live with it.* The words went through his mind, but he had to admit he grimaced inwardly at the idea of saying them to her.

It wasn't five minutes later when she repeated the motion of reaching for her absent phone. Again, she only seemed to remember when it wasn't there. Another fifteen minutes, when they were getting close to the lake, she did it yet again. And he couldn't stop himself.

"You're really addicted to that thing, aren't you?"

"It connects me to my platform," she said, sounding irritated.

"Because the world must know what you're thinking all the time?" He was poking an already aggravated woman, but his guardrails seemed to be out of whack around her.

"I notice you have one," she pointed out.

"Yes. And it's good at its function, which is communication."

"That's all you use it for? This tiny device that has more power than the computers that helped put men on the moon?"

He didn't know what was wrong with him, but the inappropriate words were out before he could stop them.

Something he rarely did anyway, but never with a client. "Maybe it's the difference between being an impressionable teenager and an adult when the first smartphone came out."

That did it. "Are you purposely trying to be offensive?" There was more than just an edge in her voice now. "The people who follow me care about the same things I do, but I sometimes have access to information they do not. And that phone is one of the main tools of my work. As much as whatever you have stored back there—" she gestured toward the back of the SUV "—are the tools of yours."

The passion in her voice echoed in the confines of the vehicle. He wondered—even more inappropriately—if she was that passionate about other things.

*You have lost your mind, Colton.*

"You're right. That was unacceptable. I apologize."

"Give me back my phone and I'll accept your apology."

"I will. We're almost there." He lifted a finger from the wheel and pointed to the right. Kanopolis Lake gleamed in the winter sun.

"Oh!" She hadn't even noticed, he guessed. "It's pretty."

She sounded so astounded he couldn't help saying, "Shocking, isn't it?"

She had the grace to apologize in turn for her tone. "I'm sorry. I just didn't realize it was there." She gave him a sideways look. "I was apparently too obsessed with my missing phone."

He almost laughed, and finally found his tact. "No comment."

But he couldn't help the twitch at one corner of his

mouth as he slowed coming into the small community on the west side of the lake. He'd always had a fondness for the place called Yankee Run, if only for the great name. But he liked the peace and the surroundings and the view, and had often thought if he ever left his modern high-tech house in Wichita, he'd move into the cabin for good.

They passed the first couple of small houses. She was looking around with interest now. He wondered if she'd ever spent any time in a place as small as this unincorporated community. He was glad of the status and size, because it meant there wasn't much to indicate exactly where they were, which he'd still prefer she didn't know, just in case.

"This is lovely," she said, surprising him. "The lake, and I'll bet the trees are beautiful and green when they leaf out."

"They are. We've got one beside the cabin that gives us a great shady spot to hang out in the summer. And the property is on a rise, so it was fun in winter if we got enough snow to sled down to the lake."

She looked at him as he made the last turn that would take them to the cabin's driveway. "You spend a lot of time here?"

"Not so much anymore," he said, "but most of the summer when we were kids."

"We?"

"Two brothers, three sisters."

Her eyes widened. "Big family."

"Wasn't planned," he said with a wry smile. "They were just going for number three and were going to stop, but fate apparently misinterpreted and thought they wanted three at once."

She blinked. "Triplets?"

He nodded. "Two boys and a girl."

"Wow. Do they run in the family?"

"Not that we could find."

He slowed, then hit the button on the remote he'd brought and the gate rumbled open. He made the turn onto the long driveway that wound through cottonwood trees to the cabin that was on a small point projecting into the lake. He'd told her they owned nearly fifty acres around the place, and if it weren't for the fact you could see the lake and the waterfront houses to the south, you'd never know there was anyone else around. If that kind of isolation bothered her, it didn't show.

He heard the crunch of their tires on gravel, to him a sound both welcoming and welcome. Dad had wanted to pave it but he'd argued him out of it. On the occasions when he had to bring someone here for work, he wanted that sound because it was a warning someone was coming, at least from this direction. That a pro would likely be coming silently through the trees or up from the lake would be dealt with in other ways.

"What about number six?" she asked, still apparently intrigued by the size of his family.

"Baby sister," he said, with an affectionate smile. "She surprised everybody five years later."

"Let me guess… You're the oldest?"

Something in the way she said it made him ask, "Why would you think that?"

"Oh, maybe your authoritarian manner?"

"That's my job right now. And I prefer to think of it as being a natural born leader."

"How about the bossy attitude?"

"You left out organized and prompt."

"I'll bet you were ordering your younger siblings around as soon as you could talk."

"You read a list somewhere, didn't you? Since we're back to assuming, that's better than being a spoiled, self-absorbed, demanding, I'm-so-special only child."

To his surprise, she burst out laughing. "Touché, Mr. Colton. I did read a list, years ago. And apparently you read the same list."

Driving slowly down the private drive, he could risk looking at her. Which may not have been wise. He appreciated her beauty, but her laugh made him want to make sure she laughed every day, which was the craziest thought he'd ever had about a woman.

"Years ago?" he asked.

"Yes. When a girl at my elementary school threw those same charges at me, I looked it up."

He drew back slightly. "What, twenty years ago?"

"Eighteen, actually. I was nine."

They were into the small grove of cottonwoods now, healthy trees so happy here that even their bare branches were thick enough to provide some shade. And in their shade, he was quickly reminded it was November. With the winter sun pouring in through the windows, it had been deceptively warm in the car.

"So you really do remember everything," he said, thinking this could be both a good and bad thing, for him and the job he had to do.

"Yes." She didn't sound happy about it.

"Even things you'd rather forget?" he asked quietly.

She gave him a rather startled look. "Yes." Her mouth—that mouth—curved into a smile that was both appreciative and sad at the same time. "And points to you. Most people don't think of that side of it."

"I will take," he said carefully, "all the points I can get."

He had the feeling that, with this woman, he was going to need them.

# Chapter 9

"This," Ashley said, "is not what I'd pictured when you said cabin."

"What did you picture?"

He'd lifted her bags out of the back of the vehicle while she stood there looking at the long, low dark brown building. Somehow, she'd had in her mind a building like, maybe her parents' carriage house. Small, with a high pointed roof. A fairy-tale kind of building. This wasn't that.

She turned to go back and pick up her bag. Glanced into the back of the vehicle and saw, as she'd guessed, a storage locker. Two, actually—one along each side of the cargo space.

She looked back at the building that seemed more small house than cabin. "No secure garage to lock it up in?"

She meant it archly, but he just shrugged. "It has a custom-built alarm system that will go off if a rabbit sneezes within ten feet of it. And," he added with a gesture up to the side of the building, "there's 24/7 video surveillance."

She drew back. "Then why the detailed check of it when we came out of the library?"

"Because some humans, the craziest ones, can be sneakier than a rabbit."

"That," she said, "I won't argue with."

He gave her a sideways glance. "I'm sure you could if you tried."

His tone was amused, not nasty, so she didn't rise to it. "I can argue most sides of most things," she said as she picked up her bag. She noted that he let her, then remembered how her parents' security people never carried anything, so their hands were free at all times.

"Even sides that oppose what you want?" he asked. He sounded as if he seriously wanted to know, and so she answered accordingly.

"Especially those. That's why I like having both sides of an issue angry with me at one time or another. I take it as proof I'm doing the right thing, not a one-sided thing."

He looked surprised, then thoughtful. "Points to you, then," he said, and went to open the door.

She walked down a rather dark but short hallway with paneling that matched the outside and a wood plank floor. And then the space opened up, and she set down her bag in amazement.

The room was like nothing she'd ever seen. The inland side of the cabin might be all solid walls, but this large space was nearly all windows—except for one wall that was almost entirely a large and quite full bookcase—

with a glorious view over a spacious deck down to the lake glistening in the near-winter sun. There was a huge stone fireplace with a heavy wood mantel at one end of the oblong room, and a kitchen with somewhat-dated tile but sleek new appliances at the other.

It was furnished with comfortable-looking, rather mismatched furniture. It would drive her meticulous mother crazy. Clearly, there had been no professional decorator in charge here. And she wasn't sure she didn't like the place better for it.

But what completely caught her attention was, of all things, the ceiling. It was made of what looked like metal tiles, or a single sheet of metal crafted to look like individual tiles, each perfectly square with a raised hammered ridge on the edges and a circular decorative medallion in the middle. The golden expanse should have been out of place, she supposed, but it wasn't. The color blended perfectly with the lighter wood of the walls, and it warmed up the entire large room.

She hadn't even noticed he'd come up behind her when he spoke. "It came from an old bank building in Braxville, our hometown. When they tore down the building, Mom bought it and had it installed here."

"It's beautiful. And unique."

"I'll give you unique," he said with a wry grin and lift of his eyebrows.

She found herself smiling at him. "Had to explain that a lot, have you?"

"How could you tell?"

"The explanation did sound fairly well practiced."

"It was easier when I was a kid. I'd bring a friend out here, he'd look up and say *weird*. And I'd say *yeah*. And that was it."

She laughed. When he wasn't being dictatorial, she quite liked him.

She walked over to the windows and looked out. "That's the tree you mentioned?" she asked, pointing at the big cottonwood to the right.

"Yep. My mom again. And my Uncle Shep. They planted it as a sapling when I was about three."

She stared at the towering tree. "A sapling?"

"Yeah. It wasn't much taller than Uncle Shep at the time. They grow really fast at first, like about six feet in a year. Only took until I was seven to be tall enough for me to fall out of and break my arm."

She turned quickly to look at him. He was smiling. "I'll bet your parents loved that."

"Mom kind of freaked. Funny, considering she's a nurse. Dad was in the middle of some project, so he didn't find out for a couple of days."

For a moment, she said nothing. She tried to imagine her father, even as busy as he always was, not finding out that she had broken an arm at seven. The image wouldn't form. He'd talked to her practically every day of her life, asking her not just about her day but her life, her dreams.

"My father would probably have wanted to cut the tree down for daring to be complicit."

He tilted his head as he looked at her, as if he were studying her. "And I'll bet you would have stopped him, saying it wasn't the tree's fault."

It unsettled her a little that he was exactly right. "Of course."

He didn't say any more about it, only, "Let's get you settled in."

This time he did pick up her bag and started up the

stairs that led up off the entry hall, directly opposite a closed door to either a closet or a room behind the expansive great room. She followed him up, brow furrowed as she tried to remember from the outside. It had seemed to her there wasn't much of an upstairs, that it had only covered about a third of the lower story.

When they reached the top, she realized that the entire space was a rather grand, spacious master suite, with a large picture window that looked out at the lake. He set her bag down on the foot of the bed while she looked around. The four-poster bed seemed huge and was covered with a blue-and-gray comforter. The blue matched the color of the lake today, and she guessed the gray matched it on cloudy days. There were coordinating drapes at the big window—the only window, she noticed—but she couldn't imagine ever wanting to close them.

"Guest closet," he said, jabbing a thumb toward a door on the back wall. "Bathroom," he added, now pointing toward a door to her left.

Curious, she went to look. "Lovely," she said, meaning it. The bathroom was worthy of the spa her mother adored to frequent. She could soak in that tub—which also had a view out to the lake, carefully angled so it didn't go both ways—up to her neck. And she stood there, staring out the carefully placed window, fighting down the ridiculous flush that had begun to rise at the thought of being naked in that tub under the same roof with this man. The realization that it was plenty big enough for two.

"Should be towels and whatever else in the tall cabinet," he said, clearly not bothered by such fevered imaginings. "My mom keeps it pretty well stocked."

She steadied herself and then turned to face him. "Shouldn't this be your room?"

He shrugged. "There's another bedroom downstairs."

"Like this?"

He smiled. "No. A lot smaller."

"Then I'll take that one and you—"

"No."

And there he was, back again, Mr. Authority. "I've slept in mud huts, Mr. Colton. As long as I sleep, it doesn't matter where."

"Noble of you. But in this case, it does matter."

The jibe stung. She hadn't said it to sound noble, just to make a point. But he seemed insistent on putting the worst spin on…everything. She'd dealt with village elders who were less cranky. With an effort, she kept her voice level. "Why does it matter here?"

"Because there's only one way to get to this room. And they'll have to go by me to do it."

She stared at him. Now she guessed she knew that door at the bottom of the stairs led to the other bedroom. "You say that as if you expect armed troops to show up."

"I don't expect them. That doesn't mean I don't prepare for them." She couldn't argue the logic of that, so didn't try. Instead, after yet again reaching for her bag before remembering the special pocket for her phone was empty, she held out her hand. "My phone now, please?"

"Oh. Yeah." He sounded rather odd, but started to reach into his pocket. He also nodded toward her bag. "No fancy designer label?"

"I thought we swore off assumptions."

"Just asking," he said. "It looks like something my sister would use, if she needed to carry but couldn't wear a holster."

She glanced at the bag, startled. "I had it made," she said briefly, managing not to frown in impatience as he pulled out her phone yet didn't hand it to her.

"Ah. Custom job."

He made it sound like that was somehow worse than carrying a big-name designer bag around. "Hard though it may be for you to believe, I actually prefer the low-key look of this bag, and I've had it for years. My phone?"

At last, he handed it over. Then he said briskly, "Get settled in. I'll go see what my partner's idea of stocking the kitchen was."

He was gone before she could answer, and she had the strangest feeling he hadn't just left, he'd escaped.

# Chapter 10

Ty glanced at his watch. If he were a betting man, he'd give her five, maybe ten minutes before she erupted.

He walked to the other end of the hall and went into the room he'd set up as an office—among other things—after he'd gone to work for Elite. He checked the comms equipment connected to their private system, sent the message that they were here and safe, then left it in monitor mode with the notification signal on. They'd agreed on periodic check-ins, but if they turned up something he needed to know, he didn't want to miss it. It was also powerful enough to send a notification to his phone, as long as he was on the property.

Then he headed back to the kitchen, wondering how far afield Mitch's idea of supplies wandered from Ashley Hart's. Since the guy's taste ran more to burgers and fries than caviar, he could only imagine. He was perusing the stack of steaks in the freezer, grinning at the addition of some bags of frozen veggies as a token, when what he'd been waiting for happened. He heard the sound of footsteps on the stairs, coming down.

What he hadn't heard was the shriek he'd almost been expecting. But then, she didn't really know. Yet.

He surreptitiously watched as she walked around the great room, with her phone held up in front of her. Ah. Checking to see if there was a signal elsewhere in the house. So she didn't immediately jump off a cliff when cut off. That seemed significant somehow.

Then she headed for the door out onto the deck, still staring at the uncooperative screen of her phone. She reached for the door handle, clearly intending on heading outside.

"Ms. Hart."

She stopped. For the first time, the phone came down. She looked back at him over her shoulder. And his heart nearly stopped. Damn, why did she have to look like… that? It wasn't just that she was beautiful, or so obviously smart, she was…she was so alive it fairly crackled around her.

"What?" she finally asked when he couldn't seem to find his voice.

He made himself focus. "Don't go outside alone."

She frowned. "I thought you said your family owned the surrounding fifty acres and the house is protected with alarms?"

"And the lake with open access is twenty-five yards away. That's an easy pistol shot." He pointed back toward the grove of cottonwoods they'd driven through. "A pro could do it from back there. Throw a rifle into the mix, and the shooter could be outside the property line and still take you out."

"If you think I'm going to sit inside for two weeks—"

She stopped when he held up a hand. "Just don't go out alone."

She turned around to face him, then. Her brow was furrowed as she looked at him. "If it is that professional you mentioned, and that someone is not even on your property to set off any of your alarms, why would you being with me make a difference?"

He hesitated for a moment, then decided on the truth. Maybe it would jolt her into taking this more seriously.

"Because he'll likely go for the bigger threat first."

"You."

"Yes."

A little to his surprise, she didn't argue the assessment. She merely looked at him consideringly. "And you accept that?"

"It's part of the job."

"Then tell me, Mr. Colton, once you're dead, what, exactly, am I supposed to do?"

Her voice was cool and calm. A little too much so for his comfort. But she did have a point. He'd planned to do this later, when she'd settled in, but the subject had come up now so there didn't seem much point in delaying it. Besides, it would postpone the inevitable blow up a little longer.

"Come with me," he said. Then added a careful, "Please."

He started back down the hall toward the office. She did follow without arguing, to his relief. He opened the office door, and nodded at her to step inside. She looked around, clearly surprised, no doubt by the rather stark utilitarian room and equipment.

"What is this?"

"Three things," he said briskly. "This room is bullet-proofed and sealable from the inside. If you have to, you head for here and hit that pad beside the door."

"So it's like a panic room?"

"Yes," he said, realizing the Harts probably had something similar. You didn't have the kind of wealth they did and not be aware you were a target for those who wanted to take it, not earn it. And somehow inheriting it seemed even worse to that sort of person, no matter that Ty knew Ashley's father had doubled the family fortune through his own efforts.

"Okay."

"Secondly—" he turned to the comms setup, pointed to a large red switch "—you flip that, push down that button and yell for help."

She seemed to consider that, as well. "What if no one answers?"

"They will. 24/7. They'll know where you are, so all you need to do is tell them what happened."

"You mean that you're dead?" she asked sweetly.

She was either the coolest customer he'd ever dealt with, or the coldest. And when he found himself thinking he'd like to have the discussion about the difference between those two with her, he knew he was in trouble. He was going to have to stay seriously on his guard.

"Exactly," he said, doing his best to sound unruffled. "You're under threat, and that's real. I didn't bring you here because it's unfailingly safe. No place is, and you need to be aware of that. I brought you because it will be harder for anyone to get to you here."

He saw her look around the office, saw her gaze snag on the first-aid locker on the wall beside the door. It was, as was everything Elite, stocked with the latest and greatest, and included a smaller portable case that held lesser amounts of everything in the main locker. Just about any kind of situation was covered, although if pressed he'd have to admit he'd only learned the minimum on some of the newer stuff. The injuries he encountered tended to be pretty basic, and if it was anything more complicated than a broken bone or a minor knife or gunshot wound, he was out of his depth, anyway.

Her gaze shifted to the locker on the other side of the door. The one with the actual lock on it. And for the first time some tension crept into her voice. He was glad to hear it. "I'm guessing the things in there are what make the things in there—" she gestured back at the locker marked with the red cross "—necessary?"

He smiled inwardly at her correct guess; there was a weapon in there to handle nearly anything. "Mostly they stop them from being necessary." Her gaze shifted to his face. He didn't remember from his admittedly somewhat hasty research that this had ever been one of her issues, but he asked anyway. "Don't care for weaponry?" His tone was just a hair too polite, but she answered evenly, with a glance at his side, where his jacket concealed his holster, that told him she was fully aware he was armed.

"It has its purpose and function." Her voice was cool again. She was back in control. "And given my family has had full-time armed security for years, it would be very hypocritical for me to crusade against their tools."

"Points to you again, then."

She met his gaze, and he didn't think he'd mistaken

the amusement in her eyes. "As someone once said to me, I'll take all the points I can get."

He couldn't help it—he let out a chuckle. "I think you're ahead at the moment."

"I shall endeavor to stay there."

She said it so snootily he knew she was putting it on. And a moment later, she was grinning at him, proving it. She was quite an unexpected package, was Ashley Hart.

*Ashley Hart, richest heiress in the civilized—or uncivilized—world, Colton. Remember that.*

"What's the third thing?"

He blinked, yanking his mind out of what was threatening to become a groove. "What?"

"You said this room was three things. You gave me two."

"Oh. Yeah. You already guessed." He walked over and pressed his thumb to the scanner on the weapons locker. A moment later, it clicked and disengaged. He pulled open the double doors, wondering if she'd freak at the sight of the rather impressive array. He looked back over his shoulder at her. Those delicately arched brows were lowered, but she didn't look intimidated, or particularly worried. Not worried enough for him, anyway. He didn't want her scared, but he didn't want her relaxing her guard, either.

Knowing the likely answer, he said, "I'll leave out something simple, just in case. A revolver, so no chance of a jam."

She came closer, scanned the racks that held everything from the mentioned revolver to a semi-auto rifle.

"Actually," she said casually, pointing at the single shotgun there, "I'd be more comfortable with the Mossberg." He blinked. She smiled at him. "Assumptions again, Mr. Colton?"

"Apparently. When and how did you pick up that particular bit of know-how?"

"My father took up trap and skeet shooting when I pitched a fit at age eight over him hunting live birds. I learned along with him."

"You any good?"

"Quite."

He studied her for a moment before he asked quietly, "Could you shoot a human being if you had to?"

To her credit, she didn't give him a snappy comeback. And after a moment, she nodded. "Under certain circumstances, I could."

"But you won't shoot a bird? A bit illogical, don't you think?"

"It's perfectly logical. The bird is innocent, being hunted while unaware, just trying to go about its life. A human has made a conscious choice."

For a moment, he just looked at her. She was surprising him on every hand. "Okay, now you're really ahead on points." He reached up and lifted the Mossberg 500 Tactical from the rack. "Twelve-gauge, five plus one, you know?" She nodded. "Want the pistol grip?"

"No. I'm not used to it, so it would just distract me."

"Good call."

When she took the weapon he held out to her, she took it with a familiarity that told him she hadn't been lying. Not that he thought she was. So far, she'd been honest to a fault. She studied it for a moment, and he pointed out a couple of things he guessed were different from the version of the weapon she was used to, for their tactical purposes.

"It fires pretty true," he said, "but we can take it out in the morning for you to fire a few so you can be sure." He gave her a wry smile. "No shooting range gear, I'm afraid. But I can throw something for you."

"That will do," she said.

"What's the difference between trap and skeet, anyway?"

She gave him a sideways look. "Testing me or do you really want to know?"

He held up his hands innocently. "I want to know. I've never done either."

"Skeet, the targets come across your field from the sides, and always at the same speed and height. Trap, they come from all directions and are moving away, not across."

"Trap sounds like it would be trickier."

"They both have their challenges." She took the box of shells he held out then and quite proficiently loaded the weapon. Then she looked at him. "Are we leaving it in here?"

He shook his head. "You might need quicker access. There's a rack in the great room."

She nodded, and soon the weapon was settled securely on the rack next to the door leading out onto the deck. It was already getting dark, the days growing ever shorter this time of year. It was also getting colder, so he set about building a fire in the fireplace. With the limited wood in the rack.

"What was that look for?"

She'd startled him. Again. He hadn't realized he'd been grimacing. "Just acknowledging that the last person here was my father."

"Meaning?"

He nodded toward the half-empty firewood rack beside the hearth. "It's sort of an unspoken rule you refill that when you leave. He never thinks about the next person who'll be here."

"Sounds...annoying."

"Yeah, well, that's my father."

"Rude or just thoughtless?"

"Oh, he's quite capable of being both. If it's not business-related, he doesn't much care. He—never mind," Ty cut himself off, wondering how on earth he'd let his father become a topic of conversation with this virtual stranger. Especially now, when Colton Construction was facing mounting problems, both personal and legal. Problems no one would appreciate him blabbing about to that stranger.

Except...she didn't feel like a stranger. He felt as if he already knew more about her, in these few hours, than he'd expected to.

Thankfully, she didn't press. Instead, she pulled her phone out once more and again started wandering the house. He knew perfectly well what she was looking for, what she wouldn't find. Finally, she made a swipe and a couple of taps on the screen, studied it for a moment and her brow furrowed in that now familiar way.

*Here it comes...*

"Okay, this is ridiculous. I can't get any kind of a carrier signal. And it's telling me there's no Wi-Fi in range."

He braced himself. Straightened up from where the fire was starting to take off. Then turned to face her.

"That's because there isn't any."

For the first time, she looked blank. Which told him a lot. "Any what?"

"Of either."

She stared at him. "You don't get a cell signal here?"

He pointed to the wall in the kitchen, where an old, rather nauseatingly yellow phone hung. "That's not there because it's pretty."

She blinked. "A landline? Seriously?"

"Very seriously. It's that or nothing out here."

"Wow." She looked back at her phone.

"Might want to turn the phone off, save the battery."

She looked as if he'd suggested she cut off a finger. "I'll turn off the carrier function, so it's not searching for a signal," she said, and did so. "But why is there no—" She stopped abruptly, and her eyes grew wider as she stared at him. "You don't have Wi-Fi, either?"

"Nope."

She was starting to look as if she were sliding into shock. "Tell me you at least have broadband?"

"I try never to lie."

She muttered something he was pretty sure there was a rude internet acronym for. "I haven't had to deal with dial-up since I was…what, seven?"

"You still won't have to."

She brightened. "Oh, that was mean. What, you have a satellite connection or something?"

"Nope. No satellite."

"Then what?"

He sighed. Loudly. Then, bracing himself for the blast, he very carefully said, "You, Ms. Hart, are offline. Completely. For the duration."

# Chapter 11

He was kidding. He was just ragging on her about her social media time again, that was all. Just kidding.

He had to be kidding.

Now she was gaping at him. While he was simply looking at her. Looking at her almost expectantly. She closed her mouth, almost embarrassed. She prided herself on her ability to keep an equanimous exterior no matter what she was thinking, but she was having trouble with that at the moment. In fact, if she were honest with herself, she'd been having trouble with it since this man had strode into her life and taken over.

"Are you saying," she enunciated carefully, "that this place does not have internet access at all? Or are you saying it does but I can't use it?"

"I believe the phrase is off-the-grid, internet-wise."

She supposed, of the two options, that was the better.

Not that either was acceptable, but she had the feeling that had he been refusing her access, she would have…

She would have given him the explosion he'd been expecting. That was why he'd looked as if he were braced. The idea that he thought her so predictable was irksome. Or worse.

So she simply asked, "Why?"

"Choice."

"To be out of touch?"

He gestured with a thumb toward that indeed unpretty yellow wall phone. "Landline."

"Yet, you have that radio set up in there," she said, gesturing toward the room with the communications equipment.

"Precaution."

"Because you're remote out here? Or is it because you use this as a safe house?"

"Yes."

She'd had about enough of the one-word answers. "What, exactly, do you expect me to do?"

"Have a tantrum? Pitch a fit, as my grandmother used to say? Addicts tend to do that."

She blinked. Maybe the one-word answers were better. "Addicts?"

"A person who is addicted—driven to use compulsively—to a habit, activity, substance…or device or platform."

She drew back slightly. "My, aren't we proficient at quoting—and editing—the dictionary."

He ignored the jab. "I'm a security expert. I don't have much patience for people under threat who insist on increasing their risk by refusing to stay off social media. Which is a dangerous thing to begin with."

"Not that you have an opinion or anything."

"It's more than an opinion. It's based in fact. Would you like a list of the victims who were injured or even killed after being unable to resist making a post that betrayed where they were?"

She didn't doubt that—she'd seen too many stories about just that. The problem was she couldn't believe this was that kind of threat. She'd grown up knowing she could be a kidnapping target, because of her family's wealth and standing, but for someone to come after her not for money but when she was trying to help, to benefit everyone?

Somehow, though, his words had taken some of the wind out of her sails. Because if she thought past her irritation, he had a point. A very valid point. Her mouth quirked, almost unwillingly. "Not to mention those who have managed to kill themselves trying to take a unique selfie?"

He looked startled, and she took no small amount of pleasure in that. And then he smiled, slowly, a slight dimple flashing in his right cheek, and that thought of pleasure shifted into an entirely different realm. She froze, inwardly. This was so not happening. Absolutely not.

"Yes," he said. "Thankfully, you're very much not stupid."

That pleasure expanded in a new direction now. Which unsettled her. What did she care if he thought her smart? Or stupid, for that matter? "Or hungry for fame?" she said hastily.

His smile turned wry. "You were born with that, Ms. Hart."

Before she really thought about it, she said, "Could

you dispense with the formality? Two weeks of *Ms. Hart* is going to be very wearing."

The smile faded altogether. "I'm not sure that would be wise."

Something knotted up in her stomach. Why would he say that? Why would he think it? The pleasure she'd gotten from his smile and his compliment had rattled her. The thought that maybe, just maybe he was feeling something similar shook her down deep.

"Why?"

It came out as barely above a whisper, and to her own ears betrayed everything she was thinking. But he answered as if it were a routine question. As if there had been none of her inner turmoil in her voice.

"You're a client, Ms. Hart. And Elite has protocols. Rules."

His businesslike tone, without a touch of regret, or anything other than a cool professionalism, chilled her emotions enough for her to say evenly, "Using my first name is against one of those rules?"

Something flickered in those dark blue eyes, and then he lowered his gaze as if he'd suddenly seen something of interest on the floor. His lack of an answer made her prod further. And she chose her words very purposefully.

"And do you never, ever break the rules, Tyler?"

His gaze shot back to her face, as if he were again startled. "Ty," he corrected, as if it were automatic. But then his voice changed. "I've been known to," he said, and there was a slight roughness in his voice that sent a shiver down her spine. She saw him take in a rather deep breath. Then, in his normal voice, he added, "And I've almost always regretted it."

"Only almost?"

"I still say that pursuing a child abductor off a roof was worth it, sprained ankle and all." This time his smile was practiced, and thus more distant. She didn't like that.

And she didn't like that she didn't like it.

*Damn. Get a grip, Colton.*

There was no reason in hell her just saying his name should have had that effect. None at all.

But it had.

He popped the tab on the caffeine-laden soda, not worrying about it because he needed to be sleeping light, anyway.

*Right. Like you're going to be sleeping at all, with her right upstairs.*

He took a long swig of the soda while staring out the kitchen window. It faced toward the cottonwoods, their winter-bare branches looking a little eerie against the night sky. He glanced at the clock on the oven, saw it was nearly an hour until moonrise. Not that it would matter much; the waning quarter moon stage they were at wouldn't put out much of that silvery light he loved.

"That's a nice smile. What brought it on?"

She'd come quietly up behind him and the smile vanished. On some level, he'd been aware, but he hadn't turned to look. Afraid to? Better not be. He was her bodyguard—damn, there had to be a better word than that—after all.

"I was thinking about the moon."

"Going to howl?" There was such a teasing tone in her voice that he couldn't help but smile again.

"Not full," he pointed out. "And it's waning, not waxing, so it'll be the end of the month before it's howlable."

She laughed. "Then what were you thinking?"

"More remembering."

"What?"

He was certain it was stupid, wouldn't be surprised if the sophisticated woman she was laughed, but he wanted to share the memory with her anyway. And he wasn't nearly as scared by that as he probably should have been.

"My mom took us all to the Flint Hills, to the Tallgrass Prairie Preserve when I was ten. It had only been established a couple of years before, and she wanted us to see what Kansas used to be. On the way back home, we had to pull over because the triplets started squabbling. I got out and walked over to look down the road, and it was just as a full moon was rising. It was huge, too big to be real, and it came up exactly where the road went over the last hill I could see, like it was leading the way, like the road was there just to take you to it. It was the most amazing thing I'd ever seen. And I think of it every time I look at the moon."

She was staring at him. Probably thinking he was the biggest goofball farm boy she'd ever imagined, far, far removed from her elite East Coast life.

"Thank you," she whispered.

He drew back. "For what?"

"Sharing that."

He was embarrassed now. Shrugged. "It's just something I remember."

"Don't belittle it. It's a memory to be cherished."

It was, to him. He'd just never expected someone like her to get it. It struck him that he was still making assumptions.

"Where was your father on that trip to the preserve?"

He managed to keep his expression even. "Working. Like always."

"Too bad. He missed something special."

*Like always.*

He quashed the sour thought as she moved, and he realized she was reaching for one of the back pockets of her jeans. She frowned, started to look around, then let out a sigh.

The phone again. She'd been reaching for her now useless phone. When she noticed he was watching, she seemed to feel compelled to explain. "I wanted to look up that preserve. I remember seeing the name when I was researching the wetlands, but I didn't follow it up then."

"Why would you?" He was trying to figure out how she thought.

"Because I like to know about things as a whole. And the tallgrass appellation was intriguing. Made me wonder if there were short-grass prairies."

"Yes. More, actually, wider-spread."

"Obviously I need to up my study of the Plains."

His mouth quirked. "Don't look at me. I think everybody should. For too many people, when they think of Kansas the only thing that comes to mind is *The Wizard of Oz*."

"I think he's been supplanted as the wizard of record," she said.

"You mean that kid with the round glasses? Yeah, I think so."

They both laughed. Hers was light, genuine, and Ty felt… He wasn't sure how to describe how he felt.

Because he'd never felt it before.

## *Chapter 12*

"That was some really good spaghetti sauce," Ashley said. She was looking at him across the table. The meal hadn't been fancy, but it had been warm and filling, and the sauce had indeed been delicious.

"Thank my mother. It's her specialty."

That surprised her. "Was she just here?"

He shook his head. "She makes it at home, a huge batch, and bottles it up."

"That's quite a process."

"She learned it from her mother, so she sees it as a sort of tribute to her to keep doing it."

"That's lovely." She gestured at the bread. "And that's one of the few times I've actually had garlic bread with enough garlic. Is that hers, too?"

One corner of his mouth went up. "No, you can blame me for that."

"Ah. A fellow garlic lover."

He nodded. "In my view, many foods are improved by a suitable application of garlic. Usually I'd tone it down for a guest, but your mom said you loved it."

Ashley drew back, startled. "You talked to my mother about my taste in food?"

He shrugged. "Of course. So besides the basics, there are bagels and cream cheese—" he gave her a smile "—peanut butter, green tea and a few other things. The purpose here is to keep you safe, not miserable." He paused, gave her a sideways look. "She did mention something about you using the garlic as an excuse to keep from kissing boys in high school, though."

Ashley felt her cheeks heat. Her mother had told him about that long-ago discussion they'd had? But she lifted her chin and shrugged in turn. "If they didn't want to kiss me badly enough to overlook the garlic, then I didn't want to be kissing them."

"Sounds like a good operational plan," he said, as if they were discussing the weather. "At least, until you run into a garlic lover."

*Like you?*

Had he done that intentionally? Made such a comment after acknowledging he was just that? Because that would imply—

She broke off her own ridiculous train of thought. What was wrong with her? She'd met this man mere hours ago. There was no way her mind should be careening off in *that* direction. She'd spent a great deal of time and energy fighting stereotypes, and she wasn't about to become one—the helpless female who falls for her bodyguard.

*Bodyguard.* What a ridiculous word, as if a person's

body was all that mattered. But somehow protector seemed...too intimate. Or too close to another kind of protection that only came up during preludes to the kind of encounter she had been wary of ever since that flirt Aiden Schmidt had proven himself the worst kind of liar.

This man would not lie. She wasn't sure why she was so certain, but she was. He might dissemble or postpone—like not telling her until they were here that there was no internet—or he might not answer at all, but if he did answer, it would be the truth. There would be no little fibs, no outright lies, no sweet nothings coming from this man. And no false flattery.

Again, she caught herself reaching for her phone. She stopped the motion with no small amount of irritation. She should have done what had occurred to her on the way to the library and run a check on Ty Colton. She'd done so on his agency, Elite Security, the moment her father had told her they'd called in the local firm. But the only person profiled on their website was the founder, Eric King, a retired Marine and full colonel with an almost staggering résumé. Which was only to be expected, she supposed.

So now all she knew was he was a partner in a private and well-respected security company—which, if it had passed her father's vetting, was no doubt top-notch, despite the troubles his family's business was having—and was distantly related to the former president. She stifled a grimace at the connection. Her parents would have had the Secret Service looking after her if they could have. For all she knew, Dad had gotten the recommendation from Joe Colton personally. She should call Dad and—

Yet again, she found herself reaching for a phone that wasn't working. Her jaw tightened.

"Dependency is a tough thing to shake," Ty said, his tone neutral.

She started to give him a glare, but it wouldn't form. Because she was starting to realize there was more than a little truth to his assessment. She enjoyed and depended on devices and the internet to stay in touch, and more importantly for her work to get out the word. She had built a large platform over the past five years, ever since she had sat down with her father and told him what she wanted to do.

But she didn't like that she had apparently become the stereotype of her generation, someone incapable of surviving without those admittedly multiple-times-removed connections. The majority of them people she didn't personally know and likely never would.

She'd never kidded herself about that. At least she thought she hadn't. But she also hadn't really realized until now just how much those distant connections, many of them hiding behind screen names they thought cute or cutting-edge, had filled her life. How often they had crowded out other things, how often she had chosen composing an important—or so she thought—post over other things she could be doing. Things involving actual human contact.

And she had to admit, she didn't like the thought.

"You really don't like social media, do you?" she asked him, even though he'd already made his feelings quite clear.

"I don't like that it allows people to hide who and what they are, which gives them the comfort of anonymity as much as wearing a mask while rioting in the streets and beating up people you disagree with, or robbing a bank."

Since she'd just been thinking something quite similar, she couldn't argue with that. "But you use the internet," she said instead.

"It's a useful, powerful tool, with proper precautions. But it's only that, a tool. Just like a vehicle or weapon." He leaned back in his chair. "Which do you think is more effective, your online interactions or the meeting you had at the library last night?"

Had it only been last night? It felt longer. Probably because her entire life had been upended by this man. But she had to admit, he'd asked an important question. "They're both important. The internet gives me a much broader reach, but the personal interaction is crucial. It makes people feel personally involved, makes them feel like they themselves can actually do something."

"What's your measure of success?"

Her brow furrowed. "Action taken?"

"Does that mean the compromise you mentioned or protests organized?"

He was making her think about things she hadn't in a while. And she found, to her surprise, she liked it. "Protests have their place. Sometimes they are the only thing that will catch the attention of those ignoring the problem. But those assaults you mentioned do not. We gain nothing by resorting to violence, except turning many who might support an acceptable compromise against us."

"What about those who find no compromise acceptable? The ones who do that assaulting?"

"Those people," she said flatly, "are living in a fantasy. And I suspect many of those who turn to violence do so because that's what they wanted to do all along."

"Well, well. Reality." His brows had risen in surprise. She counted that as a win, since he'd kept his expression so detached throughout this conversation, as if he were merely curious.

*And why would he be anything more than that? He's just trying to pass the time. This is a job to him, nothing more. You're a job to him, nothing more.*

She didn't like the fact that she had to continually remind herself of that. It made her voice a little sharp as she retorted to his reality crack.

"I do live there."

"Apparently. More than I expected." He held up a hand before she could speak. "Yes, I admit, another assumption. Don't shoot me."

Suddenly she found herself fighting a smile. Her oddly tangled reaction to him aside, she had quite enjoyed this conversation. It was always good to have to state her beliefs, if only because it kept them clear in her own mind. It was too easy to slide into the surface stuff, thinking that making a post made a difference. It might lead to that, but in itself it meant nothing without that action taken.

Later, after they'd cleaned up, she walked over to peruse the large bookcase she'd seen. She saw on a lower shelf the wizard books they'd talked about earlier and looked over her shoulder at him. "Yours?"

"Started out as mine, but all of us read them." His mouth quirked. "My mother had quite the battle to ration them out when the triplets all wanted to read them at once."

She laughed. "How did she resolve it?"

He rolled his eyes. "She made me choose. Since they were mine first."

"Oh, nice dodge!" She had the thought that she would probably quite like his mother.

"She thought so. I wasn't so happy about it."

"So what did you do?"

"I wanted to let them fight it out, but that didn't go over well with Mom. Then I thought Bridgette because she was the fastest reader so the others would get them sooner, but the guys didn't like that. So I went with a double coin flip."

"Sounds fair. Who won?"

"Bridgette."

She laughed. "So you got your second idea anyway."

"Much to her glee."

Still smiling, she turned back to the bookcase, scanning the shelves. Everything from nonfiction on one to a wide expanse of novels on the other. She saw a couple of titles that appeared to be Kansas history, but also a novel she'd been meaning to read for ages.

"No checkout required," he said from close behind her. She imagined she could feel his breath against the nape of her neck and had to suppress a shiver of response.

"Thank you," she said, hating that she sounded a bit unsteady. "I'd like something to read tonight."

She didn't hear him move, but when he spoke again, it seemed he'd backed up a step or two. And it was in that level, professional voice.

"When you go up, don't close the door."

"That seems…counterproductive."

He shook his head. "I told you, they'll have to get past me. And I need to hear, just in case somebody decides to try and scale that outside wall to your window."

She blinked. "That wall is straight up-and-down."

"Doesn't mean it can't be done. Or that a drone couldn't blast out a window and get in."

She gaped at him. "A drone? Really, Mr. Colton, don't you think that's—"

"A possibility. A distant one, admittedly, but we didn't build our reputation on overlooking even distant possibilities."

She stopped her retort before it was spoken. She'd agreed to this for her parents' sake, and she would gain nothing by arguing every little point. So she merely said, "Fine," and grabbed up the novel, thinking she would have trouble focusing on history at the moment. Then, too sweetly, she asked, "Do I have your permission to go upstairs?"

For an instant, he looked weary, and she regretted the jab. "Good night, Ms. Hart."

She was five steps up when she looked back at him. "And when do you sleep, Mr. Colton?"

"Not your problem."

"It is if you're too tired to react."

He crossed his arms and leaned one shoulder against the stairway wall, looking up at her. He was backlit by the light from the great room, and the near silhouette just emphasized how tall and broad shouldered he was. The man truly was built. She could only faintly see his face when he answered her. It didn't matter—she remembered all too well exactly what he looked like with that chiseled jaw and those blue eyes.

"I've done this job for a decade, Ms. Hart. I haven't lost anyone yet, and I don't intend to start with you. Go to bed. And keep that door open."

It was a measure of her state of mind that the thing that irritated her was that continuing *Ms. Hart.*

# Chapter 13

He'd expected her to be restless, most people were the first night in a strange place. He hadn't expected her to be up pacing the floor quite this much. She had at least done as he'd asked and left the door at the top of the stairs open. He appreciated that. But it didn't answer the question of why she was still awake at nearly 2:00 a.m.

Maybe that was her normal schedule. Maybe she was always up until the wee hours. If so, she'd probably laughed to herself when he'd told her to go to bed before eleven o'clock.

Or maybe she was still missing her phone. Maybe she really was an addict.

*Maybe she's missing something else... Someone else.*

And that was enough maybes. He got up out of the chair, an old not-too-comfortable recliner he'd pulled up close to the door of the downstairs bedroom—close so he could hear, and not-too-comfortable so he wouldn't sleep too soundly to wake up at the slightest noise—and stepped out into the dark hallway. He slid the Dan Wesson TCP he'd had on the small table beside the chair into the clip-on holster on his belt. The maker of the tactical compact pistol was a subsidiary of a Kansas City company, and he liked to keep his business local when he could. Besides, even though the 1911 model handgun had its detractors, he liked the idea of the care that went into making only a thousand or so a year.

He grimaced inwardly at the feeble trick of thinking about his everyday carry weapon in an effort not to think about what had been on his mind. Which pretty well exemplified the merry-go-round his brain seemed to be on. He made himself focus. There hadn't been anything in the file Eric had given them about a current boyfriend. A brief mention of an ex, a professor at some upscale northeast school, including the information that the breakup had apparently been mutual when the man had relocated to take a position at an even more upscale European school.

He remembered his first reaction upon reading that had been steeped in those assumptions he was trying to shake. Of course she'd dated someone like that. He'd studied the photograph of the man more out of curiosity than anything. He looked younger than he was—nearly two decades older than Ashley—with curly hair and big-rimmed glasses. He had that look Ty had always associated with the type, almost soft features and that air of superiority that seemed inbred. Assumptions again.

His second reaction—which should have been the first—was to check that they'd confirmed the man was where he said he was, and had been in the nearly a year since the split. Not that things couldn't easily be arranged from halfway around the globe, but there were no signs. There had been a few contacts between them at first, but that had faded away after about three months. And the thorough report indicated the man was now semi-attached to some distant connection to a royal family from somewhere.

But his reaction now, upon remembering that file, was different. Now he found it somehow significant that she'd chosen to stay here rather than follow the guy. He wondered if it was a sign of her love for her home or not enough love for the man.

His second thought, as he stood there listening to her moving around, was to wonder how on earth she'd managed to stay, if the Elite report was accurate—and they were almost never wrong—unattached for nearly a year. She was smart, beautiful, rich and... He fought against letting the word sound even in his mind, but it was already there. Again. Passionate.

He had about as much luck as he'd had the first time it had popped, utterly unwelcome, into his head stopping himself from wondering if that passion for her causes spilled over into her personal life.

Into her sex life. Because, surely, she had one.

He heard the creak of the third step. The one that had never been fixed, because he'd insisted it remain as noisy as possible. The family knew to avoid it if they wanted stealth, but for his purposes, it served as a makeshift alarm. His father had grumbled, but then he'd never liked the idea of using the place as a safe house, anyway. His mother had told Ty to ignore him, that the real problem was still that Ty had chosen not to go into the family business. Fitzpatrick Colton had been stunned that none of his children had made the choice he'd assumed they all would. And, of course, it never occurred to him that the reason why was his own lack of interest in them in any other way.

He dragged his mind off that well-worn path. He waited, not wanting to startle her while she was negotiating the stairs in the dark. But when she took the last step, he spoke.

"Need something, Ms. Hart?"

He heard her smothered gasp, saw her shadow spin around toward him.

"God, you startled me!"

"Why I waited until you were off the steps," he pointed out.

"Oh." He heard her take a deep breath, as if to regain what he'd startled out of her. "Thank you. I think."

He reached for the switch beside his door and flipped it. Light flooded the hallway. She squinted at the sudden flare. And then her eyes widened again, and she was staring at him so stunned that he looked at himself, wondering if he'd inadvertently grabbed a guest's left-behind T-shirt with a rude graphic without realizing it, something that might offend her. But it was, as he'd thought, his old University of Kansas shirt with the bright blue Jayhawk character on it. It was a bit small after years of washing, but there was nothing on it to make her stare like that.

*Maybe it's too flyover for her. If it were Yale or Harvard, she'd be smiling, not gaping at me.*

He, on the other hand, was having to fight gaping at her. He was sure the rather simple knit pajamas she had on weren't intended to be sexy, but on her long almost lanky, yet entirely female shape, they were. The soft cloth flowed over her, especially the soft curves of her breasts, in a way that made his fingers itch oddly.

"Did you need something?" he repeated, his voice rather harsh because he was fighting an inner battle he was quite rusty at.

"I… No," she said, dragging her gaze away from his shirt. "I just…couldn't sleep."

"Strange place."

"No, it's not that, I'm used to that, I just… I couldn't…"

"Couldn't find the off switch?" he suggested.

Her mouth shifted into a small smile. "Exactly that," she said, although something in her voice suggested to him that she meant it in a different way than he was thinking.

"I've always wondered if you turn off that switch, who turns it back on again?"

The smile widened. Damn, he liked that smile. "I've always assumed it's on a timer, and will come back on in the morning in time to start thinking about whatever it is again."

"Sort of an automated Scarlett O'Hara approach?"

The smile became a laugh. An appreciative laugh that warmed him far more than it should have. "I wouldn't have thought that was on your reading list."

"More that it was my grandmother's movie. She was born on the day it came out, so it was a big deal to her. She and my mom watch it on her birthday every year."

"That's a lovely tradition."

"Better than Oz. I can only handle so much 'If I Only Had a Brain.'" He got the laugh again. And the same burst of warmth. He put on his best glum face. "Easy for you to laugh. You didn't have your uncle whistling that at you as a kid, any time he thought you were doing something dumb."

"Actually, that sounds like a rather sweet way of guiding you."

He couldn't hang on to the glum, and his own smile broke through. "It was, in retrospect. At least he cared." He winced inwardly. He hadn't meant to let that out. So he quickly asked, "What do you usually do when this happens?" He wondered if she relied on medication, smoked pot or what.

"What I was about to do. Find a book to read until I can fall asleep."

Well, that was about as benign as it gets. "I thought you had one."

"I did, but it was too engrossing."

"So you need something boring?"

"No, because then I'll just sit there, thinking how boring this is and not get any closer to sleeping. It's better if it's something that hooks me just enough so I fall asleep almost without realizing it. Best is something I'm familiar with but still like enough to get into, just enough to turn the rest of the brain off." She grimaced. "Sorry, more than you asked. I'm tired. And frustrated."

Quickly deciding that thinking about her and frustration was something best to avoid, Ty shoved off from the doorjamb and walked into the great room and over to the bookshelves. He bent down, grabbed a hardcover volume and held it out to her. She immediately recognized the colorful dust jacket of the first book in the wizard series they'd talked about, and the grin she gave him was like a punch to the gut. And all he could think was that it was a good thing he'd kept his jeans on instead of pulling on the pajama bottoms that were much more comfortable, but much less able to hide what was currently happening south of his beltline.

"Perfect," she said as she reached out and took the book from him. He fought the urge to hang on to it—to make her ask or pull, anything to draw out the moment. He wanted more than anything to slide his hand forward just enough to brush her fingers with his, but fought down that very unprofessional urge, too.

Book in hand, she headed for the couch. She turned on the light at the end closest to the fireplace and sat. And he blurted out, "You're not going back to bed to read?"

She shook her head without looking at him, already seated and opening the cover of the tale. "If I do that, my brain knows what I'm trying to do and fights back." There was such a rueful note in her voice the corners of his mouth twitched. But at the same time, he smothered a sigh, because now there would be no sleep at all for him.

As if he could have anyway, after the sight of her in those pajamas that weren't in the least sexy.

Not in the least.

## Chapter 14

Ashley stared down at the first inside page of the book, at the name written there in a bold yet childlike hand. The combination didn't surprise her in the least. Fighting the image of the man this child had become standing there in the sudden flare of light, the T-shirt with that silly bird caricature on it tight across his chest and short enough to give her a peek at an impressive set of abs, she tried to keep her voice even.

"How old were you when this came out?" she asked, still not looking at him.

"Exactly eleven," he answered.

She smiled, the same age as the intrepid hero. She turned to the title page just as he turned to walk away, and instinctively she looked up. Immediately her gaze fastened on the back pockets of his jeans. She didn't think she'd ever seen a pair of jeans filled out better, front and back.

Heat shot through her, and her eyes widened as she forced her gaze back to the title page. What was wrong with her? She did not—ever—react to a man like this, especially a man she'd just met less than twelve hours ago. She didn't understand, and so instead of reading as she'd planned, her sometimes-riotous brain tackled the question.

It wasn't just that he was good-looking in a very masculine way, but he was bigger, more confident, to the edge of swagger. She supposed it took a very confident man to do the kind of work he did, but it was more than just that.

She heard him moving around in the kitchen and wondered what he was doing. Surely not coffee this late? He didn't seem the sort who would go for decaf. Then again, if he planned on staying awake all night, on guard, maybe caffeine was the method. But he had to sleep sometime, didn't he? Had she awakened him, or had he been still awake when she'd come downstairs?

Maybe the key was that he was so different from the men she was used to. He dared to order her around—which was, she had to admit, his job just now—when most men who knew who she was tended to defer to her, sometimes to the point of obsequiousness. Ty Colton did not. Nor could she imagine him acting in any sort of sycophantic way. She would be willing to bet he would stand up to her father in a way no one, even Simon—or maybe especially Simon—ever had.

No, Simon Karlan had turned into that sycophant, kowtowing to her father in a way that had made Andrew Hart's lip curl and her own stomach churn. In fact, if anything, it had been that memory that had been the main factor when she'd decided she was much better off without him when he left for Europe.

No, she couldn't see this man fawning over her father or anyone else. Not even the former president he was distantly related to.

She heard footsteps coming back and hastily turned a page so that at least she was looking at text and not the title page she'd never gotten past. He stopped in front of her, and she tried to mentally brace herself to look up, chanting the order not to end up gaping at that flat, toned stomach of his, or the breadth of his chest and shoulders.

When she did look up, her gaze snagged instead on what he was holding out to her. A steaming mug. Her brow furrowed. Why would you offer coffee to someone already having trouble sleeping?

"Hot chocolate," he said.

She stared at the mug for a moment, then at the strong, steady hand that held it. Managed not to let her gaze slide from there up that powerfully muscled arm. She gave herself a mental shake.

"Just how long did you and my mother talk?" she asked.

"Actually, it was your father who suggested we have this on hand in case you couldn't sleep."

She took the mug, for some reason feeling off balance by this. "I suppose you think that's silly, that my father would know that."

"Silly? Hardly. Enviable, maybe."

She took a sip and found the brew rich and sweet and soothing. And familiar. They hadn't just gotten hot chocolate—they'd gotten her favorite. He'd also made it with milk, not water, just as she liked it.

She studied him for a moment as he stood there, towering over her as she sat with her legs curled up under her. "I gather your father wouldn't be able to match that feat?"

He let out the barest breath of a chuckle. "I doubt my father could tell you what color my eyes are."

"That's hard to believe. They're rather striking."

He drew back slightly, as if she'd surprised him. She gave an exaggerated roll of her own eyes. "Oh, please. I'm sure you've had woman admire your eyes—" *among other things* "—before."

He seemed to recover quickly, and the corners of his mouth twitched. "Last client who did was old enough to be my grandmother."

She arched a brow at him. "Ageist, are you?"

"No. I don't hold yours against you."

What was that supposed to mean? Was that what all the ordering around was? He thought her a child? He couldn't possibly be that much older than she was. If her phone were working, she could find out in a moment. But it wasn't, so she had to guess, and put him at thirty to thirty-five until she could confirm. *If I ever see civilization again.*

"How gracious of you," she said, rather sourly.

"She, on the other hand, was vetting me like a stud horse, for her granddaughter."

She blinked. She felt the corners of her own mouth twitching. And then she couldn't stop it. She let out a laugh. "Well, at least she has good taste." He blinked in turn. Went very still. She felt the pressure to say something else, to make what she'd said less of a blatant compliment. Perversely, the words that came out only made it worse. "Assuming she was going for good looks and a striking eye color."

His expression didn't change. He didn't move. He stood there, towering. And finally he said, his voice oddly quiet, "What makes you think it wasn't brainpower she was after?"

She felt herself flush. But she held her head up as she answered, purposefully making it not a question, "Then she would have hit the jackpot on all counts, wouldn't she."

For a moment, he didn't react. But then a slow smile curved his mouth—that mouth—and she saw a gleam come into his eyes that made her oddly twitchy. "Your professor," he said with slow emphasis, "was a fool."

She should have been stunned that he knew about Simon at all.

Instead, she was sitting here with alternating chills and heat rippling through her as she watched him walk away.

This was crazy. It was crazy and it had to stop. Right now. The loaded conversations, the utterly unveiled compliments, the whole back-and-forth thing had to stop.

Ty drummed his fingers on the kitchen counter as he waited for the coffee machine to kick out enough to even half fill his mug. He'd tasted the hot chocolate and immediately rejected it. The soporific effect would likely do what he'd hoped it would for her, put him to sleep. But for now, if she was awake, he was awake.

But when they were both awake, it seemed they couldn't stop veering into those byways he didn't want—couldn't want—to go down.

Even waiting for the coffee was too much. He walked out of the kitchen and over to the coat rack by the door and grabbed his heavier jacket and his keys. "Going out for a quick recon," he said when he saw her look at him, even as he wondered why he felt compelled to explain when he was simply doing his job. As she no doubt knew, having grown up with security around her.

He didn't wait for her to respond but pulled the door open. Caught the sturdy stock of the Mossberg shotgun she'd handled with familiarity out of the corner of his eye. She was a bundle of contradictions, was Ashley Hart.

He stepped outside before he could change his mind. The cold air would do him good, chase the tiredness. Because he was tired, much more tired than he should have been.

*Keeping up with her wearing you down, Colton?*

He nearly laughed at his own thoughts. He took in a deep breath, watched his breath form a cloud in the light through the window from inside. If it wasn't freezing tonight, it was close.

He didn't really need to do this. All the alarms and cameras were functioning fine and would warn him if anything outside the house turned up. Outside the immediate perimeter, he'd check with the drone tomorrow. What he needed was to be a little farther from her, for a few minutes at least, and this was the only way he could do it and not slack on his job.

*Then she would have hit the jackpot on all counts...*

He felt an odd thump in his chest he would have called his heart skipping a beat if it weren't so ridiculous. He had to get his mind off this path before it became a rut he had to fight his way out of.

*So put it to work on the two dead bodies from the warehouse.*

The mystery of who they were had been solved fairly

quickly, thanks to his brother Brooks. Sadly, the female had been identified as Olivia Harrison, the mother of Brooks's now-fiancée, Gwen, and the male Fenton Crane, a PI her grandmother had hired to try to find Gwen's mother who had vanished years ago. But who the killer was, or even if it was the same person—although the methodology certainly suggested it was—remained a mystery.

He'd been hoping to dig into the case, to get to the bottom of what was turning into a scandal for Colton Construction, but instead here he was, making freaking hot chocolate for a spoiled rich kid.

Even as he thought it, his sense of fairness kicked in. She was rich, all right, beyond most people's wildest imaginings. But to his own surprise, she wasn't spoiled.

*And she's not a kid.*

Oh, yeah, don't forget that one. She was not a kid, no matter that it would be easier for him if he could think of her that way. But no, Ashley Hart was all woman. Slender curves, luscious mouth, glossy dark hair, bottomless brown eyes—yes, every inch female.

And a few male inches of his liked every bit of her. Too much.

It took two rounds of the house before the chill of the air was able to take the edge off the heat from being in the same room with her. When he finally went back, he eased the door open as quietly as he could and locked it before he even turned around.

Apparently, the combination of chocolate and book had worked. She was still on the couch but half lying down now, her head on the cushioned arm, clearly asleep. The book, while still in her hands, had fallen shut.

He stood there for a moment, simply looking at her

while silently delivering a barn burner of a lecture to himself. To stop noticing how lovely she was, to stop enjoying their bantering conversations so much, to stop wondering what it would be like to stop one of those conversations with a kiss. The Colton family might be a big deal in Braxville, in Kansas, in mid-America for that matter, but they were nowhere near the thin-air territory of the Harts of Westport. She wasn't just out of his league; she was another game altogether.

Not to mention forbidden.

She stirred slightly, stretching out more comfortably but not waking. Ty sucked in a deep breath, then walked over to his mother's favorite chair, where there was a thick knitted throw over the back. He brought it and gently spread it over Ashley. And when she smiled slightly in her sleep, released the book and snuggled into the soft wool, he took a hasty step back as an unfamiliar sensation of longing rocketed through him.

He stared a moment longer, then reached down and took the book before it fell to the floor and woke her. He turned out the light above her and walked back to his mother's chair, where there was a small lamp she could angle onto a book or the frequent needlework projects she took on. Like the throw he'd just tucked around Ashley.

He sat down, took a last look at the woman across the room, then turned on the reading light and opened the book himself. He wouldn't look at her that way again, he vowed. This woman was his to protect, but nothing more.

# *Chapter 15*

Ashley opened her eyes slowly, vaguely aware she was not in a bed. With her travels, she was used to not waking up in her own bed—sometimes she hardly remembered which place she technically called home—but she did usually make it to a bed. She blinked blurry eyes, feeling as if she'd slept more soundly than she had in weeks. Which seemed strange, since she remembered pacing the floor into the wee hours.

And then her gaze focused on the reason for her restlessness last night. The man who had plunged her into a situation she'd never found herself in before. Not being under threat. That happened occasionally. But she'd never found herself walking the floor, unable to sleep because she couldn't get a man out of her mind. Worse, a man she'd just met.

He sat in the big chair across the room, a reading lamp

aimed at the book on his lap, the only light in the room. The book she'd been reading last night, the loved but familiar story just enough to distract her whirling mind and allow her to sleep. Why he had it now, she had no idea. Perhaps he'd meant to stay awake reading. If so, it hadn't worked, because his eyes were closed and his head lolled back against the chair.

Which gave her far too much of a chance to study the strong, corded muscles of his neck and the long, powerful length of his legs, stretched out and crossed at the ankles some distance from the chair itself.

It was a very pleasant sight. And she was glad he'd at least gotten some sleep.

*Don't want your bodyguard too tired to function.*

That strange jolt of heat shot through her again as she realized other ways those words could be interpreted. Thank goodness she'd only thought them, not spoken them.

She made a note of how warm and comfy she was beneath this soft thick throw. Her pulse skipped a beat as she remembered she'd seen it before, folded across the very chair he was in now. Had she truly slept through him tucking it around her? That was hardly part of his bodyguard duties, to see to not only her safety but her comfort. So had he done it simply because beneath the tough, competent exterior he was a nice guy? Because this was, despite the use he was putting it to now, a family place? Or because—

She cut off her own thoughts before they could careen into silly territory. Telling herself not to be stupid, she raised up on one elbow to look out the window. The instant she moved, his head came up. She didn't think she'd made any sound at all, and yet he was suddenly as awake as if she'd shouted.

"Morning," he said.

Okay, that voice, that low, deep rumble shouldn't be allowed first thing in the morning. She wasn't awake enough to deal with it.

"Is it?" she muttered, glancing at the still dark windows.

To her annoyance, when she looked back, he was grinning. "Not a morning person? Although I'll grant you it is early."

"Define early."

He glanced at the windows she'd just looked at. "I'd say we're well into astronomical twilight, headed for nautical twilight."

Okay, now she was really annoyed. She sat up. "Translation, please?"

"Nautical twilight is when the center of the sun is between six and twelve degrees below the horizon and—"

She put a hand to her forehead, rubbed. "Stop. Please stop."

He relented. "I'm guessing it's between 5:30 and 6:00 a.m. Past time to get up and get to work around here."

Her first thought was to find her phone and confirm the actual time, her second was to wonder if the phone had enough charge left to keep time, since it had no network to read it from, and her third thought was a sneaky little wish that he be way wrong.

"Don't trust me?" he asked lightly.

She disentangled herself from the throw and stood up, stretching. "Did no one ever tell you it's not nice to poke at a non-morning person at…whatever hour this is?"

"Must have missed that lesson."

"We'll see how you like it when I wake you up at midnight."

Something flickered in his eyes, but he only said, "You already did."

He had a point there. But she was cranky enough not to concede it just yet. She walked over to the kitchen to where she could see the clock on the oven. And grimaced.

"How close was I?"

"Congratulations, Mister Astronomer, it's 5:52."

"Good to know."

He glanced back at the window again. "Get dressed and put your jacket back on."

She blinked. "What?"

"We're going outside."

"What?"

"Not far," he said. "Just over there."

He gestured rather vaguely toward the waterside of the house. "Why?"

"I just want to show you something."

What was this? Some kind of escape hatch or something he wanted her to know about? Someplace he wanted her to run to if something happened? With a smothered sigh and a yawn, she went back upstairs and dressed, sat and pulled her ankle boots back on, wishing she hadn't vowed last night to not be a hindrance when the man was only trying to do the job he'd been hired to do.

She went back down to find him standing there, holding out her jacket for her to slip on. "Thanks," she muttered. *For that, at least.*

She'd known it would be cold, but it was nothing she wasn't used to this time of year. Before she'd packed for this trip, she'd compared the temperature averages of her destination with her home ground, and somewhat to her surprise, they were rather similar. Wichita might have Westport beat on the record high and low ends by over ten degrees, but the average lows were within a couple of degrees.

But stepping out into the night—or early morning, apparently—chill accomplished one thing. Ten feet out, she was thoroughly awake. She would have grumbled that this better be worth it if it hadn't felt rather good. She could see the faint glint of light reflecting off the lake. She could see stars, lots of them, but also dark patches of cloud that masked them. There was just enough light to see a wide expanse of water, but without a trace of a breeze only the faintest of ripples. No city lights reflected here, and even the other buildings she could see farther south were still dark in this…astronomical twilight. She fought a smile as she drew in a deep breath of the chilly air.

"What?" he asked, and she realized she'd let out a "Hmm."

"Just thinking how, even at the same time of day—" she shot him a glance "—or night, and at the same temperature, places can smell and feel so different."

"Missing your salt air?"

"More noticing than missing," she said. "But this feels more like home than, say, Santiago's salt air, so it's not that, per se."

"How about the Amazon?"

She wasn't surprised. She already knew he—or Elite—had done their homework. His knowing about Simon had proved that. "Whole different kind of smell and feel."

They walked a little farther, then he stopped. "This'll do. Have a seat."

She wondered if this was some sort of test. Did he think her too finicky to sit on the ground? Hadn't his homework on her time in the Amazon included that she'd lived in a native hut for nearly six months?

She quickly sat to prove her point. Fortunately, the ground was dry. He dropped down beside her. And said…nothing. And she was wondering again what this was all about, this sitting here in the dark, waiting for… what?

She did noticed the sky seemed to be getting lighter. *When the center of the sun is between six and twelve degrees below the horizon…*

Maybe she should be wondering about where his job as a security expert took him instead of assuming she was the more well traveled one. She had made some assumptions of her own. Again.

"Here we go," he murmured.

She glanced at him to see what he was looking at, but he seemed to be simply staring out toward the lake. Or toward the other side of the lake. The east side, unless she'd gotten her directions seriously turned around. Which told her, belatedly, what to look for. As she thought it, she saw it, the slight demarcation between land and sky. He was staring out toward the horizon, and—

East. The faint line slowly became more definite. And then she saw the first distant change in color, from black to near black, then even lighter. The world seemed impossibly silent, as if everyone and everything was holding its breath, waiting.

And then the sky was a deep dark blue. Almost the color of his eyes. She suppressed an unwelcome imagining of what his reaction would be if she said that, that his eyes were the color of the sky just before sunrise.

The blue got lighter, the clouds more visible. "Welcome to dawn," he said, his voice so soft it seemed part of the quiet around them. The way he said it, with quiet appreciation, made the simple words sound almost... poetic. And that was something she never would have expected. "And we're not alone," he added.

She felt a jolt over his words. And then she felt an entirely different kind of jolt over the warm touch of his hand to her face as he gently turned her head toward the trees to their left.

"Down low," he whispered.

She looked and saw movement. A low slinking trot and the flick of a thick bushy tail as the creature disappeared into the trees.

"A fox?" she asked.

"Yes. An armadillo would be shinier."

He'd said it in a completely neutral tone of helpful instruction. But she was learning about him already, and knew he was teasing her. "And have a skinnier tail," she said seriously.

She saw his grin even in the faint light and felt crazily as if she'd won some prize.

*Your professor was a fool...*

His words, practically a declaration, echoed in her mind. *Stop. Don't be a fool yourself. Just enjoy the thought of Simon's face at being called a fool.*

And then everything changed again. The undersides of the clouds seemed to catch and reflect the growing light. Suddenly there was color, orange, yellow, pink, painting the clouds with the surest of hands. The horizon became a physical thing, accented by the silhouettes of trees made ebony by the brightness behind them. And then, between two of the tallest trees, the edge of the sun cleared the horizon and light arrowed across the lake, streaking it with fire.

She'd seen sunrises around the world, in some beautiful places, but somehow none had moved her more than this welcome to morning in a place she'd never thought to be. She felt a burst of understanding as sudden as that rush of light: this was what they meant by heartland.

*Past time to get up and get to work around here.*

He hadn't been teasing about that. This was the world he'd grown up in, where by dawn many had already been long at work.

And that he had wanted her to see this meant...she wasn't sure what.

"Somebody else late getting home for the day," he said, pointing now that it was light enough to see. Not allowing herself to admit she preferred the touch of his hand on her cheek, she looked. It took her a moment, so perfectly matched was the creature to the surroundings, but again it was the movement that let her focus in time to see a large bird winging silently into the trees as if that arrow of sunlight were its only predator.

"Owl?" she asked, having just gotten a glimpse of its head.

"Great horned one," he said. "There's a pair that's nested in those trees for at least three years."

"Shades of that wizard book again."

She got the grin again. And felt that same rush of pleasure that made her beyond nervous. This was ridiculous. She was here because she had work to do, work that had indirectly brought this man into her life. And when it was done, when the situation was resolved, he would be out of her life again. So becoming infatuated with the man's grin—never mind his touch—was a fool's errand. That she would never do.

# Chapter 16

Ashley Hart was a puzzlement. Or a wonder, Ty wasn't sure which. He never would have expected a woman with her background would be so taken with a simple Kansas sunrise. In fact, he'd brought her out here as much to show himself that she wouldn't be, that she wouldn't react with the wonder he always felt, as to show it to her.

She'd reacted with all the appreciation he could have wished.

*Why the hell does it matter to you? She's a client. And she'll be back on her unending world tour as soon as this threat is resolved.*

And yet, from that sound of excitement she'd made when she'd spotted the fox, the smile when she'd seen the owl, you'd think she'd never before strayed out of her own backyard. How did a woman like her, who had lived a life of old-money-style wealth, hang on to such a simple thing?

"Can we look around later?" She sounded like a little girl, excited about a wonderful new place. He hadn't expected that, either. "I mean," she added, with a touch of mockery back in her voice, "if I'm allowed outside in the daylight."

"Not alone," he said, rather gruffly at her tone.

"I assumed." The mockery was still there but vanished when she went on. "Besides, who else will show me everything, good and bad?"

"Good and bad?"

"You know, good like the fox and the owl, and bad like... Do you have snakes?"

His brow furrowed. "Of course we do." When she shuddered, he added, "Only five of the almost forty kinds are venomous. And nobody's died from a snakebite here in about half a century."

She gave him a wry smile, which he could see clearly now that there was enough light. "Thanks for the facts, but it's not my logic that reacts to them."

"Ah. Lizard brain, huh?"

"Did you have to use another reptile analogy?" she asked sourly.

He laughed. She managed a more genuine smile, but he could tell she was serious. And it would probably be wise to know more. So he asked, "How do you react? Freeze or run?"

"Both, in that order. The length of the freeze depends on how close and how big."

He wondered if she'd had to answer that before, then remembered where she'd been. "Let me guess, your least favorite part of your sojourn in the Amazon?"

The shudder was more pronounced. "Oh, yes. Do you know they have ten varieties of coral snakes alone?"

"What about the famous anaconda?"

"Oddly, they didn't bother me. When faced with that size of snake, my brain just shuts down and refuses to admit it's real."

He laughed again, admiring her honesty and that despite her fears she'd gone ahead with her venture. "Don't worry. We've mostly got prairie ringnecks, which are small, and very shy. The bluish ones are even kind of pretty. We had a big gopher snake around, although I haven't seen him in a while. But I think he's still here because the rats and voles haven't gotten out of control."

"Oh, I freely admit they have their purpose. I'm not one of those who wants them killed on sight. They're a crucial part of the system. I just don't ever, ever want to be around them. I can't even go into the reptile section of a zoo."

"Fair enough," he said. Then, not certain why, he added, "For me it's spiders. Hate those suckers."

She looked startled, but then she gave him the broadest smile yet. "How gallant of you to admit that."

Her tone was teasing again, and it made him grin yet again. He thought he'd done more of that this morning with her than he had in a month. She was surprising him, which in turn intrigued him, which in turn—

*No. Not going there. So very not going there.*

They headed back to the cabin, and Ashley went into the kitchen to fix her breakfast. He went back to the comms room—he called it that because it bothered his mother to call it a panic room—and made contact with Mitch.

"How'd the first night with her highness go?"

"Not as bad as I expected," Ty said. *And then some.*

"We'll see how you feel after catering to her for a few days."

Ty knew his buddy was just jabbing at him but felt compelled to correct his assumption. "Not sure that's going to be really necessary. She's actually fairly normal, once you get past the surface."

There was enough of a pause that he knew he'd surprised Mitch. "Whoa. Didn't expect that."

*And I didn't expect a woman who'd go all soft over a fox, an owl and a Kansas sunrise.*

"Neither did I," he said. And changed the subject before he said something stupid. "Anything new?"

"I've been keeping an eye on Sanderson," he said, naming the developer who had the most to lose if Ashley succeeded, and who had blurted out the threats against her. "Nothing unusual. He's not giving up on his project, but he's keeping his head down, too."

"No more threats?"

"No. But a little news on that front. Tech guys found out that several of the social media accounts used were from the same IP and via the same provider."

"So fake?"

"Probably like hundreds of other noisy ones, trying to make the protest against her seem bigger than it is. Or that he has more support than he does. I know social media's useful on occasion, but…"

"The usefulness comes with built-in opportunity for fakery," Ty finished.

"Yeah. You know, if it is Sanderson, I kind of feel for him. He bought that land decades ago, with these plans in mind. But then the government comes in and tells him he can't build, so it's now useless to him."

"While he's still paying taxes on it and has been all

this time. I get it. But she's not the one he should be going after."

"She's the one with the big megaphone, who called attention to it in the first place and got the hold put on his permit."

"It's what she does."

"Well, at least they didn't declare those puddles a navigable waterway," Mitch quipped.

As Ty shut down the connection a moment later, he rubbed at the back of his neck. He'd been having that sensation of being watched for at least thirty seconds.

He spun around. Ashley was there and, judging by her expression, had heard at least some of the conversation. He swiftly ran it back in his head, spared a moment of thanks that she hadn't been there when Mitch called her "her highness." He'd have to remind Mitch she could be within earshot. Of course, Mitch would just tell him to shut the damn door, but he had the feeling that would just rouse her curiosity, and what he was communicating wasn't what he wanted Ashley curious about.

*Put a lid on it, Colton. And nail the sucker down.*

"Your partner doesn't seem to like me much."

"He's never met you."

"That doesn't seem to stop him from having an opinion."

"Does it stop anyone?"

She sighed. "I suppose not. By the way, I did not agree with that previous interpretation of wetlands. Which I've made clear in the past."

"Declaring a mud puddle in someone's backyard a wetland does not make it one?" he quoted.

She drew back slightly. "You really did do your homework. That was a long time ago."

"The more I know, the better I can do my job."

She studied him for a moment. He didn't know what she was thinking. But he supposed a woman who ran in her circles, and who gave testimony in front of government committees, was probably fairly skilled at hiding her thoughts. Her emotions, not so much. Something about what he'd said hadn't pleased her.

But whatever it was, she shook it off and said only, "Can we go outside now?"

He looked at her, considering. Which he knew irked her. The whole permission thing was obviously bothering her. "I was about to do a drone check of the property, but a personal one wouldn't hurt."

"Drone?"

He nodded. We've got a small one, with a good camera. Actually belongs to my Uncle Shep, but he lets us play with it."

"The uncle of the tree planting?"

"Yes. He just moved back to Braxville recently, so he's spent some time here." He looked her up and down. "Got any sturdier shoes?"

She looked down at the ankle boots she'd had on yesterday and had pulled back on this morning because they were handy. "Don't like them?" she asked, that edge of sweetness back in her voice that he was learning didn't bode well.

"Whether I like them isn't the point. Whether you can walk on uneven ground with them and they'll hold up to mud and rocks is. And if you want to risk…whatever those cost doing it."

"They weren't that expensive," she protested.

"Honey, I don't even want to know what you consider expensive. Do you have other shoes or not?"

She didn't say a word, but turned and went back down the hall, her every step declaring she was once more not happy with him. She disappeared up the stairs, and he let out a long audible breath.

He glanced at the weather station on the wall above the radio. Still in the low forties. He walked into the bedroom he was using and picked up the extra magazine for his TCP. He clipped it on his belt and shifted the weapon itself slightly. Tried not to think about needing it, but knew there was no guarantee, even out here. They were isolated, yet not unreachable. Not to someone angry enough.

Back out in the great room, he took his jacket off the rack by the door and pulled it on. After a moment's thought, he grabbed one of the knitted wool hats from the basket below the rack.

And the entire time tried not to think about what had seemed to flash in her eyes when he'd called her *honey*.

# Chapter 17

"Better?" Ashley asked sweetly.

The irritating man glanced down at her hiking boots. If he was surprised by how heavy-duty and well-worn they were, he didn't say so. Which irritated her in turn, because she had a sharp answer about more assumptions ready to fire at him. Her work often required her to walk through wilder places, and she'd learned early on to be always prepared.

"They'll do," he said. Then he held out a heavy knit hat. "Here. This'll help until it warms up more."

She glanced pointedly at his bare head. Tried not to notice the way his hair still managed to look tousled even though it was fairly short. She liked the way it kicked forward, thick and dark. But then she liked a lot about this man. In looks, anyway. Any woman would, she consoled herself.

*Just like any woman's heart would have kicked up the pace if he called her honey?*

He noted her look, reached down to a basket and pulled out another similar hat. "Happy now?"

"No, but that's not your job, is it?" For an instant, the briefest flash of…something flared in those dark blue eyes. The first, totally insane thought that hit her was that he was wishing that it were his job. Making her happy. Rattled at her own reactions more than anything, she looked down at the hat she held. It felt indeed warm. And soft, almost luxurious. "This is luscious. What's it made of?"

"You'd have to ask my mother. She's the knitter."

"Oh? She made this?"

"And that blanket thing."

The throw he'd tucked so carefully around her. She shoved aside the memory and said only, "She does beautiful work."

"She's a beautiful woman. Inside and out."

He said it without the slightest bit of hesitation or male embarrassment, and since there was absolutely no sign he was a mamma's boy, she liked that. A lot. She let that show in her smile. "I hope you tell her that."

"Often. We all do."

They stepped outside. It was still chilly, and she tugged on the hat. So did he, and she noticed he gave it an extra pat when he had it down over the top of his ears. Because his mother had made it? She found that sweet, as well. Mr. Ty Colton—cool, competent, slightly bossy security expert—had a soft spot, after all. That it was for his mother, she found charming.

*If you want to know how a man will treat his wife, watch how he treats his mother.*

The old saying popped into her head out of nowhere. And nearly stunned her. What on earth was she doing thinking about *that?* She scrambled for something else to say, before she let something inescapably stupid out.

"What about your father?"

How quickly the very male shrug came back. "He is who he is."

"And from what you've said, not the warm and fuzzy type," she said, recovered now as they went down the steps of the deck.

He let out a short sharp laugh. "Not unless you've got a great lot or building he wants for sale. He's all business, all the time."

"My father used to be like that."

"Used to? I'd have thought with an empire to run, he still would be."

She gave him a sideways look at his use of the word *empire*, but decided to let it go since he was smiling. Also she quashed the unexpected thought that she would forgive a lot for that smile. She suddenly remembered the conversation with her mother when she'd called to tell her that her father had hired a security firm.

*Eric King is a solid, honest contractor, and he's promised he'll put the man your father asked for on it. Cooperate, Ashley.*

His best man. She glanced up at the man beside her, all too aware of his size and obvious strength. Too aware of the way he moved with that easy grace and power. Too aware of those dark blue eyes framed by thick dark lashes.

*Too aware of how his freaking hair grows.*

Somehow she didn't think that was the kind of cooperation her mother had meant. But then her mother hadn't seen Ty Colton. And Ashley couldn't even imagine a woman who wouldn't be hyperaware of this man.

It was just that she never was. She never reacted this way to a man. She might be intrigued, or curious, even admiring. At least she could learn something from a man—that had been what had lured her into the relationship with Simon—but her on-all-levels awareness and fascination and, she had to admit, physical response had never happened before.

She'd been so lost in her thoughts she hadn't really noticed they'd walked out onto the small dock on the lake. The lake that was much larger than she'd thought, although she'd only glanced at a map since her goal was miles away from here.

"What kind of fish are there?"

He looked a little surprised but answered without comment. "Walleye, few kinds of bass—we usually have luck with whites right out front here—crappie, and catfish, of course." He gave her a sideways look, then. "If you're into bottom-feeders."

"One of the most amazing fishes I've ever seen is a catfish. From Thailand. A glass catfish."

"Okay, you got me."

"It's tiny, two or three inches. And it's completely transparent. All the organs are clustered up near its head, so the entire body is just skeleton-like. It's quite remarkable. And even more interesting, they only settled its true taxonomy fairly recently. They thought it was the same as another larger species—are you laughing at me?"

"No," he said instantly. "Just admiring—okay, maybe envying—your recall."

He said it so easily, with no hint of the jab she often got when people accused her of being a walking encyclopedia of useless trivia. "Sometimes I wish I could shut it off," she answered honestly.

"And the rest of the time?"

"I rely on it."

He nodded as if he'd expected that answer. She looked out at the water again, thinking that this was the easiest exchange she'd ever had about her ability to remember even the most minor facts.

"Lots of boats out there."

"Trout season opened last Sunday. Lot of folks headed toward the seep stream, since they stocked it at the end of last month."

"There's a dam, right? It's not a natural lake?"

"Dam's about five miles down." He nodded, toward the north. "Smoky Hills River comes in right up there."

She glanced in the direction he'd indicated. "Could we walk there? To where the river comes in?"

"It's about a mile and a half, to the start of the delta flats."

"So not that far, then."

He glanced down at her well-worn boots again. "Guess not," he said with a grin.

She smiled back at him. "Then can we?"

"Are you actually asking me permission?"

"I'm asking the man who knows the way," she pointed out.

To her surprise, he laughed. And once more it seemed her every nerve tingled in response. "Good—and practical—point." He seemed thoughtful for a moment. "Let me scout it out first, after the rain we had last week. There's no real trail, and I haven't seen it in a while."

"I don't need a trail. I've hiked in many places without one." She frowned. "I don't have my compass with me, though."

"I have one. But I'm thinking more about any threat."

For a moment, she'd actually forgotten. Why she was here, why she was with this man at all. "You really think…somebody might be out there, lying in wait or something?"

She hated how small her voice sounded. But being so completely out of touch had apparently affected her more than she would have expected. When she went to places where she knew ahead of time there would be no internet or phone communications, she mentally prepared for it. But she hadn't expected that here, so she was having a little trouble adapting.

*You're really addicted to that thing, aren't you?*

Maybe he was more right than she wanted to admit.

"I was thinking more about snakes," Ty answered her, giving her a look too innocent to be true. Quickly her mood shifted and she laughed.

"In that case, have at it."

"I'll be back in under an hour. Lock the door and keep the shotgun handy until I do."

She purposefully fluttered her eyelashes at him. "Oh, dear, how will I know it's you?"

He grinned. Damn him. "You mean besides the wall of windows?"

"I wouldn't want to shoot you by mistake."

He gave her a long look. "I have the feeling if you ever shot someone, it would not be by mistake."

She didn't know why that pleased her. Why she was feeling pleased at all during a conversation about shooting someone. But she was. It unsettled her enough that she questioned just how much she wanted to do this.

"If this is too much trouble—"

"It's fine. I need to do a wider recon, anyway." He walked into the kitchen and grabbed a couple of bottles of drinking water. Then he went to a small cabinet on the other side of the door out onto the deck and opened it. He reached in and pulled out a small loaded backpack, tucked the water into side pockets, and slung it over one shoulder. When he saw her looking at it, he shrugged. "Better to lug it and not need it than the other way around."

She wondered what was in it. First-aid things, she supposed. Survival gear, although why he would need it here, and this close to the cabin…unless he got hurt. A slip and fall was always possible, and if he broke an arm or leg out there, he'd be screwed with no phone service. Of course, the likelihood of big tough Ty Colton needing help was silly, she supposed. But still…

Even as she thought it, he reached back into the cabinet and brought out two hand-sized walkie-talkies. He turned knobs on both, then handed her one.

"It gets a little spotty at the river because of the terrain, but up until then it should be clear."

She let out a relieved sigh. "Good, so you can call for help if you need it."

He looked utterly startled. With a bemused smile he said, "It's for you to call for help if you need it."

She watched him go, feeling a bit bemused herself at the fact that they had each been thinking of the other. Of course, it was his job just now to worry about her.

But that didn't explain why her first reaction had been to worry about him.

# Chapter 18

Upon getting back to the cabin, Ty was surprised to find that she'd set out snacks for them. "How long are you planning on being out there?" he asked, masking his amusement at the array. More water was good, but she'd found his stash of energy bars, grabbed a couple of apples from the bowl on the counter and thrown in a couple of candy bars she must have had herself. She'd also apparently had a small folding backpack in her luggage, because it was also on the counter.

"Better to lug it and not need it, I believe someone said?"

He smiled at that. And noticed yet again he'd done more smiling in the last twenty-four hours—almost—than he had in weeks. There hadn't been much to smile about with all the chaos going on around Colton Construction. Nothing like finding a couple of bodies sealed up in one of your old buildings to put the blight on your outlook.

"Sounds like a smart guy," he said, glad to see that she took it as he'd meant it, jokingly.

"So, we're clear to go?"

He nodded. "Nothing out there but some wildlife. Didn't see a single snake, by the way."

"Thank goodness."

He walked into the kitchen, over to the erasable note board on the fridge. He unclipped the marker and scrawled a note.

"Tree down?" Ashley asked, having followed him in and read past his shoulder.

He nodded as he put the marker back in place after noting the location. "First one of us with the time and energy will cut it up for firewood. Which is good, because we'll need more by next year. If we spend much time up here this winter, we'll go through what we've got."

"Can't you buy more?"

"If we can find some local wood, but out here most people use up their own. The motto is buy it where you burn it. So people don't bring in new invasive species or transport new pests." He gave her a sideways look. "But you probably know that."

"I knew about the federal policy, but I confess, not the motto. Sounds effective."

"Personally, I think the photos of forests peppered with dying trees are more so, but the words do stick in your head."

She seemed to hesitate, then said, "You don't disagree with my goals, then."

*Uh-oh.* He resorted to his usual response in tricky

areas like this. A shrug. "Doesn't matter if I disagree. Nothing to do with my job."

"But you follow the policy?"

"It makes sense."

"And if it didn't?" Another shrug. "So you do disagree?"

"Doesn't matter," he repeated.

"I'm curious."

"Then you'll have to stay curious," he said firmly. He was *not* going to get into a debate with a client. If he made her mad, she'd be less likely to cooperate and that could be dangerous. "You ready for this hike?"

To his relief, she let it drop, although something in her expression had him thinking the reprieve was only temporary. She hadn't gotten to where she was today, an advocate with a reputation for getting things done, by letting things slide. And he doubted many people told her no, anyway.

He tucked the snacks into an outside pocket on his backpack, and she did the same. She also slid her phone into the back pocket of her snug jeans. The pocket that curved over her delightful backside.

*Lucky phone.*

The errant thought put an edge in his voice when he said, "If you're hoping for reception out there, don't count on it."

Her chin came up. "I was thinking about photos. Do you have a problem with that?"

"Not as long as none of them see the light of day before the threat has passed." He hesitated, then added, "You do realize this is a risk, going out like this?"

She met his gaze. Then she sighed. "This is selfish

of me, isn't it? Putting you in a position where it will be harder to do your job?"

Her sudden, unexpected admission wiped away the rest of his warning. "Worry about the risk to you, not my job."

Her mouth quirked. "Kind of entwined, aren't they?"

He shrugged. "You're in danger. But you shouldn't have to be a prisoner. So be aware but let me do…what I do. Oh, and about those pictures, I'd prefer you didn't advertise the exact location to the world. We'd like to keep this little corner as it is."

"So you do believe in preservation? Or only of what you yourself own?"

"I do believe in preservation, and right now that means self-preservation, so we're not having this discussion."

"Coward."

He didn't rise to the obvious bait. "You'd better hope not."

"Point taken," she admitted. And she didn't quibble about him leading the way. But then he already knew she wasn't foolish, just determined. And maybe the tiniest bit spoiled. Nothing like he would have expected, of course. Those assumptions again.

Once they'd crossed the cleared area around the house and got into the trees and underbrush, the walking grew harder. But she didn't comment and got through easily enough. He was hyper-attuned to their surroundings, on guard, but he still noticed she often turned sideways to avoid breaking branches and managed to avoid stepping in places that were more muddy and neatly dodged rocks. She obviously hadn't lied; she was used to this.

And she was smiling. Constantly, although it wid-

ened whenever they encountered wildlife, and turned
to a delighted grin when he stopped her and pointed out
a couple of black-tailed prairie dogs, which she'd never
seen before.

"They don't hibernate?" she asked, watching the two
small creatures in the distance.

"Not fully. There's a stage in between they go into at
night in the winter, to lower their metabolism."

"Torpor," she said. And then laughed as the animals
called out to each other. "They really do bark!"

"Hence the name," he said.

"What else have you seen out here?" she asked as
they walked on.

"Year-round? The usual. Lots of squirrels, gophers
and rabbits. Raccoons, we've got a ton of those. Foxes, as
you saw. Badgers. Coyotes occasionally. And last summer I swear I saw those last two working together."

"Working together?"

He jerked a thumb back toward the prairie dogs.
"Hunting those guys." She winced, just slightly. "Don't
like the laws of nature?" he asked.

"I try not to dwell on things I can't change and focus
on things that I can," she said, "and I understand the food
chain and its necessity in the natural world."

"Harder when the prey is little and cute, though." Her
gaze sharpened. "At least, it is for me," he added.

And again, quickly, she went from the edge of offense
to laughter. "I thought you were jabbing at me again."

He shook his head. "Hey, I'm as big a sucker for a
cute, furry face as anyone."

She looked back toward the prairie dogs, or rather
where they had been. They'd vanished now—maybe
those barks had been a warning. He made a mental note

of that. There was nothing here that would be truly dangerous to humans, but a hungry coyote was always something to be aware of.

"How did they work together, the coyote and the badger?"

He kept it as bloodless as he could. "The prairie dog's instinct is to burrow away from the fast coyote, who can't really dig deep, and run from the slower badger, who can. The badger scared one into running, then the coyote pounced."

She looked thoughtful. "That makes sense. Each using their particular skills." Her brow furrowed. "But did the coyote share? That seems unlikely."

"No. But I assume it works in reverse, that the coyote scares the prey into the burrow for the badger to dig out, often enough to make the partnership worthwhile for both."

"So even though they're competitors…"

"Yep. We could learn from them, I think."

"I wish we would," she said with a sigh. Maybe she wasn't quite as innocently optimistic as her parents feared, because that hadn't sounded at all confident.

They were some distance farther on when she stopped again. He turned back and saw her tilt her head as if listening intently. He smiled. "Meadowlark. Our state bird."

"It's a beautiful call. Your favorite bird?"

"Well, as a born and bred Kansan, I should say yes, but I'm more of a raptor guy."

She smiled. He was really getting to like that smile. "Why am I not surprised?"

"Of course, I do have a soft spot for roadrunners, ever since I saw one once, down near Coffeyville."

"Too many cartoons as a child, perhaps?" she asked innocently. Too innocently.

"Don't tell me you watched cartoons?" He said it with as much feigned shock as he could manage. "A woman with your upbringing?"

He got the laugh again. "We're just shattering assumptions all over the place, aren't we?"

"Well, there's the little fact they feed on spiders, too. Oh," he added, giving her a raised brow, "and snakes."

"My new favorite bird." She was still laughing, and as they started to walk again, he had the craziest wish that she wasn't a client, that they just…were. Together. Under other circumstances.

But they weren't. She was a client. A job.

And even if she weren't, she was way, way beyond his reach.

## Chapter 19

This was not fair.

This was so not fair.

She'd spent her entire life from the time she was old enough to understand assumptions and clichés, fighting against becoming either. Besides teaching her to beware of those who would pursue her for her name, wealth and of late fame, her parents had taught her early on that people would assume things about her because of that wealth. That many would have a picture in their mind, a clichéd perception of who she must be without having ever met her.

That was why she had built some very sturdy walls around her heart and emotions, why she didn't trust easily. Why she had worked so hard, studying, learning, so she could never be written off as one of those famous sorts who mouthed off and revealed a lack of knowledge about most things. The biggest cliché of the social media age, she often thought.

And now she was turning into a living, breathing cliché herself. The woman in danger who fell for her bodyguard.

She'd met a lot of people in her travels. Many kinds of people. A lot of them had been men.

But she'd never ever met a man like Ty Colton. And she wasn't sure if that spoke more to the circles she'd been running in or the man himself. She had a feeling it was some of both. Simon, for instance, had always looked upon men who focused on fitness of body with a certain disdain. It did not matter, he'd often said, usually with a sniff through his elevated nose, if the body was fit when the brain was not. Because she'd been flattered by the brilliant man's attentions, she had stopped herself from asking if that meant the reverse was also true. Funny, she'd never quite thought about Simon this way before. Never realized that in his own way, he had quite limited his own life.

She tried to picture the professor out here, striding so confidently yet carefully through thick underbrush and sometimes muddy terrain. The image that formed was laughable. She had never done that, laughed at Simon, even though his lack of stature and solidity had earned that from many of his students—behind his back, of course, which had only made her rise to his defense.

Ty didn't need any defense. He had muscles her ex could only dream of, shoulders broad enough to be a cliché in themselves. And the sight of his butt in those jeans explained completely why Simon had never worn them.

Ty was so hyper-alert and aware. He seemed utterly focused on their surroundings yet at the same time he was aware every time she stopped to look at something, or slipped slightly, or even turned her head. Simon would be oblivious, except perhaps to complain about the lack of a paved trail, which was about where his adventures into anything outside city skyscrapers ended.

To be fair, because she always endeavored to be, she tried to picture Ty among those city skyscrapers. She had the feeling he would be just as confident there, although perhaps not quite as comfortable in a stylish suit. For some reason, the image of him in formal wear, a tux even, formed in her mind, and for a moment it was so vivid she forgot how to breathe.

His head snapped around, and she realized she'd gasped aloud. "You okay?"

He stopped, and she nearly ran into him. Spent a moment wishing she had kept going. Wondered how it would feel to go into his arms willingly.

"Fine," she said, embarrassed now.

"Need to rest?"

"No, I'm good. Really. I was just…thinking."

His mouth—speaking of things that made her forget how to breathe—quirked upward at one corner. "Are you ever not?"

"Rarely," she admitted.

He gave her that look that told her she wasn't the only one thinking. But she doubted very much he was wrestling with the same kinds of thoughts she was. The same kind of revelations. How had just being with him, pried by force from her phone and other connections, so rattled her mindset? She had the oddest feeling, something almost bedrock—or that she'd thought was bedrock—was shifting, changing. And it was because of him.

Which made her edgy, because to him she was just

a client, and likely one he found problematic, given his reaction to a simple social media post. Although in retrospect, if she worked off the assumption the threat was real, she could see his point.

And she hadn't liked how twitchy she'd gotten since access had been removed. Hadn't liked the thought that perhaps she really was addicted. She vowed then and there to cut back. To enforce personal restrictions, to have times when she put the phone away.

He was indulging her with this hike, however. Although he didn't seem to be minding it much. Even though he'd made the same trek once already today. *To make sure I'd be safe. The man is a professional. And part of that job is probably making clients feel comfortable, at ease. Remember that.*

He led her up a mild but rather rocky slope, and they came out on an outcropping of the orangish rock that she'd seen in the area. And below them was the spread of the area where the river met the lake, water running to the lake here, marshy flats there. An ideal place for the plant growth so crucial to migrating wildlife.

They sat on that outcropping, and she had to admit she was ready for the break. He seemed unaffected, and she wondered if he did this regularly, or if his fitness came from gym workouts.

They'd been sitting quietly, looking out over the view for a few minutes when he spoke again. "Do you ever change your mind about something?"

Her brow furrowed. "Of course. If the circumstances or the information I have changes, or is proved wrong."

"What if it's something you've…taken a stand on? Publicly."

"Then I have to admit I was wrong, or misinformed,

as publicly as I took that stand, and explain why I changed my mind."

"You *have* to?"

"Well, yes. To be fair."

"And that's important to you. Being fair."

She almost snapped out a rather peevish "Of course," but something about the way he was looking at her made her pause. The answer she finally gave him was much more than she usually said.

"Life itself is so often unfair—especially to the smaller among us, like those prairie dogs—so I feel it's up to us humans to at least try to even it out."

He nodded back the way they had come. "Those prairie dogs build entire cities underground, a network of burrows with rooms at different depths for different purposes. They've got fine-tuned hearing so they can hear a predator's approach even while underground. They've got those warning barks. Nature equipped them pretty well for survival."

She knew she was staring at him. She hadn't expected him to reel off all that…knowledge. "If you care enough to learn all that, how can you think it's wrong to protect their habitat?"

"I don't. But I also think that while we humans may be at the top of the food chain—unless we do something stupid—we're just as much a part of the system as any other animal. And I don't appreciate those who believe we should be completely removed from it, as if we have less right to be here than those below us on that chain."

"I've never believed that. But I do believe that with that status at the top comes responsibility."

"I wouldn't disagree with that." He shrugged again, that very male gesture she was coming to envy. "I guess

I'm just more of a conservationist. For all of the planet's inhabitants."

"And I wouldn't disagree with that," she said quietly. That got a smile that did crazy things to her insides.

After a moment, he pointed across the river to a clear area on the other side. "If this was spring, you'd be looking at a field of sunflowers."

"So they really do grow wild here?"

"And cultivated."

"Before I started researching," she said, as she took out her water bottle for a sip, "I would have been among those who assumed Kansas was completely flat."

He gave her that sideways look. "Sure you want to admit that to a native Kansas boy?"

"I'm not embarrassed to admit my ignorance, as long as I'm working to alleviate it."

"Why does that sound like something you'd say in one of your speeches?"

She couldn't stop her laugh. "Because it is?" It got her another smile. And she wished she could stop feeling like she'd won some kind of prize every time that happened.

"We're used to it, even though we're only the twenty-third flattest state. But most people's idea of Kansas comes from *The Wizard of Oz*, or *Little House on the Prairie*. Personally, I prefer being Superman's home state."

She found herself laughing yet again. "I don't blame you."

They sat quietly for a while, just looking. Which he seemed content to do. She was vaguely aware that the warmth built by the hike was seeping away and the ground was cold beneath her, but it wasn't yet uncomfortable.

"Well, well," Ty murmured, "hello there."

He was looking upriver, and she shifted her gaze that direction. She didn't say anything, but once more he was obviously aware of her movement, because without looking at her, he added, "Find the tallest tree on the left bank, then look straight right to the one jutting out over the river."

It took her a moment, but then she spotted the large bird perched on a branch. Had it not been barren of leaves she never would have seen the distinctive white head and tail.

"A bald eagle?"

He nodded. "We have a nesting pair in the area. They're usually at the seep stream about now. They figured out trout season long ago."

She laughed. He smiled. And for a split second, she wondered if he felt the same way when she laughed as she did when he did. *That sounded silly even unspoken.* Searching for something to say that wouldn't betray that silliness, she asked, "Do you usually go fishing when you're here?"

He kept his gaze on the regal bird. "Not my first thought this time of year. But I keep the license updated. And I heard a rumor there are a lot of white bass right out in front of the point just now."

"Do you want to go?"

He looked at her then. "This isn't a vacation trip."

She sighed. "I know that. But I like fishing."

He blinked. "You do?"

"Must you always sound so surprised?"

"That was nothing personal. Well, except that you're female. I don't know that many who like fishing."

"Maybe you need to meet more females," she said

rather sourly as she lifted her bottle for another drink of water.

"Now you sound like my mother."

That caught her off guard, and the laugh that burst from her, then caused a spew of water. He gave her a look she could only describe as that of a rather mischievous little boy.

And another of her inner walls melted away.

# Chapter 20

"Do I need a fishing license?" Ashley asked. She shifted the pole she was carrying as they walked toward the lake, a much shorter distance than yesterday's trek.

Ty raised a brow at her. She still wasn't taking this threat seriously enough for his taste. And he was a little edgy—again—after a second restless night. Not because of her being restless, because this time she'd gone to bed and stayed there, but because... Hell, he didn't know why he hadn't been able to settle. He'd learned to gauge his limits, and figured he had another night like that in him. But after that he was going to need some serious sleep or he was going to be tired enough to possibly miss something.

Unless something happened, of course. Then adrenaline would kick in and carry the day. At least, it always had.

But she was looking at him in honest inquiry, as if she'd never thought of the ramifications. Which was another surprise. He would have thought, her parents being who they were, she would have had security precautions hammered into her practically from birth.

"And how long do you suppose it would take for word to get out that Ashley Hart of the Westport Harts bought a fishing license in tiny Yankee Run? You might as well post our coordinates to the world."

She grimaced. "Just trying to obey the law, Mr. Colton."

"I told you, I've got one," he said. "And this is a unique situation." *Not to mention I can't see even the state government seriously going after the sole Hart offspring.* "But we'll take the heat and pay the fine if you get caught. Or catch anything," he added, in an exaggeratedly teasing tone.

"If? Humph," she retorted, her nose so far in the air he knew it had to be intentional. She had a sense of humor, did Ms. Ashley Hart of the Westport Harts. And wasn't afraid to poke at her own image. He liked that.

He liked a lot about her.

And he hoped he didn't regret this. But while going out on the water in the small runabout in the boathouse would have been akin to stepping out onto a sunlit stage with a target on them, they were fairly sheltered here on the point. Visible from certain angles on the lake but masked to a great extent from others, and almost completely hidden from anyone who might be trespassing on Colton land. They'd have to get really close before they could see them, and if they managed that without Ty hearing them coming, he deserved what he got.

But she didn't.

He'd never failed on a protection job, even in a couple of near-miss circumstances, once when he'd spotted the threat in time and gotten the protectee to safety, and once when he'd taken out the armed suspect. He'd earned Eric's pleased approval, something he treasured because of his respect for the man. But somehow this time was different.

The thought of failing to protect Ashley made him feel crazy tense. If he did fail, and if because of that she was hurt or worse, he somehow knew that would be a shift of the ground under his feet so large he wasn't sure he could withstand it. He'd never felt this before, and it made him nervous, edgy, and complicated things even further.

And he'd known her exactly twenty-four hours. How the hell had this happened in twenty-four hours?

How the hell had it happened at all?

He tried to focus on what they were here for. "We're lucky it hasn't gotten too cold yet, or they'd be really sluggish, and clustered in deep water."

"So they're prepping for winter?"

"Feeding up," he said with a nod. "Just in different places. Springtime, you can catch them as fast as you can reel in and recast just about anywhere. It's like a frenzy." As they reached the lake's edge, he scanned the water. There were several boats off the point, so the fish must still be striking.

"Is that a problem?" Ashley asked, looking at the other anglers.

At least she'd thought about it. That was progress, he supposed. "No. I know who they are."

She blinked and turned to look at him. "All of them?"

He nodded. "They're all locals or regulars I've seen before. Typical, this time of year." At her expression, he couldn't help chuckling. "You hang out in big cities too much," he teased.

"There are advantages," she said, "but disadvantages, too. I like the idea of knowing all the people around you."

Yet again, she surprised him. But he kept it to himself as he pointed at a spot a few yards out in the water. "There's some brush right around here that ends up underwater when the lake's full, like now."

"Good hiding place," she said.

"It's a little tough to cast out that far from here onshore, but it can be done."

"Shall I take that as a challenge?"

He gave her a sideways look. "Not from me. I don't generally fish from here. I'm too lazy when there's a perfectly good boat around."

Something shifted in her expression, and he couldn't read it at all. "Sorry to disrupt your routine."

His words could have been taken as a complaint, although he couldn't see why she'd think something like that would be important to him now, on the job. But something in the dark depths of those chocolate-brown eyes had him grabbing for a response. And the moment it came out, he regretted both the words and the rough note that had come into his voice.

"There's nothing about you that's routine."

To his relief, she didn't reply to his ill-advised admission. She just gave him a curious look, as if she weren't quite sure how to interpret what he'd said. He couldn't believe that. Hell, she was probably more than used to guys hitting on her. She probably—

*Damn.*

Hitting on her?

*Client. Protocol. Rules of conduct.*

The warnings pealed out in his mind. And once he'd led her to the spot where she could cast out a lure and still be mostly hidden, he backed away from her. Again, she gave him that curious but unrevealing look.

He scanned the area behind them, listening carefully. There was a slight breeze today, but nothing that would have masked the approach of anything the size of a human being.

He turned back in time to see her finish rigging the pole and the bright spinner lure he'd suggested she try first. She'd done it competently. More than competently.

"Who taught you to fish?"

"My father, first. He likes sport fishing, although he's more of a salt water guy."

*Of course he was. Probably prize marlin fishing or something.*

But she'd said first. "And second?"

"A tribal member in Alaska was generous enough to share some of their knowledge with me. Once I proved I was up to it, of course."

She flicked a glance at him with those last words, and he suspected she thought she was having to prove herself again. And he supposed, in a way, she was. She was certainly shattering most of those assumptions of his.

"Why were you in Alaska?"

"I spent a couple of months visiting an isolated area that needed a medical clinic built, so the one doctor they had would have a central location and facilities." She smiled then, as if that memory were a special one. And that made him want to know more. As if what was special to this woman was important to him.

"You spent two months there?"

"I hadn't planned to, but Dr. Kallik changed that.

She's brilliant. In those two months, she taught me a lot about rough-and-ready medicine." She gave him another sideways glance. "I even assisted her on a couple of operations, when she needed more hands."

He nearly gaped at her. Yet he could see it—she was cool, calm and brilliant herself. What other unexpected skills did she have?

His mind immediately careened into the gutter and he clamped his jaw tightly to keep from letting something beyond foolish tumble out of his mouth. He watched her silently. She was obviously familiar with the equipment, and while her first cast was off a bit, the next was better. But she still wasn't happy with the location. He saw her studying the top of the brush that stuck up out of the water, and the next thing he knew she startled him completely by wading hip deep out into the water.

"If I'd known you were going to do that, I would have brought waders."

"I'll dry," she said briefly, clearly unconcerned.

Chalk another one up in the surprise category. Ashley Hart was just full of them. She didn't look at him but was completely intent on her next cast. This one she apparently put where she wanted for she let it drop. He would have, too, if he'd hit that spot.

There was something about her intensity, her focus, that had him thinking odd things. Like about the amount of research she must do to be as knowledgeable as she appeared. About her apparent ability to see both sides of an issue, even one where she had strong feelings or convictions. About the love in her voice when she spoke of her parents, as if they were an ordinary, loving mother and father instead of one of the richest couples in the world. Although that, he supposed, said as much about them as her.

He nearly laughed at himself when he felt a jab of envy. His own father had been far too busy and involved with the business to take his son, or any of his kids, fishing. His mother told him he'd always had plans to teach him, but after the triplets had been born his dad had, understandably Ty supposed, focused utterly and entirely on making enough money to support a family that had suddenly numbered seven.

Then he slid into simply watching her. He didn't know how much time had passed when a faint rustle behind them snapped him out of his fascinated scrutiny, of her focus, her concentration, the grace of her movements, the curves of her slender body. His head snapped around toward the sound, and a moment later, he saw a pair of gray squirrels busily foraging for the nearing winter. He scanned farther, saw nothing, went back to the squirrels. He heard the same sound again, as one of the animals dug through some downed leaves.

Breathing easily again, he turned back. He glanced at his watch as he did so, startled to see well over an hour had gone by. He looked up as Ashley let out a whoop of triumph. In short order, she reeled in a respectably sized white bass. His instinct was to help her unhook it, but he quashed it. He had the feeling she wouldn't appreciate help she didn't need. He did dig a stringer out of the fishing gear bag he'd brought along.

"Move fast," he suggested. "If they're striking, they're hungry."

"So am I." She was grinning so widely he couldn't help but grin back at her.

She did as he'd suggested while he put the fish on the

string and dropped it back into the water. She caught three more in short order, while Ty stood there marveling at the pleasure she took in the simple act. And she never even blinked at handling the fish. Clearly, she wasn't afraid to get her hands dirty. Or her feet wet.

"Nice work," he said as they packed up the gear. "We'll eat well tonight."

Her brow furrowed. "I don't know much about bass, but I've heard…"

"People who don't like the taste don't know how to fix it. More exactly, they don't know how to trim it." She arched those delicate brows at him. He grinned at her. "You caught 'em, I'll cook 'em."

"You cook?"

"Only things I've hunted down myself, like any good caveman," he said, deadpan.

She burst out laughing. Yeah, he liked that. Too damned much.

"Then the real question is, who gets to clean them?" she asked.

"We'll split them up."

"Before we split them up?"

It was his turn to laugh, and she looked just as pleased as he'd felt when she had. With the feeling that he was wading into water much deeper than the thirty-five feet of the lake, he turned and led the way back to the cabin.

## Chapter 21

"Any reason not to use this?"

Ashley blinked. She'd been watching with fascination as Ty worked. He seemed at home in the kitchen—this one, at least—and it was a pleasure to watch. Of course, he was a pleasure to watch anyway, doing anything.

Except ordering you around, she reminded herself sternly. And, if she were honest, it also bothered her when he left the cabin periodically, with his usual cautions and reminders about how to contact Elite in case of emergency. He was doing regular reconnaissance, which reminded her of why she was here. Why that was upsetting, beyond the obvious, she didn't want to think about.

*What, you want to pretend you're just off on a vacation with him?*

But now he'd stopped in the middle of prepping what would apparently be a sauce for the fish, holding up a bottle of white wine. It took her a moment to realize he was asking if she had any problem with alcohol.

"Oh. No." She wondered why he'd asked, if it was routine or if he suspected she had a problem. She did not. She almost had, when she'd been at college and it had been rampant, but she hated the aftermath so much she rarely drank more than a couple of drinks in an occasional evening.

She'd watched with interest as, after they'd cleaned, scaled and filleted the fish, he'd shown her the reddish flesh along one edge. "That's what gives it the taste some people don't like," he'd explained, and trimmed it away.

Now he poured about a cup of the wine into the pan and raised the heat. He'd sautéed the salted and floured fish in the skillet and then covered it while he peeled and cut up garlic and a lemon, half of which he squeezed for juice, the other half he cut into thin slices. He didn't consult a recipe, so he'd clearly done this before.

"Have to settle for dry oregano, since it wasn't on the stocking list," he said, as he added butter to the pan, then the seasonings.

"It already smells wonderful," she said.

And when she took her first bite, her eyes widened. "Oh. My, that's good."

"Must you sound so surprised?"

It was such a perfect imitation of her own intonation earlier that she nearly burst out laughing. "Touché," she said, and took another bite. The flavors were an amazing blend, and the fish light and flaky. "Except for my mom's swordfish, this may be the best fish dinner I've ever eaten."

"Considering where you've likely eaten, I'll take that as a great compliment." Then, with a warm smile, as if he'd liked that she'd given her mother the exception, he added, "And I'm sure your mother's swordfish is amazing."

"You—" She cut herself off in more than a little shock when she'd been about to say, *You'll have to try it sometime*. She never ever broached that subject with a man. Never brought up the possibility of taking him home to meet them. It was part of her vetting process. If a guy asked to meet her parents within the first three months, she knew he was after something.

But that was a guy she was dating. Not a guy her parents had hired to protect her.

"She loves to cook," she said instead, rather inanely. "I think she looks forward to their cook's vacation more than he does."

She was watching his face to see if he reacted to the fact that her parents had a full-time chef. He didn't. Normally she would have thought he'd developed an excellent poker face for his work, but she'd seen him surprised—and annoyed.

The real question was, if he did have that poker face, why was he letting her see that surprise, that annoyance…that humor? He wasn't at all the stiff-lipped sort she was used to on her parents' security staff. Yet he seemed no less trained, and certainly no less capable. Perhaps the more personable, more human approach was part of his style, to put clients at ease.

That he was always on the job was pounded home when, after the kitchen was cleaned up in a quick joint effort and he'd started a fire in the fireplace, he left again, this time stepping out into the fading light of dusk. She wondered if he really expected to find something—or someone—or if it was just part of the routine. Part of being thorough.

When she heard him coming back, she quickly sat down near the crackling fire, so he wouldn't come in and notice she'd been pacing the floor the entire time he'd been gone.

"Ever thought about a guard dog?" she asked when he came in.

"Often," he said as he shed his jacket. She looked away from the weapon on his belt. She wasn't repelled, it was a tool of his trade, nothing more, but once again it reminded her of why they were here. Why they were together at all. "My boss is thinking of adding one or two to the staff."

"My parents have a pair at home. They're wonderful."

He walked over and laid another log on the fire, then sat in the chair opposite her nearest the hearth, probably for the warmth after his trek outside. "What are they?"

She quashed the silly wish that he would have sat next to her on the couch and answered evenly, "Malinois."

He nodded. "Good dogs. Smart, strong, quick and if need be, lethal."

"You forgot beautiful and intense."

He smiled. "That, too."

"It always amazes me how they can go from playing to on duty in a split second." *Kind of like you.*

She inwardly rolled her eyes at herself as she compared him to a dog. Then again, every adjective they'd applied to the animals applied to him, too. And she didn't know which unsettled her more, the lethal if need be part or the beautiful part.

Of course, what unsettled her most was the thought that the lethality might be necessary. She wasn't used to walking around worrying about everything around her, watching constantly for anything out of the ordinary, looking for threats. And she didn't like it. But she also knew the fact that nothing had happened was no guarantee nothing would. There were times when, as much as she had come to like this place, she understood that isolation wasn't always a good thing. Because the only targets out walking around were her, and Ty.

"What's Wichita like?" she asked abruptly, before she said something seriously stupid.

"Biggest city in the state. Started as a trading post on the Chisolm Trail. Incorporated in 1870. Nicknamed Cowtown, and Wyatt Earp was the law there for a while."

She blinked at the four-sentence history lesson. "Wow."

"But now," he went on, stretching out those long strong legs, "it's the Air Capital of the World."

"Air capital?"

"Beechcraft, Cessna, Stearman all started production there in the early days. Learjet, Airbus and a few others followed."

"I had no idea." She studied him for a moment. "I suppose that doesn't surprise you."

He shrugged. "I only know it because I live there, and was born in Kansas. Ask me about, say, Cleveland, which is about the same size, and all I'd know is it's on Lake Erie and home of the Rock & Roll Hall of Fame."

"More than some would," she said with a smile.

For a brief moment, he stared at her, and she wondered why. Then she saw a muscle in his jaw jump and he looked away, into the fire.

*Into the fire.*

She'd heard the phrase countless times, in various

contexts. But at this moment, sitting here with him, so close and yet so distant, she could only think of one. She'd been raised to have the courage of her convictions, but also to be beyond cautious about people who would mask their true goals behind a facade of friendship or caring. She'd been burned more than once, but she'd learned. Every time she'd learned, become even more cautious, until her walls were high and solid.

Yet here she was now, part of her wanting to leap right into the fire she sensed between them, the fire hotter even than the one he was staring into. She'd been attracted to men before, but she rarely allowed it to take root because so many times it went sour, or she found out they'd had a plan all along, that usually involved access to Hart money.

It had never been as powerful as this. So powerful all her usual walls and defenses seemed useless. All her self-lecturing, all her telling herself it was the circumstances, the imposed isolation that was causing these feelings were failing miserably.

"What was it like, growing up an only child?"

She gave a start, both because of the abrupt and unexpected question and because his voice had sounded just like hers had when she'd asked about Wichita to keep herself from saying something she'd regret. It took her a moment to formulate a reply, which in itself felt odd. She usually had quick answers to almost everything. This man truly did discombobulate her.

"Good and bad," she finally said. "Good because you got all the attention, bad because you got all the attention."

He smiled at that, and the odd tension eased a little. "I get that. Being one of six gave me a lot of cover."

"It was hard," she confessed, "being the sole focus of all their hopes and expectations. At least, until I realized that their biggest hope trumped all the rest."

"Which was?"

"For me to be happy." She was a little stunned. She almost never talked about that with anyone.

He looked at her steadily then, one corner of his mouth curving upward. "Consider another assumption blasted. Your parents sound great."

"They are." That, at least, she could say with full faith and force.

"And they must be incredibly proud of you."

"They are," she repeated. "Even if this isn't the path they would have chosen."

His mouth quirked higher. "I know that feeling. But my old man wasn't as understanding. Which may be why none of us went into the family business."

Her mouth quirked in turn. "Our family business seems to be being the Harts of Westport."

He laughed, and Ashley felt that quick jolt of pleasure yet again.

If this kept up, she wasn't going to have any guard-rails left.

Ty wasn't sure what he'd expected. He didn't really think she had exaggerated her skill, but he was having trouble reconciling his image of Ashley Hart, heiress, with the woman he was watching now. The woman who was consistently hitting the blocks of wood he was tossing, no matter what direction or height he threw them.

The sound of the shotgun echoed through the bare trees, and he could only imagine every living creature within a mile taking cover. They didn't hunt much out here, but the sheer volume alone would send him running to hide if he were, say, one of those little prairie dogs.

He waited while she reloaded. Then she nodded, and he started tossing again. And as before, she didn't miss. In fact, the only time she'd missed at all was in the beginning, when a bird had broken for cover just as he tossed the second block. She'd yanked the shotgun off target, he guessed, to be sure she didn't hit the bird by accident.

He had a sudden vision of an eight-year-old Ashley fearlessly confronting her father, demanding he stop hunting living birds. He could just see her looking at him, the pain of what he was doing reflected in those deep brown eyes. And he wondered how many people around the world would never believe that Andrew Hart, head of the global Hart empire, would give in. To a little girl, even if she was his daughter and his only child.

He believed it. Because he already knew that when determined, Ashley Hart could be a nearly unstoppable force.

He also knew, with wry acceptance, that his own father would never give in like that, unless it was something he wanted to do anyway.

This time when she had emptied the weapon, she stopped, took out the ear protection he'd retrieved from the locker in the SUV and turned to look at him.

"You're as good as you said you were," he said, figuring she'd earned it.

She smiled so widely it made his chest tighten a little. "Your turn," she said.

He laughed. "Not my thing."

"Do you hunt?"

"Not much anymore, unless there's another reason."

Her brow furrowed. "Like what?"

"Renegade coyote. Rabid skunk. That kind of thing."

"Oh." She looked down at the Mossberg, then back at him. "Not birds?"

He gave her a rather sheepish look. "Nah. I like them too much. So I'm a hypocrite who eats them, but I don't want to be part of the process."

To his surprise, she smiled. "I'm afraid I'm with you on that. You sure you don't want to try?"

"I'd embarrass myself."

"I could teach you."

His entire perception shifted in that moment. An image formed in his mind of Ashley standing close behind him as she showed him how to aim, to fire…things he already knew but had never done in this particular exercise.

And he knew from his own instant, fierce response to just that imaginary vision that the answer had to be no.

And he spent a good portion of the hours of darkness regretting that.

"Why do I get the feeling you didn't call just to say hello?"

Ty grinned despite the fact that his brother Neil couldn't see him over the old landline. "Come on, what's the good of having a high-power attorney for a brother if he can't give you a little helpful advice now and then?"

"You know what I make per hour to dispense helpful advice?"

"You want to charge the brother who saved you from drowning when you were five?"

"Yeah, yeah. One of these days I'm going to call that paid back."

"I'll consider it a big installment if you can tell me

how we can put this jerk who's after Ashley away for a long time."

There was a split-second pause before Neil said, "Ashley?"

*Uh-oh.* He knew instantly that he should have kept it professional, referred to her simply as a client or protectee. Neil was just too damned good at reading people, even if he only had a voice to work with. He scrambled to cover.

"We decided it would be wiser not to throw around that particular last name," he said.

"Hmm." The non-word fairly echoed with his brother's lack of acceptance of the excuse. But to Ty's relief, he let it go. "You do realize I'm not a prosecutor?"

"Please. Who would know better how to destroy the perfect defense than the guy who builds them?"

That got him a laugh. "Are you sure it's who you thought it was?"

"It's not confirmed," Ty had to admit. "He's been lying low since we pulled her off stage." He'd talked to Mitch early this morning, before Ashley had come downstairs. Wearing that damned silky-looking robe thing that made her look like some forties movie star or something. And he'd waited until she'd gone back upstairs to dress to call Neil, denying even to himself it was so he wouldn't think about that sleek fabric sliding off her sleek body.

"Maybe he thinks he won when she went quiet."

"Maybe. But she won't stay quiet, so we need to be ready."

"Stubborn, huh?"

"Determined. And dedicated."

"Was that actual admiration I heard in my hard-to-impress big brother's voice?"

He opened his mouth to refute it, but the words wouldn't come. "She's...not what I expected."

"And I gather in a good way? Sounds like it's getting personal, bro."

*No. It can't. I'm not that stupid. Am I?*

"Can we dispense with the analysis and get to an answer?"

"All I can say is that where it stands right now, if it is him, at most he'd likely get off with a fine and probation. He's done nothing but mouth off, so far."

"So far," Ty said grimly. "If he gets angry enough, he could follow through and come after her physically."

"If he does, you'll keep her safe," Neil said, with such certainty that Ty couldn't help but feel warmed by his brother's faith.

"Yeah," he said. "I will."

And it was a vow to her as much as to himself. He would keep her safe. The world needed more Ashley Harts, not less.

## Chapter 22

"You have to do it anyway, right?" Ashley asked as she stood looking at the downed tree he'd made note of when they'd first arrived.

Ty sat on the thick trunk and grinned at her. "I was thinking I'd leave it for my little brother Neil," he drawled lazily. "So he doesn't get soft sitting in that office all day, wearing those expensive suits."

She laughed, because she knew he was anything but lazy. And when looked at in the larger scheme of things, he was working very hard at making this as easy as possible on her. Including trekking out every day because she wanted to learn about this place she'd never been, when it would obviously be easier to do his job if she stayed safely inside the cabin. She studied him for a moment, trying to picture him here as a kid. She wondered if he'd ever had an awkward stage, or if he'd always been…

"What?" he asked at her look.

"Just pondering the sibling thing again," she said hastily, trying not to betray that she'd been mentally drooling over him. Again. "And what I missed, being an only."

"Maybe you gained just as much," he pointed out.

"Did you all compete?"

"Sometimes. Unless someone outside came at one of us."

"Came at?"

"You know what I mean, when—" He stopped, and his mouth twisted wryly. "No, I guess you don't." He looked thoughtful for a moment. "When she was thirteen, some older kid started harassing my little sister Bridgette. She's the girl of the triplets."

"Older kid?" Possibilities tumbled through her mind, none of them pleasant.

"Yeah." His lips quirked in that way she was coming to quite like. "He was thirteen and a half."

She smiled. "What happened?"

"I found her hiding and crying one day, and it seriously pissed me off. So I went after him."

"How old were you?"

"Sixteen." He gave her a sideways look. "And I'd already hit six feet tall. He wasn't much over five. I picked him up and took him behind a dumpster for a chat."

Her eyes widened at the image that made. "You must have scared him to death!"

"That was the intention. He made Bridgette cry."

Ashley felt a wave of something warm and almost wistful. "I… That's wonderful. You must have been a great big brother."

He shrugged. It seemed to be his reaction to compliments. "Anyway, that's what I meant. We might be at odds with each other, but to the outside, it was all for one and all that."

"Sometimes I do truly wish I hadn't missed out on that dynamic."

"It had its moments." His mouth quirked again. "Looking back, I think he probably had a crush on her, but I didn't recognize that then."

*Do you now? Recognize crushes?*

Her breath jammed up in her throat, and she quickly turned away, masking it as looking toward the sky, which was rather gray today, as if rain were on the way. She was not used to this, not at all, and it was very unsettling. She heard him move, looked back just in time to see him stand, that tall powerful body moving with a grace and ease that made her pulse kick up all over again.

"Are you sure you don't want to cut this up?" she said quickly.

"Not my job right now."

No, she was his job right now. Job, not…crush. "What if I stay here with you?" *Oh, now that sounded disinterested.*

"You'd end up being put to work."

She was startled at how much that idea appealed. "I'd like that. A lot. I need something physical to do." She nearly groaned aloud at that. But he didn't make any suggestive comment. Because it never occurred to him that *something physical* could mean…something else?

And so an hour later—after he made yet another check of the property—he was armed with a chain saw and an ax and, wearing a pair of goggles, attacking the dead tree. The moment he started trimming the smaller branches, she started gathering them up and piling them a few feet away. He looked over at her, then nodded.

And before he went back to work, she thought she saw a trace of a smile.

They continued the process, and she had the silly thought that they worked well together. She guessed she was trying to focus on that rather than notice he'd pulled off his jacket as he worked. He was into the bigger limbs now and cutting them into smaller—fireplace-sized, she realized—lengths. She started stacking those, trying to keep it neat until he shut the chain saw off and spoke.

"They'll need to be split anyway, so don't worry about neatness yet."

She turned around to look at him. And nearly choked as he raised an arm to shove the goggles up to his forehead so he could wipe his face. In the process, his shirt lifted and gave her a full view of what she'd only suspected all along: a perfect set of abs.

She looked away quickly before he lowered his arm and caught her gaping at him. Went back to her stacking before her rattled mind recalled what he'd said to her. She tossed down the logs she'd been about to place neatly on top and turned to go get more. And ran smack into those abs as he brought over more wood.

"Whoa," he said, twisting to drop the logs to one side rather than have them hit her, then grabbing her as she wobbled forward. The motion pressed her harder against him, and suddenly she couldn't seem to remember how to move. Nor could she look away. She just stood there, looking up at him, barely capable of breathing, let alone moving.

The only saving grace was that he didn't move either, for a long silent moment. And when he did, it was to slowly, as if against his will, lower his head. Then his gaze shifted from her eyes to her mouth, and her pulse began to race and her lips parted and he was—

He jerked away. Took a swift step back. Started to speak but stopped, and she saw him swallow. Then, in a voice that had no intonation at all, he said, "Let's wrap this up. Rain coming in."

It took them another half hour to get everything he'd cut moved to the pile for splitting. And she spent every minute of it telling herself that he had *not* been about to kiss her.

Ashley turned a page, listening to the rain that had started last night, just as he'd predicted as they left the half-finished tree yesterday. She was more than a little surprised at herself. And it wasn't just her unexpected reaction to Ty, although that was surprising enough. It was that she was actually enjoying this.

They'd been here five days now, isolated, in a place with no internet, no connection with the outside world except for seeing the occasional boat going by and that ancient landline phone. There were books to read and movies to watch—on DVDs—but no streaming, on-line research and no social media. And yet she wasn't climbing the walls. In fact, she was more relaxed than she could ever remember.

Well, except for the Ty-making-her-pulse-race thing. And that near kiss she kept telling herself hadn't been that at all.

She'd spent days quietly reading with Simon, but even that was different. Because he had seemed startled when-ever he'd looked up and noticed she was there. With Ty, it seemed every time she looked up, he looked at her within seconds, as if he somehow knew when her attention had shifted. As if he was utterly, completely aware of her no matter what he was doing.

*That's his job.*

It had become a mantra, repeated to herself time after time as she tried to convince herself it was nothing more, that she was imagining that…something that seemed to flash in his gaze for an instant.

They'd spent the nicer days outside, and he'd seemed okay with letting her simply explore their property however she wanted, as long as he'd checked it first, either personally or with that little surveillance drone he handled with such skill. If she had questions about something she saw out there, be it wildlife or vegetation or terrain, he always had the answer.

She wondered if there was anything he wasn't good at.

And that gave rise to a flood of heated thoughts that made her consider walking out into that cold November rain just to cool off.

She stole a glance at him, certain she must have mistaken the times before just as she had mistaken what had happened out by the downed tree. He was once more in the chair opposite her favored place by the fire, reading a rather thick tome that he said belonged to his uncle— she presumed the uncle of the tree planting he'd told her about—on naval history. He seemed intent on it, and she was about to look away, convinced now her imagination had just been overactive, when he looked up at her.

"Sorry about the rain. Feeling antsy?" he asked.

*Yes, but not because of the rain.* "I'm fine."

"Sorry you can't talk to your folks."

He'd explained yesterday morning, with regret she didn't doubt was real, that while this line was secure, he couldn't guarantee the other end would be except for

Elite, his police detective sister, Jordana, and his criminal attorney brother, Neil, who also had access to secure, monitored lines.

"They know you're okay," he had relayed from Mitch, who had spoken to her parents. Then, with a slightly puzzled look, he added, "And they said to tell you to remember Ashworth."

As it came back to her now, she sighed. She hadn't wanted to explain then, but it had been nagging at her ever since. She closed her book. "Ashworth," she said, "is the private school my parents sent me to when I was a kid."

He didn't even blink at the abruptness of it or the delay. "I know."

Of course he did.

He didn't push or pry, just waited silently, giving her the option to go on or end it. It occurred to her that he did that often, gave her the choice, whether it was where to explore outside, what movie to watch or this. Making up for the choices she didn't get to make? Interesting thought. But then she found many, many things about Ty Colton interesting.

"I didn't want to go. But it turned out to be the best thing in the end."

"Why didn't you want to go?"

Interesting, she thought, that that was his first question, not about the school or why it had turned out for the best. "I didn't want to be…different."

"You're Ashley Hart. You were always going to be different."

"I know that now. At aged ten, not so much." She gave him a curious look. "And you're a Colton. Everywhere there's a branch of your family, they're in the middle of things." Surely that meant he could understand what it was like? He was connected to the former president, even if it was distantly. "Didn't you find that difficult sometimes?"

"That's one thing about us heartland folks. We generally take people at their own worth—or lack of it— not their name."

She caught herself sighing again. "That sounds…wonderful. Hard to believe, but wonderful."

"Hard to believe in your world, maybe. That's one reason I stay right here. So I can just be myself."

"I envy you that," she said softly. The longing that filled her at that moment surprised her both by simply existing at all and by its power.

Then, with a rather crooked smile she found oddly endearing, he added, "I'm not saying the name isn't a factor, but I've always looked on it as something to overcome, not trade on."

And that, she thought, said a great deal about the kind of man he was. "Your parents must be very proud of you."

He looked a little startled, as if he weren't quite sure how to take that. "My mother is. My father…not so much."

She would have smiled at his echoing her own words if what he'd said hadn't been rather sad. She'd gathered his father irritated him, but how could any father not be proud to have a son like him?

"I'm sorry to hear that," she said, meaning it.

He shrugged. She wondered if it was because he didn't want to talk about it, or because it didn't really matter to him. She hoped it was the latter. And wondered if his father had any idea what he was missing.

## *Chapter 23*

Ty stood looking out the window, rubbing his unshaven jaw. The weather was still spotty, the weather-alert station was predicting it would get worse as a large front approached, and they were warily monitoring an unsettled jet stream. But he thought they could risk a walk outside, at least out to the point and back. She hadn't complained, but they hadn't been out in a couple of days, and to his surprise, he found he missed trekking around with her.

Of course, if she knew that what sleep he'd gotten last night had been decorated with dreams where he hadn't pulled back from her, where he'd gone ahead and kissed her and his world had gone up in flames, she likely wouldn't come anywhere near him.

"Cliché much?" he muttered under his breath.

"Problem?"

He nearly jumped as she spoke from right behind

him. *Some bodyguard you are.* He didn't look at her. He didn't dare. Because he was afraid those dreams would somehow show in his eyes.

*And when did you turn calf-eyed, Colton?*

The self-lecturing wasn't working too well. He made himself answer casually. "Thinking about a walk out to the point, if you wanted to go. I think the rain will hold off for a while."

"I'd like that," she answered quickly.

"Gear up, then," he said. "I don't know how long it'll hold."

She was ready more quickly than he would have expected, but he'd already seen she wasn't one of those women who took hours to get ready to simply step out into the world.

As they walked, he updated her. "Elite has been watching Sanderson steadily. He's been relatively quiet. No more direct threats."

She seemed oddly troubled by what he'd thought would be good news for her. "Indirect ones, then?"

"Not really. He's changed tacks, it seems. Maybe he realized he went too far."

He half expected her to suggest that this was overkill then, that she didn't need to be tucked away here, didn't need to be protected. By him.

But she didn't. Instead, she merely asked, "What's he doing now?"

"Now he's touting the benefits of his development in the way of jobs, housing, bringing money into the economy."

He'd intentionally kept his tone neutral, but she reacted rather defensively. "And you agree with that?"

"I agree those are valid points and should be considered. Looking for a fight?"

To his surprise—again—she gave him an almost sheepish look. "I sounded that way, didn't I?"

"Pretty much."

"Sorry. I don't want to fight." She lowered her gaze to the narrow trail they were walking. "Not with you."

She said those last words so softly he wasn't sure he was supposed to hear them. But hear them he had, and it knotted him up inside. He didn't dare risk answering her. Because he was starting to realize just how much trouble he was in here.

Then they were at the point that jutted out into the lake north of the cabin. He showed her to his favorite spot, where the sandstone had been shaped by wind and water into a serviceable place to sit and look out over the lake.

"This is lovely," she said, as she sat on the stone, apparently not caring that it was wet in spots from the earlier rain.

"I did a lot of my teenage thinking here."

"I can see why." She gave him a sideways look and a smile. "Although some would say the terms *teenage* and *thinking* are mutually exclusive."

"Not me," he said, holding up his hands in mock defense. "I did a lot of thinking." He couldn't hold back a grin. "Of course, most of it was crazy wrong, but it was thinking."

She laughed, and he had the thought he'd rather hear that laugh than just about anything. And that had him remembering that moment again, when he'd nearly kissed her.

*Talk about crazy wrong thinking...*

"That's Kanopolis State Park over there," he said

abruptly, pointing across the lake and not caring if he sounded like a tour guide. Not now, when he was trying not to look at her, at that luscious mouth that was too damned tempting. "It was the first state park in Kansas. They've got a full-on prairie dog town over there, makes ours look like an outpost." She smiled at that, and he went on. "And some serious hiking trails. About thirty miles' worth. Horsethief Canyon'll kill you on a hot day."

"Sounds challenging."

"The wildlife viewing area is a lot easier. And fun, really."

"What kind of wildlife?"

"Anything from woodchucks to wild turkeys. Porcupines. Mule deer."

She looked at him rather intently for a moment, he wasn't sure why. "What's your favorite?"

He had to think about that for a moment. "Bobcat, maybe. Or kestrels. I like the way they hover like oversized hummingbirds."

She laughed at that. "So, the higher-ups on the food chain you were talking about, then?"

His brow furrowed. "I hadn't thought about it like that, but I guess so. I admire getting the job done." He gave her a sideways look. "I suppose you're more for the prey than the hunters?"

"I think an eagle—or a bobcat—on the hunt is a beautiful thing. But I also think the mouse has his place."

"Then we agree," he said quietly.

She smiled at that. "I'd like to see this refuge sometime."

*And I'd like to take you there.* He bit back the thought before it made it into words. "It's a great place. Two ponds, a marsh, a bunch of photo blinds and an observation deck." He raised a brow at her. "But what I think you'd like best is what it used to be."

"What did it used to be?"

"A motorcycle racetrack."

She blinked. "What?"

He nodded. "It hadn't been in use in a while, so some area folks donated the money and it was converted to a natural sanctuary."

"That's wonderful!"

He'd known she'd like the idea, but he hadn't quite expected the delight that shone in her eyes.

And he couldn't quite stop the wish that he could put that look in her eyes in another, much more personal way.

Usually in a place like this, Ashley would be more aware of her surroundings than anything else. She would be looking at everything, plants, animals, birds, smiling at the familiar while searching out those she didn't know, filing the image of them away in her brain to research later. Normally she would have pulled out her phone and done it right then, but to her surprise, she didn't miss it. She had belatedly realized that her prodigious brain gave her an advantage others might not have: the ability to remember exactly what she'd seen later and track it down.

Usually in a place like this, her focus would be on where she was, not who she was with.

But nothing with Ty Colton was usual. Not for her. And that was unsettling enough that it had her completely off balance. Which in turn was startling enough that she didn't quite know how to deal with it.

She tried to focus on other things. What he'd told her about the sanctuary they'd built over there in the state park. But that just made her think about how he'd known what that would mean to her. So she tried thinking about the fact that the creatures he admired most were the predators, and what that said about him.

*I admire getting the job done.*

So did she, didn't she? Her entire life was about getting the job done; it was merely a different sort of job. She—

"I wonder," he murmured, staring out over the lake as if he were seeing something else entirely.

"You wonder what?" she asked after a moment when he didn't go on.

He still didn't look at her, but he answered, in a tone that sounded like her father when he was thinking out loud. "If Sanderson would be willing to move his development back a little, and maybe put some effort into improving the wetlands, or maybe building a sanctuary of sorts, or a bird study center. Maybe the county would trade him some land to do that."

She nearly gaped at him. That was exactly the sort of compromise she always worked toward, and he'd come up with it just like that.

"He could make it a selling point," he murmured, even more quietly now, brow furrowed, still staring out over the water. "Give buyers a stake in preserving the wetland, maybe even put part of homeowner's association fees toward maintaining them. I'm sure there are people who would buy into it just for those reasons." For another long moment, he kept looking out over the lake. Then he gave his head a sharp shake. And glanced at her. "Sorry," he muttered. "Just thinking out loud."

She was certain she was still gaping at him but couldn't help it. "Don't apologize. It's a perfect solution. Exactly what I work toward." He smiled then, looking pleased, although there was a touch of surprise in it. "Do you think the county would do that? Could they afford it?"

"No idea," he answered. "There might be some Chickadee Checkoff funds available, since it's essentially to protect wildlife." She was familiar with the term in some states for the checkboxes on tax returns that sent taxpayer donations to specific causes. "Problem would be convincing them, since everyone thinks their cause is the most important."

She smiled at back at him. "I'm very good at convincing." She was looking right at him then and didn't—couldn't—miss the flare of something hot and almost intimate in his eyes.

"I know you are," he said, and his voice sounded as his gaze had looked. A strange combination of heat and chill swept over her, and feeling a shiver go down her spine at the same time, her cheeks flushed. It was an experience she'd never had before.

But she'd never met a man like this one before. And certainly never one who did such crazy things to her, when they'd never even kissed.

Yet.

The single short word echoed in her mind. And she knew that on some level her mind had already decided it would happen. She also realized that if left up to him, it would not. Because he wouldn't. He would see it as a violation of his duty. She almost blushed all over again at the thought, which seemed old-fashioned to her very modern mind, but she couldn't deny it was very appealing.

It also meant it would be up to her.

A challenge. She was always up for a challenge.

# Chapter 24

Ty was actually grateful for the new boat that cruised into sight off the point. As he'd told her, this time of year, there were more locals and regulars out than strangers, but this was a brand that was chiefly used by a boat-rental operation near the park.

He watched the small vessel for a moment, noticed the turn and the overcorrection as it tried to get closer. Unfamiliarity with the controls, or maybe boats in general.

It was enough.

"Time to head back," he said, still watching.

"What is it?"

"Time to head back," he repeated, turning and taking her elbow in case she wanted to argue. Even as he thought it, she denied it.

"I wasn't arguing, but why? That boat you were staring at?"

"It's a rental."

"Is that unusual?"

"Sort of. It's from a place that closes down to just a few boats this time of year, so they can repair and maintain the rest of their fleet." He glanced at her, then. "I used to work there summers, and some of those renters brought boats back in sorry shape."

She looked out toward the newcomer. "Like this guy, who can't figure out the controls?" No, she didn't miss much. He'd just had the thought when he heard her breath catch. "You think he's here…because of me?"

"I think we don't gamble he's not."

To his relief, she didn't make a case out of it and started back the way they had come. He felt a little easier once they were out of sight from the water, knowing that if it had been someone intent on her, they'd been far enough out and the boat's driver awkward enough that they likely hadn't had a chance to verify it was her.

She seemed intent on the walk, but he knew all too well by now that that agile mind of hers never rested. She would be hell on wheels to try to keep up with.

Why he was even thinking that escaped him. It certainly wouldn't be his job to keep up with her, not after this was over. Since she'd only promised her parents two weeks, it soon would be. Although he had a feeling if Elite could show a valid actual threat, her parents would at least try to convince her to extend the situation. He didn't know whether to hope for that or not.

*Of course not, you idiot. You want her in danger?*

No, he didn't. But he wasn't looking forward to the end of this job, either. He'd gotten too much enjoyment—something rare enough for him to be notable—out of the quiet hours they'd spent reading, or the time spent hiking, fishing or just talking.

Of course, it would be entirely different on the outside. In her normal life, she'd be on the go all the time, jetting here and there, mostly glued to that phone of hers, or being interviewed or making speeches or giving talks on her favorite causes. There wouldn't be many quiet, peaceful hours of the sort they'd shared under these conditions. No, her life was not only different, it took place in a different world, and one he wanted no part of.

*As if that were an issue. It's not like she—*

He heard her let out a little cry in the same instant he saw her start to fall backward toward him as she apparently slipped or put her foot down wrong. He reacted instinctively, instantly grabbing her and stepping forward at the same time. She stayed upright but ended up pressed solidly against him.

"Oh," she said, rather breathlessly.

*Yeah. Oh.*

He thought it as his body went on full alert. The jolt of adrenaline when he'd thought she would fall had shifted to other purposes, and when he felt the taut, luscious curve of her backside pressed against him, there was no denying where it had gone.

He should let her go, step back, yet the simple act seemed beyond him at the moment. And so he held on, until she turned in his arms, obviously unaware of what the added friction was doing to him.

She stood there, looking up at him with the oddest expression. Warm yet cautious, shy yet intent. And that smile, that slight curve of those soft lips he just knew would be warm and pliant, was the sweetest damn thing he'd ever seen.

And then she was moving, still pressed against him but stretching up, her slender body sliding over him in a way that made newly awakened parts start demanding.

"Ash…"

He couldn't even finish her name, because he'd known where she was headed. Again, he gave his body the order to step back, to get his hands off her. And again, it ignored him, far too enamored of the feel of her to give it up merely because he knew he should.

Then she was kissing him, and it was more than even his recently vivid imagination could ever have produced. Her mouth wasn't just warm and pliant. It was luscious, sweet and at the same time fierce and demanding. And when he felt the tip of her tongue brush over his lower lip, it sent a shudder of sensation through him and he was lost.

For a moment, Ashley was afraid she'd miscalculated. Or else she'd stunned him, which was more acceptable than thinking he hadn't wanted this at all.

But that was her last coherent thought. In the instant after she had her first delicious taste of him on the tip of her tongue, he broke and was kissing her back. She knew he had wanted this, and if his intensity was anything to go by, he'd wanted it as much as she had. That made her want even more.

She hungrily deepened the kiss and savored the low groan that ripped from his throat. Her head spun, but she didn't care, as long as he didn't stop. The ground seemed to shift, until that slip and near fall she'd manufactured might become the real thing. It built and built as she probed, tasted, relished. Only a need for air, after longer than she would have thought possible, made her pull back enough to catch a breath.

His fingers tightened on her shoulders, as if he were afraid she would bolt, which made no sense since she'd started this. With full and aware intent. But without any idea what it would really be like, with no clue about the way it would erupt into a searing blaze. How could she have any idea, when she'd never felt anything like it in her life?

Her first thought, when friends told her of their own experiences, was that the accounts were exaggerations. That while you could feel attracted, even fiercely so, to someone, the tales of fire and soaring sensation were hyperbole. But then she would think of her parents, and their decades-long love affair, and the fact that despite their wealth, all they had ever told her to do was to find the kind of love they had and be happy. The more disconcerting fact was that they both insisted that they'd known their destiny before they'd even spoken, the moment they'd spotted each other across a college lecture hall.

That she was thinking that now, after a kiss that had shaken her from head to toe, was beyond unsettling. If Ty hadn't looked as stunned as she felt, she didn't know what she would have done.

He started to pull back, or at least tried to, but it seemed he was no more able to move away than she was. She caught a glimpse of his eyes, a darker blue than ever, heard him suck in a breath so deep it hinted that he'd needed it as badly as she had. Then his head came back down, his mouth captured hers, and she felt an entirely different kind of thrill, which made no sense to her either. Why would it be different? Why would him kissing her instead of the other way around be so very…special?

Then she was lost again in that flood of sensation, that rippling heat, until she was clutching at him almost wildly, wanting more, ever more. Right here, right now, on the cold ground, she didn't care. She had to have more. She had to have it all. With him, it had to be all.

When he broke the kiss, her head kept spinning for a moment. She heard a low, faint "Damn," and it took her a moment to register he'd actually said it. She felt a shudder go through him, ending with his hands tightening on her shoulders once more. And then he stepped firmly, purposefully back away from her. If she hadn't had the prominent evidence that he'd been as aroused as she had been pressing against her abdomen seconds ago, she might have felt hurt.

"That should never have happened," he said stiffly. "I'm sorry."

She, who had an answer for every situation, didn't seem to have one ready for this. It took her a moment to remember how to speak, anyway.

"I…believe I'm the one who started it."

"Doesn't matter. I should have stopped it."

She should have realized he would react this way. If she'd learned nothing else about Ty Colton this week, it was that he took his job—protecting her—very seriously. And obviously, in his mind, that included protecting her from him. Even if she didn't want that particular protection.

"I'm very glad you didn't," she said softly. "I wouldn't have missed that for the world."

He looked startled that she'd said it, but when he looked away, as if he couldn't meet her gaze any longer, she thought she saw the slightest curve of one corner of his mouth. As if he were pleased but didn't dare show it.

"It's getting late. We'd better get back." His voice was so rough she knew she'd been right. And that was enough.

For now.

## Chapter 25

Ty's jaw was getting tired of being clenched so much. This was ridiculous.

On their hike back to the cabin, they had reached the spot where the tree had gone down, and he thought that grabbing the splitting ax and tackling that big pile of logs would be just the thing to take the edge off. Too bad it was already getting dark. Besides, he couldn't leave her alone for as long as that job would take. Which of course compounded the problem.

Yeah, he'd made a mistake, a huge one, letting that kiss happen. He'd compounded it by initiating one himself. But that didn't mean he had to spend every minute obsessing about it. He could stop that. Use some of that stubborn he was known for. Hadn't his boss told him one of the reasons he took him on was that he was stubborn enough to stay out of the Colton family business?

*And damn lucky you did, or you'd be a suspect in that mess instead of trying to unravel the truth about it.*

Not that he'd gotten much unraveling done since Eric had dropped this job on him. He knew his sister Jordana was still digging, and that she wouldn't stop until she had the truth; she was nothing if not determined. Eric himself said she was the kind of determined he always looked for when recruiting. Ty had always admired the way she'd stood up to the old man, and when he'd told her that, she'd said she admired him for the same thing.

"I guess we did stand up to him, didn't we? He was about as happy about you joining the Navy as he was about me going with Elite."

And in the end, they respected each other for taking the harder path because it was the right thing for them.

But he kind of doubted Jordana envied anyone these days. She and Clint had worked things out and she was happier than he'd ever seen her. He'd always told her he thought the Chicago businessman was a good guy, and the way he'd handled the chaos that the current Colton mess had brought into his life had only proved that in Ty's book.

But that hadn't slowed down her dogged investigation in the least. Still, Ty was bothered by not being hands-on himself, despite the fact that technically he had no legal standing. Because he knew that in a private capacity, both he and Brooks could sometimes get people to open up in ways the police could not. Something about that lack of arrest powers made people more willing to talk.

But he wasn't out there working on it. He was stuck here. Stuck with the woman he'd thought would be the proverbial spoiled little rich girl but who instead had intrigued him at every turn. Including physically, he reluctantly admitted. It was a line he'd never crossed while working before, yet now he wanted not just cross it but obliterate it. And that shook him to the core.

"That's quite a frown."

A snap of adrenaline shot through him. That was twice now she'd come up on him and he'd been unaware. Which meant he'd been unaware of their surroundings, too, out here in the open.

*Idiot. Get your head in the game, Colton. You're supposed to be protecting that body, not lusting after it.*

This had to stop. Both times she'd surprised him, it had been because he was so deep into thinking about her that he'd been oblivious. In this case, he'd been reliving that kiss, again and again in his mind. And that, obviously, was not something he could admit to her. He could barely admit it to himself.

Backtracking in his thoughts for an answer to her comment, he said, "Just thinking about a family problem."

She studied him for a moment. Not that he knew that from looking at her, since at the moment he didn't think he dared. But he'd swear he could feel her gaze on him as they started walking again.

"The bodies they found or the cancer cases?" she asked. He stopped dead, turning his head sharply. Stared at her. "I told you I saw something. Now I remember what it was. Researching the area, I saw some of the stories, about both," she explained.

"And the idea that those cancers are somehow connected to Colton Construction is right up your alley, isn't it?"

His voice was sharp, and he was a little surprised at himself. He'd sounded more than just edgy because he felt like he'd been slacking off on the job at hand. He'd been worried about the whole situation, yes, but he wasn't used to feeling defensive about the family business, and didn't know why he'd retorted like that. Except she got to him in many ways he wasn't used to.

"I have some knowledge and experience with such cases, yes," she said easily, as if he hadn't snapped. Then he realized she was probably used to dealing with upset or angry people about these things. "And the fact that in the study I saw, all the men who've become ill worked for the same company at the same time, at the same building site is highly suggestive."

"I'm sure." He'd thought the same thing, and again wondered why he was feeling edgy about her putting it into words. Sure, he'd always defend his family, but that she was saying what others had, what he himself had considered seemed different somehow.

"There could be many causes," she said. "Contaminated building materials, lack of careful workplace practices."

"Right."

She tilted her head as she looked at him. "I'm not making accusations. It's far too early for that, and it may well be your family's company has nothing to do with it. It could be something that had already been in place, nothing they were responsible for. For example, if something had once been built there using arsenic-treated wood before it was banned. The arsenic can leach into the soil and contaminate it, and there would be no way to have known without testing."

By now he wasn't surprised at her knowledge about similar situations. It had become clear she was no figurehead, no front or money supplier who talked big, spent money, but knew nothing. She did, as she'd said, her homework, and she learned and remembered.

What surprised him was her willingness to proffer an explanation where Colton Construction was absolved.

*Someday maybe you'll get it through your head that she's not what you expected, in any way.*

Someday? He was thinking as if it would matter on that future someday. As if when this was over she wouldn't simply go back to her world, and he would stay here in his.

He was calling himself all sorts of stupid when they finally cleared the trees. And he stopped dead again. Glanced at his watch, wondering if it was off. It was barely past sunset, so he'd thought the deeper darkness had been the trees. Even leafless, the big cottonwoods cast shadows.

But now, for the first time since they'd left the point he got a clear look at the sky to the west. The storm clouds had arrived and were piling up in a way that told him that the predicted strong frontal system was approaching. But it wasn't that that had the hair on the back of his neck prickling, it was the sky itself.

Green.

There was no mistaking the tint of green in more than one place.

"Come on," he said, "we need to get to the cabin."

"Why the rush?" she asked, although she picked up her pace to keep up with him. And she could do it, with those long legs of hers.

He gave himself a mental slap. Now of all times he needed to focus. "I don't like that sky," he said.

She looked. "It does look strange." Her brow furrowed. "Why does it look green?"

"We can have the science-versus-folklore argument about that inside, but for now just accept it doesn't mean anything good and keep moving."

He was thankful she didn't argue. They kept going, and he kept giving the sky wary glances. They were halfway across the clearing the cabin stood in when the hail started. Sudden and hard, the frozen pellets came down like a vertical avalanche, bouncing as they hit the ground. And them.

"Now we run," he said. And grabbed her hand. He told himself it was simply to be sure she kept up, but he didn't even believe it himself.

They ran. The hail was getting larger, harder, and there was already enough on the ground to keep it from melting quickly.

"It's moving fast," she exclaimed, and he heard the first tinge of concern in her voice.

"Yes."

He left it at that, seeing no need to voice his particular thought yet. But by the time they reached the deck of the cabin, it was more than a thought, it was apprehension. The moment they were close enough, he heard it, the blaring sound from inside. He swore, low and harsh.

"What?" She sounded worried for the first time. Distracted, she slipped on the step up to the deck that was slick with the icy pellets.

He grabbed her, kept her upright as he said with angry disgust, "We get about one a year in November, and it has to be freaking here and now? Keep moving." His gut was yelling *run* but the deck was as slippery as the steps, and he didn't want to deal with a broken limb on either of them.

"What?" she repeated, her voice rising a little. He

stalled until they got inside. He closed the door behind them. "Ty? Tell me what that sound is."

He tried to ignore how much he liked her using his first name. And finally turned to face her, the alert ringing in his ears.

"It's a tornado warning."

# Chapter 26

A tornado. In Kansas. Ashley couldn't help it, she laughed. "Seriously?"

"Very." There was no denying the grim tone of his voice. He was already headed down the hall toward the panic room.

She could tell now that they were inside that that's where the whooping alert sound was coming from. She followed. This was one phenomenon she had zero experience with. She'd been through hurricanes, earthquakes, even a volcanic eruption once, but she'd somehow managed to never encounter an actual tornado. The closest she'd ever been was one of her mom's favorite old movies—and not the one involving the flying monkeys.

He looked at the weather station in the array of electronics. Swore again. The landline phone in the room rang. He grabbed it. The conversation was short.

"Looking at it. Yes, too close. Going now. Hope so."

He hung up and spun around. "Come on. We're heading for the cellar."

She blinked. What cellar? "But shouldn't we stay here in the safe room? It's solid and—"

"Aboveground. They're saying the one that touched down in the area was an EF3 to EF4. This whole place could be gone."

Fear spiked in her at those words. She decided it would not be wise to argue with him, not over this. He was Kansas born and bred, and obviously knew what he was talking about.

"I'll just go grab my—"

"No! No time. Tornadoes this time of year tend to move faster. We have to take shelter now."

His urgency drove her fear higher. She was close on his heels as he ran back down the hall. They went through the kitchen, he grabbed up his keys from the counter, then yanked open a door she had assumed was some kind of cupboard or pantry. But it was a stairway going down to the cellar she hadn't known existed. It was, oddly, mostly underneath what had to be the deck area.

He insisted she go first, and he closed the door as she started down, casting them into pitch-black. But then he apparently hit a switch because light flared. As she reached the bottom, she looked around.

She didn't know what she'd expected, but this wasn't it. It was larger, maybe twenty by twenty, with walls of what appeared to be solid concrete, broken up only by a set of steps on the far wall, leading up to what looked like an exit hatch of some sort. The heavy metal hatch had a small window that looked like it had been made for an airplane and able to withstand just about anything. There were shelves with what looked like emergency supplies along one wall, in addition to a counter with a sink and a microwave. On another wall was a small television and what looked like a duplicate of the weather station upstairs. There was a small couch and some upholstered chairs in front of the TV, and a table with several chairs near the makeshift kitchen.

That was all she had time to notice before a movement Ty made drew her attention and she turned in time to see him swinging a door shut at the bottom of the stairs. This was no ordinary door; it was thick, solid and metal, not wood. And it closed with sliding bars from the inside of the door that entered openings in the wall itself. It looked as if it could withstand a direct hit from a bomb.

"Why do I feel as if we're going into lockdown at NORAD?" she said nervously.

Ty gave her a look that was at first startled but then, unexpectedly, he grinned. Suddenly her fear ebbed a little. "That's actually where my Uncle Shep got the idea," he said. "He had the chance to go on a tour there once when he was in the Navy."

"That hatch his idea, too? It looks like it could be on a submarine."

The grin widened. "Exactly. It was made by a company that does just that. He wanted the window so we could at least get a peek outside without having to go out there. And it lets a little light in when the power's out."

"Your uncle sounds like quite a guy."

"He's the best," Ty said simply. And he said it, she noticed, with much more warmth than he'd ever spoken of his father. Then he gestured toward the back corner of the room, where she saw now there was a second small room, rather grimly built of cinder block. "That's the bedroom and the last resort," he said. "If it gets really bad, that's where you go."

She walked over and looked into the corner room. It looked like a jail cell with the narrow bunk, but there were bottles of drinking water lined up on the shelves opposite. And a large white case with the too-familiar red cross on it, which only added to her unease.

"Define really bad," she said, nerves kicking up again.

"If you feel the cabin lifting."

She stared at him. Was he serious? Dear God, he was. She looked at the very heavy beams above them. Then back at him as he walked over and turned on both the second weather station and the television, tuned to a twenty-four-hour weather channel.

"How far away?" she asked, staring at the map.

"The one that touched down was just west of the dam." Her breath jammed up in her throat. "That's four miles from here, which is a long way, in tornado terms. Bigger concern is where there's one…"

"There can be more," she finished, looking upward again.

"Yes."

As she looked up, she remembered what she'd noticed before. "Why is this mostly under the deck rather than the house?"

One corner of his mouth curved upward in that way that made her want to kiss him all over again. "Good catch. It's so that if it gets really bad up top, we don't end up with a refrigerator on our heads."

She blinked. Then she smiled back at him. "I am forever amazed at the power of the human survival instinct."

"That was my father. He does know the construction business."

There was respect in his tone, if not warmth. At least not the kind of warmth that had been in his voice when he'd spoken of his uncle. The Coltons must have a complicated family dynamic. She supposed that with eight of them, it couldn't be any other way. She wondered if all of them had the same rather stiff relationship with their father.

She made a mental note to give her father a hug when this was over. Even if he had annoyed her with insisting on this protection measure. Then again, if her father hadn't insisted, she never would have met Ty. And that somehow seemed a much greater loss than having her life restricted for a while. Truly, she hadn't felt restricted since they'd gotten here. In fact, until this storm had begun, she had barely thought about being without her phone. Her thought had been to retrieve it before they came down here, but that had been habit as much as anything, since it wouldn't change the fact that there was no reception.

But now it occurred to her that she wished she did have it, just in case. She could write notes on it, to her parents, her friends. Or texts that could be found later if the worst happened.

"You're looking pretty grim."

She nearly jumped. She hadn't realized he'd come up beside her. "I...was just thinking."

"Well, there's a news flash," he said, and the way he said it made her smile again. "About what? Being stuck in a storm cellar?"

"A pretty nice storm cellar. I would have pictured something rather dark and dank."

"It'll be dark if—" he grimaced "—make that when the power goes out." He glanced around. "But it is nice. Dad built it, but furnished and stocked it to my mother's specifications. She's all about taking care of people."

Ashley's smile widened. "Good nurses are like that. My mother's the same."

"But that's not what you were thinking about."

She'd hoped to divert him, but she should have known better. This was not a man who would be diverted unless he wanted to be. "No. I was thinking about…leaving notes for my family and friends. Just in case."

For an instant, he simply looked at her, but then he took a step and wrapped her in his arms. "Hey, hey, don't be going there. We'll be fine."

She should pull herself together. She should tell him she was all right. She should stand on her own two feet as she always had.

But this felt too darned good to do any of that.

*Just for a minute or two. I'm allowed that much, aren't I?*

She felt a shiver ripple through her. She knew it was a reaction to him, to him holding her like this, but he tightened the embrace and murmured more reassurance. Which only intensified her response to the strength of him, the heat, the caring.

For a long moment, they stood there, and she felt his cheek come to rest atop her head. It felt strangely intimate, as intimate almost as that kiss. And then he went tense and his head lifted. She looked up, saw him staring at the television screen. She hadn't been paying much attention to what the meteorologist had been saying; it had become background noise as she explored the cellar. Now she turned her head to look, but before she could register what she was seeing, the screen—and the cellar—went dark. She wasn't startled. She'd expected the power to go out after what he'd said, but...

"What is it?" she asked. "What did she say?"

"Another touchdown, just north of Yankee Run."

She felt a chill. It was such a cute little town. She'd hate to see it badly damaged. Did everyone have a cellar like this, or at least something? She hoped so. She'd hate to think—

It hit her then. North of Yankee Run.

*They* were north of Yankee Run.

# Chapter 27

This time when she trembled, there was some genuine fear in it. She might not have been through a tornado before, but she'd certainly seen enough images of the aftermath and damage they could leave behind. She told herself to trust his word that they would be all right. And in fact she did trust him, more than she ever would have expected. But still...

A loud crash from outside made her jump, even though it hadn't sounded too close. He tightened his arms.

"I suppose you're not in the least afraid," she said rather wryly.

"Worried," he conceded. "Although come to think of it, it might do my father good to have to rebuild this place. Give him something else to think about."

She supposed he meant both the bodies found in the Colton building and the cancer cases link. She found it rather touching that despite the fact that they didn't have the close relationship she and her own father had, that this was what he thought of. "I'd hate to think of losing that amazing historic ceiling."

"That'd really bum out my mom. She loves that thing."

This time the crash was even louder, and much closer, and a little yelp accompanied her jump. She heard the blare of what she guessed was the SUV's alarm faintly over the wind. Ty reached into his pocket and a moment later that noise amid all the rest stopped. But he didn't let go of her, and she gave up all pretense of not wanting or needing the comfort. She did need it, and she surely, surely wanted it.

"I think," he said, having to lean down to say it against her ear so she could hear him as the howl outside intensified, "we'd better hit the bunker."

She shivered again. She wondered for a moment if he would have retreated to that final shelter if she hadn't been here, but decided she didn't care. She'd feel better knowing they were as safe as possible. So she didn't resist and they headed across the cellar and into the bunker.

And then the already fierce howl became thunderous. She remembered hearing that tornados sounded like a freight train. What they hadn't said was it made you feel as if you were stuck on the tracks watching it bear down on you. It got, impossibly, even louder. Genuine fear plunged through her as he pulled her into the cinder block shelter. She held on to him, more like clinging to him, and she didn't care.

"It's okay, Ash. We'll be okay."

She heard the words, but it felt strange. She was certain he normally would have said them quietly, comfortingly, but he had to shout them for her to hear. And two things hit her simultaneously. One, that she would accept the usually hated shortening of her name from him, and second, that if he'd told her instead that they were going to die, the thing she'd regret most at this moment was that they'd never gone beyond those kisses.

An instant later, she felt it, that lifting he'd talked about. She bit back a little scream. And then startlingly, his mouth came down on hers. As if he'd read her thought, or as if he'd had a similar one himself, a regret that they'd never explored what lay beyond the amazing fire they'd kindled with just a kiss.

He plundered her mouth and she let him. Then she probed further herself, letting the thrill of the taste of him, the feel of him, the heat of him push back the fear. It was fierce, and fast, and held a sense of urgency she'd never felt in her life. She didn't just want, she simply had to have him. When his hands slid down from her shoulders to her waist, to pull her closer, she realized from the prod of rigid male flesh against her that he was as aroused as she was. And suddenly nothing, not who they were, not even the storm outside mattered more than having this man completely.

She became some wild thing she didn't recognize, pulling at his clothes, hastening to shed her own. Some part of her half expected him to stop her, to rebuild that wall he persisted in putting between them, but he never faltered. *Decision made*, she thought dizzily as his hands cupped her breasts and his fingers toyed with her nipples, sending fire shooting through her to pool low and deep.

And then she had his shirt off and she felt a new spike of heat at the sight of that broad strong chest and flat ridged belly. She was only vaguely aware of ridding herself of the remaining barriers of cloth, and they went down to the narrow bunk in a tumble. It didn't matter that it was narrow, because they were already so tightly together there seemed like more than enough room.

It was mad, it was wild, it was almost desperate. She couldn't reach enough, couldn't touch enough, couldn't stroke enough. And when he finally levered himself over her and paused, she arched her hips and reached to guide him, giving the answer to the question she couldn't have heard, anyway.

He drove home in a thrust as powerful as the storm outside, and she cried out with the sheer pleasure of it. Nothing mattered but this, and she vaguely realized that this was the human instinct that should amaze her, the human instinct she'd never completely understood until this moment, with this man.

Sex had been pleasurable for her before, but they'd surpassed that level with that first kiss. This was something much, much more, something bigger, something transcendent.

When he shifted to take one nipple into his mouth and suckle it, then flick it with his tongue, her body careened out of control. She felt as if she were headed for some crazed plunge into the unknown. Then came the explosion, and she knew what had come before had been only a prelude.

She let herself scream because she couldn't help it, but it was drowned out by the storm.

Ty wondered if he'd ever heard such silence in his life. He knew it technically wasn't silence. There were noises—mostly things falling, it seemed like. Creaking as things settled. He knew it just seemed like utter, total silence after the roaring sound last night that had come closer and closer until it was deafening. The total darkness of the storm cellar intensified the feeling, and had seemed to magnify the already deafening roar.

The sound, and the rumble he could actually feel, that had brought real, genuine and thankfully rare fear with it, fear that he and Ashley wouldn't survive the hit that sounded nearly direct.

But they had survived.

Oh, boy, had they survived.

His body was still feeling the aftershocks of that moment, a moment he would have sworn had come at the peak of the tornado strike that he knew had been far too close. The moment when she had moaned out his name as her nails dug into his back, and her sleek, hot body had clenched around him, driving him over the edge into some dizzying, swirling place he'd never been before. The pulsing throb had gone on and on, until he couldn't even hear the howl going on above them over the hammering of his pulse in his ears.

And now, in the silent darkness, his instinct should have been to emerge, to check the damage, but all he wanted to do was stay right here, buried in the heat of her, and start all over again.

It was dark out, anyway. Better to wait until morning, right?

Even as he silently admitted he was using the dark as an excuse, she arched up to him, wrapped her arms around his neck and pulled him down for yet another of those deep, lingering, luscious kisses. They proved just how long he'd neglected this aspect of his life by the way he responded to her instantly.

More quickly than he would have thought possible, they were soaring toward that peak again. And then in that utter and complete darkness, savoring the sweetness of holding her close, he finally slept.

It was still fairly dark when he awoke, but his inner clock was saying it was morning. Early, but morning. He'd taken off his watch for some reason—

Memory slammed home. He'd taken off the watch for fear it would scratch the beautiful, delicate silk of Ashley's skin. Ashley, who was curled up beside him, with seemingly every inch of that naked skin against his own.

Where was the damned watch? He needed to know what time it was, needed to know if it would be light out yet, needed to check in with Elite and let them know they were all right, needed to get topside and assess, needed to find out if there was anything left standing up there.

He also knew he was focusing on all of that to avoid the huge, looming and utterly beautiful mistake he had made.

Ashley stirred. He started to pull away, as he knew he needed to. But her arms were around him, holding him close, and he couldn't quite bring himself to detach. Not yet. Just one more sweet moment.

But the longer he stayed here, nestled against her, the more interested his rebellious body became in a rematch. And while someday, far in the future, he might be able to write off last night as an adrenaline-induced, fear-heightened lapse in judgment, doing it again now that the immediate threat was over would be something else again.

But damn, she felt good. In that instant when he'd first exploded inside her, he wouldn't have cared one bit if that twister had landed on top of them. He half felt like it had anyway, because it had been like nothing he'd ever experienced in his life. And no matter how he tried to chalk that up to a long dry spell when he'd had neither the time nor the inclination to go after no-strings sex, there was a small voice in the back of his head stupidly chanting that this was what it was supposed to be like.

"Hi," Ashley whispered, "and wow." And damned if her tone didn't match that stupid voice in his head.

"Yeah," he muttered. What he wanted to say was, *Last night was incredible, let's do it again. And again and again and again, endlessly.* And that realization shook him enough to finally make the move.

He lifted himself off her, trying not to look at her slender naked body in the faint light as he stood. Not that not looking helped. He was hard all over again, and under current circumstances, it wasn't something he could exactly hide. Then she reached for him, her slender fingers curling. The memory of the first touch of her hands on him, those fingers encircling, stroking, caressing his rigid flesh from tip to bottom, nearly made his knees buckle. Knowing her first touch would incinerate his willpower, he took a step back and away.

He saw her puzzled look. "Ty?"

She'd lifted up on her elbows, and the movement drew his eyes to the soft rounds of her breasts, where he had nuzzled and stoked, and to the rosy tips he had suckled and flicked with his tongue until she had cried out. He felt a surge of heat that nearly staggered him. He covered it by backing up another step, safely out of her reach.

She sat up, then. "Ty?" she repeated. "It's all right. I mean…if you're worried, I'm on birth control. There are crazies out there, so my parents insisted, just in case."

He hadn't even thought of that. Stupidly, it had been the last thing on his mind.

For a long silent moment, he just stared at her. The

faint light from the hatch window barely gave him enough light to see her outline. But he didn't need any light at all. He knew that limber, lanky shape intimately now, and it was etched into his memory with such depth he knew he'd carry it forever.

Along with the knowledge that this had been the biggest professional mistake of his career, probably his life. Because he already knew he was going to pay the price for this one forever.

"What's wrong?"

"This," he answered hoarsely. "This was wrong. A mistake."

She went very still. "A mistake," she said, sounding as if she were enunciating each word with exquisite care.

"Yes. It should never have happened. It was incredibly unprofessional of me, and I apologize."

She was on her feet in an instant. "You *apologize*? After...*that,* you apologize?"

"Yes. I'm sorry. You have every right to make a complaint to my boss and—"

For the first time since he'd known her she swore, rather colorfully. "The only thing I have to complain about is myself, apparently. For being stupid enough to become a living, breathing cliché, the poor little woman falling for her bodyguard."

Her bodyguard. That was what he was. All he was. But then the rest of what she'd said hit. Falling for? She'd fallen for him? That was crazy. She was a Hart, and no matter the local standing of the Coltons, and the higher standing of other branches of the family, she was way out of his league. They weren't even on the same playing field.

Hell, they weren't even playing the same game.

# Chapter 28

"My friends will laugh themselves silly," Ashley said, not caring how harsh she sounded as she gathered her scattered clothes.

"Ash—"

"Just shut up, will you please? I find I desperately need to get dressed." And as she did so she found she needed to revoke the permission she'd silently given him. "And don't call me that. It's Ashley to you." Deep down she knew she would never forget how he'd whispered it in the darkness, or how he'd groaned it out when he'd gone rigid as he pulsed fiercely inside her. "Or perhaps we should go back to Ms. Hart."

He went very still. She told herself she didn't care. When she wobbled pulling her right boot on, she saw from the corner of her eye him moving to help and she waved him off. If he touched her again she was afraid she might lose her resolve. And wouldn't the world just love to hear about the lofty Ashley Hart begging a man to…

She'd almost thought the words *love her*. And that made her angrier still. It wasn't that she'd never begged before, she had. But she'd begged for her causes, for people to see reason, to listen to each other, to understand. But a man? No. Never. When Simon had left, she hadn't asked him to reconsider, hadn't even asked him to take her with him. So why could she picture herself begging this man all too well?

"Ashley," he said, "please understand—"

She threw up a hand to stop him. "Oh, I do. I get it. It was…it was storm-induced madness and I was handy, right? Meaningless."

He let out a short, harsh laugh. "Meaningless? Is that what you call something I'll never ever forget? Something I'll torture myself about for the rest of my life?"

She stopped with the other boot in her hand, straightened to stare at his shadowy shape. She hated that she couldn't see his face clearly, his eyes. It was lighter than it had been even a couple of minutes ago, but his back was to it, casting his face in shadow.

"I've achieved greatness now, haven't I?" She hated the way she sounded, the way the pain echoed beneath the sarcasm. "I've become someone's greatest regret." She yanked on the other boot, then straightened again. "There are some people, some I even know, who would pride themselves on that. I've never been one of them."

She determinedly did not look at him as she tightened the laces and then tied them. She was aware he was getting dressed himself, and forced herself not to steal even a split-second glimpse. She didn't need to. Every line of his powerful body was etched into her brain, probably permanently. And whatever her future held, if ever there was another man in it, she doubted very much if he would ever measure up to this one.

He finished dressing, and out of the corner of her eye she saw him reach for the weapon that she only now realized he'd put on the floor within reach last night. Ever the bodyguard.

Then he stood looking at her for a silent moment. "Ash," he began, and his tone was full of so much regret it was the spark to her fury. If she were the type who resorted to physical violence, she would have slapped him. Hard.

"I told you not to call me that! You don't have the right anymore."

He went very still. And when, after a moment, he spoke, that cool, detached professional she'd first encountered in the hotel lobby was back. In force. "You're right, Ms. Hart. I need to go topside and assess damage. Please stay here and—"

"I'm not staying down here, wondering."

"I need to make sure there are no hazards, things that could fall—"

"The tornado hit some time ago." And what should have been terrifying had turned out to be the sweetest moments of her life. But what she had wanted more and more of, he apparently didn't want at all. Didn't want her. She hated the way even her thoughts sounded whiny. Made herself focus. "Wouldn't everything that's going to fall have done so already?"

"There could still be things that could be dislodged and cause injury. I'll take a quick look first."

"And if you get killed by a falling chimney, what am

I supposed to do?" she asked, her voice dripping with false sweetness.

"Just stay put," he said, not even blinking at her snark about his possible death. "Elite will be out here soon if I don't report in."

He walked out into the main cellar. When she stepped out behind him, she saw that he was headed not for the stairway up into the house but the hatch, where the morning light was getting brighter. This had the effect of making it look as if he'd stepped into a spotlight. Her breath caught as the light poured down over his tall, lean body, reminding her too, too vividly of that body naked in her arms, against her skin, driving into her with sweet, luscious force, driving her upward to an explosion she thought would likely ruin her for any other man.

She shoved the very thought out of her mind as he started up the steps. "Why *that* way?" she asked and was pleased to hear she'd managed an almost matter-of-fact tone.

"Because I can at least see this is clear. There could be anything piled up against the inside door."

Meaning the whole cabin could be in rubble. She felt a qualm at the thought of him losing this place that had clearly been a family refuge. The thought of that unique hammered-metal antique ceiling being scattered to the winds, lost forever, made her unaccountably sad. She had felt...not just safe here—and she knew that was more because of Ty than the place—but comfortable. At home. She liked the simplicity of it, the lack of flash and glamour and the focus on comfort and relaxing. She even had come to like—well, not like, but at least not mind—the being cut off part. It had taken her a while, but eventually she had stopped unconsciously reaching for her phone all the time. If nothing else, this had taught her just how truly addicted she was to the darn thing. She was going to have to work on that, when this was over.

Over.

If the cabin was gone, this part would certainly be over. She wondered what would happen next, but didn't give it a great deal of thought. It occurred to her that Simon would have insisted they stay here in the cellar, where they had food, water and were relatively safe, until the authorities rescued them. But Ashley had spent a lot of time in parts of the world where there were no authorities interested in rescue and had learned you needed to at least try to help yourself. She knew perfectly well she'd be doing exactly what Ty was doing, in that case.

She didn't dwell on that, either. She was too busy watching as Ty undid the rather aggressive-looking latches that held the hatch in place. The man was a pleasure to watch move, no matter what he was doing.

*Right. And he regrets what he was doing with you last night. It was wrong, a mistake, it never should have happened. He couldn't make it any clearer.*

Some reasoning part of her, the part she seemed to have trouble hanging on to around him, understood. He was a professional, he had a job here, and that job did not include getting involved with…the subject. The client. Her. But neither of them had asked for this. And she, at least, had certainly never expected to react to the man the way she had. As if he'd been what she'd been waiting for her entire life. Even if that was how she felt, it would be crazy, suicidal even, to show that so soon. She'd known the man less than…ten days. What was that, a fraction of a single percent of the days of her life?

She gave her head a shake before her brain could

dart down that rabbit hole. She watched as he swung the heavy hatch open, and more light poured in. It seemed the calm after the storm had arrived, and with it clear, or at least bright, skies. But she felt no relief, no joy of survival. Because as he started up and out, as she watched that long, lean, powerful body move, all she could think of was what else he'd said, and the wrenching tone in which he'd said it.

*Meaningless? Is that what you call something I'll never ever forget? Something I'll torture myself about for the rest of my life?*

"Well, Mr. Ty Colton," she murmured when she knew he couldn't hear, "I may just have to make sure you really do never ever forget."

# Chapter 29

Ty was a little surprised when he clambered out of the hatch and found the cabin still standing. Not undamaged, but still standing. A quick scan of the surroundings didn't show anything immediately threatening, so he called back down into the cellar, "It's okay, if you want to come up."

He was startled when she popped up beside him a split second later. Obviously she'd already been on her way up.

"Good," she said, with surprising cheer. "I didn't really want a chimney to fall on you. It would spoil all my plans for later."

His head snapped around and he stared at her. That sounded like... It couldn't mean what it sounded like. But she was smiling, a rather private, knowing smile that made him wonder if maybe it had meant exactly what his clearly overstimulated—and attracted—brain had provided, complete with full-color images.

He fought down the surge of heat that rocketed through him at the idea. The thought of having her again, the light of day gliding over that silken skin and lithe, limber body was enough to make him want to head back down to that bed right now.

Finally deciding anything he said in this moment would likely get him in trouble, he said nothing and tried to focus on inspecting the damage. The chimney was indeed still standing, although the roof around was missing a lot of shingles. The deck furniture was gone, except for the big table, that was dangling over the edge lopsidedly. One of the large front windows was a spiderweb of broken glass radiating from the probable impact point of the branch he saw lying on the deck. But a look through the unbroken window showed that, save for some things knocked over and another broken window in the kitchen, things appeared fairly stable. And the door to the cellar was clear.

"It looks good. Can we go in?" Ashley asked.

"I want to check the propane tank first. I don't smell anything, but I want to be sure. And look for any power lines down that might cause a problem when the power comes back on."

She nodded. "I'll do that."

She turned away, as she went pulling some sort of elastic band out of a pocket and tugging her dark brown hair back into a tail. Practical, but all it made him want to do was pull it back off again so he could thread his fingers through that soft silk. Which made him think of it trailing over his body as it had last night, stroking him in a way he'd never known could curl his toes.

*Damn.*

He headed for the big propane tank at a much faster pace than he'd intended, because he was sure if he didn't get away from her, he would say something stupid. Not that anything he'd say could be stupider than what he'd done, but at least he could avoid compounding the issue.

Once he was as certain as he could be that the tank and the lines to and from it were intact and no explosion was imminent, he just stood there for a moment, pondering the unpleasant fact that he didn't want to go back to the house. He didn't want to face her. He had no business even worrying about that when he needed to be assessing damage and reporting in.

Lecturing himself every step of the way, if only because it kept him from remembering last night, he went. Ashley appeared completely able, unlike himself, to focus on what should be first on the list.

"The structure looks fairly good. Besides the roof damage, there's some siding missing on the north side and another broken window in the kitchen. And that," she said, gesturing at the deck railing he'd already noticed was missing. "I haven't looked inside yet."

He nodded, not trusting himself to speak, and headed for the door to the cabin. Once inside, he was relieved to see that except for some debris in the living room near the broken window, and the same in the kitchen, things looked pretty intact.

*Me, not so much.*

He didn't look at her as she followed him into the kitchen. He picked up the landline phone. As he'd expected, it was dead.

"No flying refrigerator," she said.

"Not this time." He supposed he should be glad she

could joke. Or not. He wasn't sure. He wasn't sure of anything right now, and that was a state he was unaccustomed enough with to be beyond unsettling.

"How long does it usually take for the power to come back on?"

He didn't look at her. Didn't dare. "Depends on how much damage was done. There were likely places that got hit much worse than we did."

"Just wondering if we should keep it closed to retain the chill for a few hours, or give it up and eat everything."

He still didn't look at her. "Whatever you want."

"On the other hand, you could simply stand there and radiate chill," she said sweetly. "Everything would be frozen within an hour."

His head jerked around then, almost involuntarily. Just in time to see her turn on her heel and walk into the living room, where she began to pick up some things that had been knocked over.

"Don't mess with the broken glass." The words were out before he could stop them, and before he could think about the wisdom of speaking in the tone of an order to an already-pissed-off woman.

"Why?" she asked, and her voice was even more deadly sweet now. "Afraid I'll cut your throat with it?"

He let out a long breath. "I wouldn't blame you if you tried."

She straightened, indeed holding a shard of glass that would do the job. "I won't say it isn't tempting at the moment. But while I may have made a mistake about your feelings, I knew my own, and the decision I made last night was mine."

He stared at her. It was a moment before he could get

any words past the tightness in his throat. "The only mistake last night was mine. I should never have let it go so far."

"It? *It?*"

He'd handled many things in his life, faced more than a few tough situations in his work, and yet he felt utterly incapable of dealing with a woman this angry. Especially since he deserved every bit of it.

"I need to check in," he said roughly, and headed down the hall. With his luck at the moment, the battery backup on the comms had failed along with everything else, or something else would go wrong.

But it hadn't, and there was an undertone in Mitch's voice that told him it was a good thing. "Man, the boss has been walking the floor since sunup. The chopper's just about in the air."

"Stand down, we're okay. A little damage to the cabin, but it's still standing. Power's out, so we'll need to re-locate."

"I'll set up the secondary location," Mitch said. "How soon you figure on leaving?"

"Right now, but I don't know what shape the roads will be in."

"You had better," Ashley said from behind him, "think about what shape your car is in first."

He frowned and turned to look at her. Damn, that was stupid of him. He'd assumed it was the wind blowing things around that had set off the alarm. But if the car was actually damaged, that was going to make things trickier. They might need that helicopter evac after all. "Hang on, Mitch," he said, as his partner started to speak.

"I didn't get to that part of my outside look around," Ashley said.

*Before what had happened last night had caused a different kind of heat between them.*

"What part?"

"A tree came down, partly on your car." For a moment, sorrow seemed to show in her expression. Sorrow that they might be stuck here, together awhile longer? No doubt. Before he could speak, she added softly, "The tree."

It took him a moment to realize what she meant. That it was the big cottonwood, the one Uncle Shep had planted. And a whole new possibility for why she'd looked sad popped into his head. He was probably gaping at her, but he couldn't seem to help it.

"Ty?"

Mitch's voice snapped him out of his daze. "I'll get back to you," he said. "I need to see if we have transport or not."

A minute later, he was on the inland side of the cabin, staring at the mess the big tree had made coming down. The only good things he could see were that it hadn't come down on the cabin, because it would have likely destroyed the upper floor, and that the main trunk hadn't hit the SUV. As it was, several large limbs had. The windshield was cracked and the hood had a serious dent that ran from one fender to the other.

"I'm sorry," she said quietly. "I know that tree meant something to you, to your family."

He didn't know what to say to this woman who moments ago had been furious with him. This woman who had both frustrated and inflamed him. Who had both made him angry and sent him to physical heights he hadn't even known were possible.

The woman he never should have laid a hand on, let alone everything else he'd done to her and let her do to him.

Emotions he wasn't used to dealing with roiled inside him and needed an outlet. He walked over to the front of the car and grabbed a branch to test the weight. It wasn't going to move easily. He went over to the main limb that was on the car and could barely budge it thanks to the resistance of the wide groove it had made in the hood of the vehicle.

"Maybe you should try starting it before you kill yourself trying to get that tree off of it."

He looked at her across the damaged hood, through the branches of the downed tree. Her expression was as neutral as her voice had been. His mouth quirked. "Good point," he conceded.

He didn't make the mistake of thinking she wasn't still angry with him, but for the moment they seemed to have a truce. He dug into his pocket for the keys as he walked toward the driver's door near where she stood.

He was nearly there when a sharp crack split the air. That was no tree limb breaking. He whirled as two more came in rapid succession. A metallic bang told him something had hit the vehicle.

No question.

Shots.

# Chapter 30

It happened so fast Ashley was barely able to process it. Ty dived across the three feet between them. He took her down to the ground, the thud nearly knocking the wind out of her. Then, her mind still that half second behind, she realized he was shielding her with his own body.

He'd drawn his own weapon as he did so. He fired a couple of rounds in the direction the shots had come from. The shots were impossibly loud, and she couldn't help wincing. Ty's free arm tightened around her as if in reassurance. And then he all but forced her up to her knees, pushing her to crawl to the relative shelter of the SUV. She had to tug at her blouse, which seemed to have caught on something, the way it was oddly clinging. Then she winced again as Ty shot once more.

For a moment, nothing happened.

"Come on," Ty muttered from where he was crouched beside her. "Shoot back, jackass."

Ashley nearly gasped. "You want them to shoot again?"

"I need a read on exactly where he is."

So he'd been hoping to draw return fire. It made sense, but didn't make her any happier.

All the while, Ty's attention was fixed across the clearing. And stayed there when he asked, "You remember how to work the comms?"

"Of course. Do you want me to go call for help?" Her mind was already racing. She'd go around the side of the house, away from the shooter, and go in the side door she'd noticed. If it was unlocked, there was that. She—

"Not unless you have to," he said, cutting off her rampaging thoughts. He gave her an odd sort of smile, then, to her surprise, reached out to touch her cheek. But shortly after, he was all business again. "Keep the engine block between you and the clearing."

It was clearly an order, and while she understood the physics of it, she didn't understand why he—

He was moving, in an oddly fluid sort of crouch, toward the back of the big SUV. Away from her. The pistol he carried was in both hands, in a grip she was certain meant he was planning to shoot again. Surely he wasn't going to go out there? She nearly screamed at him not to be stupid.

"Ty!"

He glanced back. "Stay down!"

And then he stepped out from the cover of the vehicle, weapon raised. And in that instant it came to Ashley so clearly it was undeniable. This was not a man who would ever, in anything, sit and wait to be rescued. He would take action. In this case, he would take out the threat, or die trying. It was why he'd reminded her about the communications setup.

And that moment when he'd smiled and touched her had been a "just in case."

Another shot rang out. And in one smooth, practiced motion, Ty adjusted his aim and fired. Once, twice. She heard a yelp from the direction of the trees across the clearing. A moment later came the sound of something—someone—running through the trees and underbrush.

"Run, you bastard," she heard Ty mutter.

But he didn't move for a moment, and she understood he was waiting to see if there had been more than one shooter. Standing there in the open, a target. And again she wanted to scream at him. And when no further shots came, she breathed a sigh of relief.

But then she saw the way his shirt was clinging to his side, as if wet. And her thoughts started to tumble in rapid succession. She looked down at her blouse, where it had been oddly clinging. Saw the wet red smear. Touched it, but felt no pain. Looked back at Ty.

His blood. It was his blood. God, he'd been hit. Shot. And since there was blood on her, it hadn't been now, when he'd stepped out from behind the car.

He'd been shot when he'd thrown himself over her to protect her. He'd been shot then, but he'd just kept going.

Even as the pieces fell together for her, he swayed on his feet. He reached out and touched the back of the SUV for balance. She wondered if he even realized yet. He'd probably been running on pure adrenaline, and when the crash came, coupled with being wounded, it would be ugly.

She ran to him. "Let's go inside."

He looked at her, shook his head. "I should go after him."

"In what?" she asked, gesturing at the pinned, damaged vehicle. "We need to make contact, like you said. They can look for him." He wasn't moving. Stubborn, stubborn man. So she pulled out the one tool she was certain of. "Please, I'd like to go inside. I'd feel safer."

"Oh. Sure."

He was starting to sound a little foggy, and she knew the crash was imminent. And yet he put an arm around her as if to support her, when at any moment he was going to go down like the proverbial ton of bricks. And when he did, he'd be stuck where he was, because there was no way she'd be able to move an unconscious six feet two inches of pure muscle.

She let out an inward sigh of relief when they made it back inside. She kicked the door closed behind them, very aware he was leaning more heavily on her with every step. It was then that he looked downward, touched his side with his free hand. Looked at his bloody fingers. Then he glanced at her, saw the blood on her blouse. His eyes widened, and there was pure distress in his voice when he said her name.

"Ash? You're hurt?"

Was it possible he still didn't realize? "It's not mine, hero."

She grabbed a towel within reach from the kitchen counter and folded it quickly, then pressed it against his side to at least slow the bleeding that seemed frighteningly severe to her. He swayed, and she abandoned any idea of getting him to the closest bed. The couch was only three feet away. It would have to do.

"You're all right? You're sure?"

She didn't know what to think. Was this just professional concern? It didn't seem like it. It seemed a lot more personal. Especially from a guy with morning-after regrets.

"I'm sure. Sit down—actually, lie down before you fall down."

"I need...to..."

"Down," she repeated firmly. He was getting so vague it was scaring her even more. Once he was on the couch, she was swamped by the realization it was all up to her now. She was aware on some level that this was not something that normally bothered her, and on an even deeper level why it was bothering her now. She really had let herself fall for this man, and angry as she'd been at him this morning, she couldn't just shut that off.

"Call," he began, but his voice was getting fainter.

"I will," she said. "Bleeding first. I'm going to go get the first-aid kit."

She ran down the hall to the safe room, grabbed the white box that was a duplicate of the one on the shelf in the bunker. The bunker...the bed. She fought off a flood of memories from last night. There was no time now, even if it had been the most amazing night of her life.

Back at his side, she opened the lid. The briefcase-sized kit was well organized and equipped.

"Pack it," he said, his voice fainter yet.

"I know." She'd never actually dealt with a gunshot wound, but she'd helped Alaskan Dr. Kallik with a knife wound and a deep accidental stab with a spear, and figured the principal would be similar.

*Except for the bullet part.*

She'd deal with that later, right now getting the bleeding stopped was paramount. The bullet, infection, all of that had to wait. She dug into the first-aid kit and spotted what she'd hoped would be there. She should have known Elite—and Ty—would have the latest advances for emergencies; her father would settle for nothing less. She knew about the new purpose-specific packing gauze that held small specially designed sponges that expanded and put deep, solid pressure throughout a deep puncture wound. It was better at stopping bleeding than anything else she'd heard about. It was not a pleasant process, for either the person doing it or the victim, but it worked, and nothing else mattered.

And if he bled out and died, she would never get over it.

He groaned the moment she started, but bit it off and clenched his jaw.

"Hang on, Ty," she whispered, as she proceeded with the ugly job of stuffing gauze into a deep open wound. Damn, she could feel the bullet. It wasn't really that deep, and it felt…misshapen somehow. And she could feel a sharp edge, doing more damage even now.

She swore, something she rarely did. Even in his condition, Ty noticed. "What?"

"I can feel the bullet. It's… It feels mashed."

"Ricochet," he got out through gritted teeth. "I heard the smack when it hit the car."

"The edges are making it worse," she said. "Every time you breathe."

"Just as…soon…keep doing that," he said, and Ashley felt a wave of emotion for this man who could joke even now.

"I could get it out, if I just had something bigger than tweezers to grab it."

"The kit."

His voice wasn't nearly as strong as it had been just a moment ago. Hastily Ashley dug into the first-aid kit.

Found, amazingly, small forceps. When she turned back, his eyes were closed. And he looked ghastly pale.

"Stay with me." And she didn't even care about all the ways those words could be interpreted.

His eyes fluttered open. His right hand moved, and lightly grasped her wrist. Her gaze shot to his face. He held her eyes. "I trust you."

The words echoed in her head. *I trust you.* Even after this morning, when she'd been so furious with him, when just an hour ago she'd been yelling at him, he trusted her. Trusted her to do what was necessary, even if the task was ghastly.

Which told her he knew her better than she thought he did.

Then his fingers tightened a little. "Last night...still should never... But I'm not sorry."

He said it with more energy than she would have thought he had. And apparently it was the last he had, because the moment the words were out, his eyes rolled up a little and he passed out.

# Chapter 31

It was way too bright in here.

Ty's first thought when he tried to open his eyes floated around in his head for a moment before things settled. He tried raising his eyelids again, wondered why they were resisting, and if he'd have to pry them open manually.

"Come on, honey, come back to us now."

The soft coaxing voice was loving, and familiar.

Mom.

He smiled before he managed to get his eyes open at last. There was another moment or two of blur before things swam into focus. She was right there, as she had always been, her blue eyes warm with love and concern. Her dark auburn hair, usually up in a tidy knot, had a few strands hanging loose, as if she'd been in a hurry. Which was odd, because she was usually fairly fastidious about that. It struck him belatedly, as he also noticed the furrow between her eyebrows, that she'd been anxious.

It all tumbled together now, the sounds, the smell, the rails on the bed… Hospital.

"Hi, Mom," he managed, although his mouth and throat were dry.

Relief changed her expression immediately. She leaned forward and, unable to deliver her usual hug, simply grabbed his hand and squeezed. And he saw tears starting to streak down her cheeks.

"I've been so worried about you, Tyler," she said, her voice as tight as her grip on his fingers.

"I'm…fine." His brain was kicking into gear now. Shot. He'd been shot. He tried to move, and pain shot upward from his side.

"Hold still," his mother ordered. "You nearly bled to death, and you've been out for two days. Thank goodness for Ashley Hart."

His eyes widened. "Two days? Wait, where is Ashley? I—"

"She's safe." The second voice came from the foot of the bed and his gaze shifted. Jordana. "Mitch said to tell you she's safe, at one of the Harts' other houses. Mitch wouldn't tell even me where."

"Need-to-know basis," Ty muttered. But damn it, *he* needed to know. He needed to know where she was and that she was safe.

"Right," Jordana said. When she went on, it was in the concise manner of her job as a detective, although Ty was pretty sure he heard in her voice the urge to read him the riot act for getting hurt and no doubt scaring them all. "Mitch also said they have no idea who the shooter is. Elite had Sanderson under observation, and there's been no variation in his routine."

"He's not stupid."

"Unlike your chosen career," his mother said, apparently deciding that now that he was awake and at least coherent she could let her upset out a little. "I do wish you'd reconsider that."

They'd had this discussion often, and Ty understood that it was his mother's fear for him driving her now. He squeezed her hand and didn't respond to her words.

"Your girl's pretty smart, though," Jordana said.

"I know," Ty said, not even caring what it might betray that he accepted his sister's assessment. Although he did wonder if she'd meant it generically or if she'd somehow guessed how he felt about Ashley. This was Jordana, and she was pretty darned smart, too.

She went on. "She not only saved your sorry butt with that field surgery of hers, she saved the bullet she pulled out of you. It's pretty messed up, being a ricochet, but Yvette's got what ballistics they could get, and is running it through every system known to man or she'd be here."

He tried not to think about what Ashley had had to do and just be glad she'd had the knowledge—and the guts—to do it. "Good," was all he said.

"And," his mother added, "she chewed your father out rather fiercely."

Ty blinked, wondering if he was on the verge of passing out again. "She...what?"

"He was quite taken aback. She told him he was a fool if he didn't see the amazing man you are. If he wasn't prouder of you than anything he'd done in his life."

Ashley had said...that?

"And that," Jordana said with a grin, "pretty much told us where you two stand."

"Indeed," said his mother with an approving smile.

There was a flurry of footsteps at the door to the room. Ty looked in time to see Fitz Colton stride in, with Brooks and Neil at his heels, and some steps behind them Uncle Shep. His father looked strained. Older. Worried. He rushed to the bedside.

"They said you were awake. You scared the hell out of us, son."

He sounded genuinely concerned. They'd been at odds so much about Ty's refusal to go into the family business that most of the time they maintained a sort of armed neutrality. Maybe Ashley—damn, she'd really gone after the old man?—had gotten to him.

"Amen to that, jerk," Brooks said, with a swipe at his arm.

"Ditto," Neil agreed, only his light smack hit Ty's left knee. And off to one side, Uncle Shep smiled warmly and nodded at him.

Ty was more than a little moved by the solid presence of his family. The only one here who hadn't spoken was Bridgette, and when he looked at her, he saw the shadow in her blue eyes. Not only had she buried one man she'd loved, she'd gone through her own life-threatening experience just last month, and he saw the understanding in her gaze. Later, they would talk. And as if she'd read his thought, his sister nodded.

He glanced back at his father, again noticed how worn and tired he looked. He would also have to ask Bridgette about how far she'd gotten in her own investigation, into the link between Colton Construction and the outbreak of cancer cases among the workers. But maybe not with his father right here. He shifted back to Jordana, and thought about asking what the status was on the investigation into the bodies. Damn, there was too much going on, when all he wanted to do was find Ashley and see for himself that she was all right.

But before he could do or say anything, a wave of weariness engulfed him and it all faded away again.

When he woke up again, the fogginess had lifted. And...he was moving. Not he himself, but the bed. Gurney. Whatever it was. Down a hallway.

"Hey, welcome back."

His gaze snapped to his right, and he smiled at the tall slim blonde walking alongside him. "Hey, sis. What's up? Find something?"

"Still old cut-to-the-chase Ty, huh?" Yvette wrinkled her nose at him in obviously mock irritation. "Much as I love my work, I wish my family would keep me a little less busy."

"Wouldn't want you to get bored," he said. He glanced up at the orderly pushing the gurney. "Where are we going?"

The man smiled at him. "Your own spacious, private suite."

Ty blinked, and his brow furrowed. Yvette laughed. "Guess you wore out your welcome in ICU, bro."

He looked back at the orderly. "What would it take to get you to steer this thing out the front door?"

The smile became a grin. "More than you got on you, dude."

Given that he had nothing but the damned hospital gown, Ty couldn't argue that. But that realization brought home something else. He looked back at Yvette. His little sister might not be a field officer, but she'd been with the

Braxville PD for nearly a year now. She'd get it. "Speaking of that, where is my…stuff?"

"We've got your clothes and wallet," she said, "and Mitch has your gear."

She put the slightest of emphasis on the last word, and he knew she'd understood he meant his weapon. He nodded, relieved.

The process of moving into the bed in the regular hospital room proved to him, much as he hated to admit it, that heading for the front door would have been a bad idea. When at last they were alone, his sister looked at him seriously. "You scared the heck out of us, Ty."

"Not my intent."

"I didn't get to meet your Ashley, but when I do, I'm giving her the biggest hug in history. She saved you. And had the smarts to preserve the bullet."

*Your Ashley.* Damn, he liked the sound of that. And he'd give just about anything to see her. Anything except her safety.

"Something you're not telling us, bro?" Yvette asked, one brow arched.

Guessing his thoughts must have shown in his face, he hastily said, "Nothing."

"Try that on somebody who didn't just see you go all soft."

"That's a pretty unscientific assumption," he said, hoping a teasing jab at her particular skill would divert her.

"You want the lecture on micro-expressions?" Yvette countered coolly. "Not to mention I have years of experience reading you."

"She's a client."

"Uh-huh."

"Just tell me what you came up with," he said, feeling a bit exasperated. And frustrated at being stuck here, when he should have been out looking for the shooter. And the person responsible for those two bodies sealed up in a Colton warehouse.

"The bullet was already deformed from the ricochet." She gave him a serious look. "Which is also why it cut you up inside so badly. But also why it didn't go as deep as it could have. And it took some doing to get a valid result on the characteristics."

"Which were?"

"Aside from the lands and grooves, it was a .45 ACP."

He winced. "Then I was damned lucky it wasn't a direct hit."

She nodded. "Bad enough as it was. But there's one more thing." She paused, as if for effect. "It had a left twist."

His brows shot upward. There was only one major US manufacturer whose weapons didn't use right-twist rifling in their barrels. "A Colt?"

"Looks that way. Unless it's a British import."

"Narrows it down." In fact, he had a Colt .45 himself, but it was a historic, collector-type weapon he rarely shot. "Couple that with the fact that he wasn't a great shot with it. Maybe he borrowed the gun."

"They find it, I'll match it," she vowed. "Nobody shoots my brother and walks away free."

It hurt to lift up enough to grab and hug her, but Ty did it anyway.

## Chapter 32

Ty threw a shirt into the duffel, paused, thought about where he was headed and added a heavy sweater and a pair of gloves. Every time he turned he could feel the tug on his injury, but he didn't let it slow him down. Just as he hadn't let the doctor's orders change his plans.

He'd been laid up in that damned hospital for nearly a week. He'd been up pacing the floor of his room since six this morning, but with typical efficiency, it had been nearly noon before his release orders had finally come through. He'd considered just walking out without the paperwork, but he didn't want his boss chewing him out for making Elite look bad.

It was enough that a shooter had gotten to them, although Eric had dryly stated he figured a tornado touchdown was a good enough excuse. Although that still didn't explain how the shooter had found them in the first place. Ty knew no one at Elite would have let that out, so somebody else had to have slipped up. The family should know better than to talk about his work when he was on a case, and his parents were the only ones who'd known why he wanted the cabin, anyway.

He didn't bring up the subject with his boss, knew he didn't have to; he would be already on it. He spared a thought for how lucky he was, even though he'd gotten himself shot. Lucky to have work he loved and a boss he both admired and respected. Eric had not only driven to Braxville to check on him, he'd waited around so he could give him a ride home to Wichita. Ty guessed there weren't a lot of bosses who would go to that extreme. And after learning where Ashley was—at her parents' ski lodge in Beaver Creek, Colorado—in the interest of not having to defy him as well as the doctor, he hadn't mentioned his plans. Or much of anything else.

He'd let Eric talk, noticed he'd once more seemed impressed with Jordana after speaking with her outside the hospital room. He had found Ty's mother warm and charming, but was unimpressed with his father. And unsurprisingly, as former military himself, had liked Uncle Shep, although he'd also noticed the slight tension in the family when the former Navy man had been present.

But he'd underestimated his boss's perception, because the last thing he said to him after he dropped him off was, "Don't do anything stupid, Colton."

"Not today," he'd answered, unwilling to go any further.

"Good. There's nothing that won't keep until you get a decent night's sleep."

Only the knowledge that the man was right, he wasn't up to the task at the moment, had kept him home last night. But with his plans firmly in place, he'd slept well, awakened early and was almost ready to roll.

He was grabbing his winter jacket out of the closet when his doorbell rang. He pulled his phone out of his back pocket. The phone he'd been tethered to since he'd gotten it back from Jordana, searching for any mention of Ashley, since he hadn't heard one word except from Mitch through Elite, that she was all right. Her followers were questioning her absence on social media, although it appeared they were determined to follow through on the demonstration she'd organized at the wetlands near Lake Inman, where Sanderson was planning his development. But she herself hadn't posted, which surprised him a little. He'd thought once she had a signal again she wouldn't be able to resist making up for lost time.

Maybe she had taken his warning seriously. He'd like to believe that.

*Right. If she took me—or what happened between us—so seriously, she'd have at least called.*

He knew Elite would have hustled her off to another safe site, and apparently Eric had agreed the Colorado location was safe enough, so he'd never expected her to visit him in the hospital, but a call would have been possible. If she'd wanted to.

Which made his plans a bit problematic. But damn it, this was his job, no matter how tangled he'd let things get. Her safety was his responsibility. *She* was his responsibility.

Not to mention that she'd likely saved his life. Even the doctors had agreed on that, that it would have been a lot more touch and go if she hadn't had the knowledge and the nerve to do what she'd done.

The doorbell came again, and he shook his head

sharply. Looked again at the phone he'd grabbed and then forgotten as his thoughts spiraled. Maybe it was whatever drugs they'd given him in the hospital that was making it hard to focus.

Even as he thought it, he knew better. It wasn't hard to focus. It was just hard to focus on anything but Ashley.

He tapped the screen and called up the cam at the front door. Was surprised to see Jordana standing there, looking worried. What was she doing here at six on a Saturday morning? He tapped for the speaker. "Come on in," he said, as he unlocked the door.

He started that way, hearing his sister's swift steps across the entryway floor. He made sure he was walking normally, and that the ache in his side didn't show on his face. She'd tell him to take a pain pill, and that wasn't in the game plan.

"You're a ways out of your jurisdiction," he said jokingly as he got to her, to further stave off any fussing over him. She did look him up and down, but apparently that he was upright and moving was enough.

Or that what she had to say took precedence, he realized as he looked at her expression.

"It's Dex," she said bluntly.

He blinked. "What's Dex? Besides the guy who insulted Gwen and who makes promises Dad has to keep."

"The gun's his."

Maybe the drugs they'd given him in the hospital were still in his system, because he was having trouble processing. "Wait...you're saying Dex shot at Ashley?"

"No. He shot *you*. Yvette matched the slug to his .45."

Ty drew back slightly. Too quickly, and the tug on his wound made him wince. "Why the hell would he—"

"I think he's behind the bodies in the wall."

Ty stared at her. He knew his sister was good, very good, but he was going to need more to just buy this wholesale. "Give it to me," he ordered, his voice tight.

"He had access to the building from the beginning. He asked Dad if he could use the cabin, and Dad told him you were using it for work."

Ty winced again, mentally this time. "Damn. I really don't want that spread around, that we use the cabin as a safe house. I thought Dad realized that."

Jordana gave him a rather odd little smile. "He does. But he was bragging about you, and it slipped out."

Ty knew he was gaping at her now. "Bragging? About me? I don't believe it. The old man's never forgiven me for going with Elite."

"That doesn't mean he's not proud of what you do, bro," Jordana said quietly.

He was going to need time to process that particular revelation. He focused on the immediate problem. "Just because he wanted to use the cabin—"

He stopped when she held up a hand. "Dad also bragged that you were getting close to finding the truth about the bodies. That being private, you weren't hamstrung like we are sometimes. And that you'd never quit until you did."

If there'd been a chair handy, Ty would have collapsed into it by now. Not because of his injury but in shock. His father had never said anything like that to him. He'd never had the slightest idea he was proud of him, of his work, he'd only known that he was unhappy he hadn't gone to work for Colton Construction.

Jordana apparently read his expression. "Come on, firstborn, you know you're the favorite." She let out a sigh. "Which is a lot better than being the misfit."

"Who's the misfit?" he asked, mystified.

She grimaced at him. "Me, of course. Not the oldest, not one of the triplets, not the baby. I'm just…there."

Ty stared at her. "You're the best cop on the force, one of the best in the state. Even my boss is impressed with you. If Dad's not prouder of you than any of us, he's a bigger fool than I think he is."

To his surprise, his sister blushed. "That's what Clint says."

Ty smiled at that. "I knew I liked that guy." He had approved of Jordana's romance with the Chicago businessman from the beginning.

But he supposed it was a measure of how far he was off his game that he had to work to concentrate on the sense of what she'd said about the cold case that had thrown the family into chaos.

"So you think Dex killed Fenton Crane and Olivia Harrison, and tried to kill me because he thought I was getting close?"

She nodded, and looked at him even more intently. "And I think he would have killed your client, too, to make it look like she was the target and throw off suspicion."

The thought of Ashley dead chilled him. The thought of her dying because of this mess his family was in and his failure to protect her made the chill arctic. He was supposed to protect her, and instead she ended up saving him.

He shook it off. He had no time for even self-recrimination now. "How sure are you of this?"

"Very. For one final reason."

"Which is."

"Dex has dropped off the map."

"Damn. Damn, sis."

"Yes."

"Have you told Dad?"

"Not yet." Again, she gave him that assessing look. "I thought you'd want to let the Harts know right away."

Ty nearly groaned aloud. "That our family mess nearly got their daughter killed? Yeah, I can't wait to have that conversation."

"I got the feeling you were a bit more personally involved than that."

He looked into those blue eyes so like their mother's, and couldn't lie to her. "Yeah. Well. My mistake."

"Are you sure it was a mistake?"

"Geeze, Jord, she's Ashley freaking Hart of the Westport Harts. Yeah, I'm sure."

"I seem to remember you telling me to go for it with Clint," she said neutrally. "He may not be Hart-level rich, but it's the same principle. So I'll say the same to you, bro. Go for it. If you lose, you'll only be where you already think you are now."

His sister, Ty thought as he got behind the wheel of his own SUV this time, had a way of putting things that made sense. *You'll only be where you already think you are.*

A little over an hour later, he was through Salina and on I-70 heading west. Just over five hundred miles to go. He had grudgingly sworn to make himself stop now and then to rest a little and eat, although it took some self-convincing. He didn't want to end up in a ditch, or later off the side of a mountain, if he pushed too hard. Or worse, take some innocent bystander with him. And he had to admit, after a week of hospital food, a little gorging on fast food was necessary.

He was crossing into Colorado before noon. He was sure now it had been the right decision to drive rather than hassle with flight schedules and rental cars. It probably would have taken him just as long either way, and this way at least he could decide when he needed to stop for a rest. He ignored the ache in his side as best he could, used the pain to keep himself alert. And pondered Jordana's news.

Dex? He'd always thought the man a little smarmy, a little too charming. Many women seemed taken by him, in any case. And he took advantage. Personally, he'd thought Dex's wife, Mary, was deserving of much better treatment by her non-prince of a husband. It had been one of those not-so-secret things that no one talked about because they didn't want to hurt her, since she was so nice.

But…a double-murderer?

Neither of the victims in the walls had been shot, but he didn't think Dex carried a weapon around; Ty would have noticed. That wasn't the sort of thing he missed. Then again, this had been three decades ago. He had no idea what Markus Dexter had been like then. At three years old, he'd only known he didn't like the guy much, but his wife was nice.

When he got back, he was damned well going to find answers. And he'd use whatever resources he had, whatever methods—some of which Dad had been right about when he'd said he wasn't as hamstrung as the police— to do it. The family's future depended on resolving that double murder.

But his future depended on reaching Ashley.

# Chapter 33

The lodge was a timber-frame-style building, large but managing to be unpretentious at the same time. There were balconies all around, no doubt giving great views down the valley one way, up the mountain on the other side. That was the focus—the location, not the home itself. It suited the Harts, because it seemed they were everything Ashley had said they were. Kind, loving, generous…and crazy, utterly in love. He'd learned a lot about body language and signals in his career. Everything about these two declared they were a unit, inseparable.

When he'd arrived, they were just getting out of a large luxury SUV, returning from a day in Roaring Springs, another resort town to the west. They had gone to look at a location for a resort catering to people with disabilities they were considering investing in. They'd invited him in, gushing out enough thanks to make him uncomfortable.

"We ran into the local sheriff there," Andrew Hart said, as they stepped inside. A quick glance around showed him the interior was fairly unpretentious, confirming the focus was on nature outside, and Ty was even more impressed than before. "Trey Colton. Any connection?"

"I… Yes. Distantly." He tried for a smile. "I think we're all over the place."

"Well, he was a very nice man," Angela Hart said.

"And tough enough for the job, I think," Mr. Hart added.

He could see Ashley in both of them. She had her mother's hair, the same rich shade of brown and sleekly straight. But she had her father's eyes, that deep dark brown, with the same quickness and intensity. The problem was they were embarrassing him a bit with their effusive thanks and praise. He wasn't real happy about how this whole thing had gone down—the fact that he had slept with their daughter aside—and wasn't sure he deserved any of it.

"Ashley insisted we go take the meeting," her mother said, as if feeling she needed to explain why they weren't here with her.

"Of course," Ty said.

"Our personal security detail is watching her," her father added. "They know the house and the area."

"Is she all right?" The words tumbled out of his mouth before he could stop them, and he wondered if his anxious tone would register. Wondered if—and what—Ashley had told them.

He'd had a long time to think while trapped in that

hospital bed. One of the things he'd focused on was the discussion he'd had with his sister Jordana when she'd come back from Chicago, trying to hide her heartbreak over Clint. All because Clint had never really told her how he felt about her. Jordana had told him how that had made her feel. Which in turn had led him to picture that morning after in the cellar, from Ashley's point of view.

*This was wrong. A mistake.*

How would he have felt if Jordana had told him Clint had said that, the morning after their first time together? He would have wanted to shoot the guy.

Memories of harsh words spoken had tumbled through his mind in an endless loop.

*It was...storm-induced madness and I was handy, right? Meaningless.*

*Meaningless? Is that what you call something I'll never ever forget? Something I'll torture myself about for the rest of my life?*

But the phrase that tortured him was the one where Ashley had in essence done what Clint had not. She'd admitted to her feelings.

*...falling for her bodyguard.*

He didn't know how much damage he'd done. He didn't know if anything could be salvaged from the wreckage he'd caused. He only knew he had to try. He tried to pull himself together.

"I think I should ask are you all right?" Mrs. Hart asked, eyeing him with concern. "I can't believe you drove this far a week after being shot."

"You and my mother," Ty said wryly, then feeling a little explanation was required, added, "She was a nurse, too, although she mostly teaches now."

She seemed surprised for a moment, and Ty realized

it was probably because he'd known about her work. Did Ashley never tell people things like that? He'd understand it if she didn't. They probably always had to be on guard about people using any information they could find against them.

Andrew Hart didn't appear surprised at all. But then he was focused on only one thing. "Is there any progress on identifying the shooter?"

Ty braced himself. He hadn't been looking forward to this. "Yes. And my family and I owe you an apology."

The man's brow furrowed. "Your family?"

"It appears the shooter wasn't after Ashley. He was after me."

Mrs. Hart gasped, but Ashley's father held his gaze levelly. This was the man who had built upon the fortune left to him, not merely lived high on it. "You'll pardon me for saying that the name Colton seems to attract…"

"Chaos? I wouldn't argue that," Ty said wearily. He could feel the cost of the exertion to get here creeping up on him. "And that's why the family apology."

He dreaded the next part, admitting that being with him had put Ashley in danger. That Dex likely would have killed her, too, to make it look as if she had been the target and he himself just collateral damage.

"I understand," Mr. Hart said, now with an edge in his voice as his gaze flicked to his wife and then back to Ty. "All of it. And let's leave it at that, shall we?"

Ty stared into eyes so like Ashley's, deep brown, alert and doing nothing to mask the intelligence behind them. The man did understand. And he didn't feel his wife needed to know how close their daughter had come. At least not now. But Ty had the feeling that if the mother was as smart as the daughter, she'd figure that out on her own.

"Yes, let's," Mrs. Hart said. "You didn't know at the time, and you acted to save Ashley, taking the bullet that could easily have struck her," her mother said briskly. "And for that, we will be eternally grateful."

"May I...see her?" God, thirty-three years old and he felt like an awkward teenager asking a girl's parents' permission to take her out. He was just thankful they had no idea of the extent of his unprofessionalism. Yet.

Of course, if Ashley was still furious with him, as she had every right to be, they would likely never know.

"I'm sure she'll want to see you. She hated leaving you in the hospital," her mother assured him, and led him over to what appeared to be the main stairway. She gestured upward. "Turn right at the top of the stairs. Her room is all the way at the end." She smiled. "Ashley likes to look out at the mountain. Says she sees more of the local wildlife from there."

"That...sounds like her," Ty said, his throat tight.

Something must have crept into his voice, because Mrs. Hart's expression changed, her eyebrows lowering slightly. "Do we need to talk, Mr. Colton?"

He thought of everything Ashley had said about her parents, how much she loved, admired and respected them. And he knew he couldn't lie.

"That," he said, "depends on Ashley."

"In that case," her father said, "you'd better go up and see her."

He wondered, on his way up, how much longer he could stay on his feet. It was catching up to him. He could feel it. But the thought of seeing Ashley kept him going. He could crawl across the Sahara if he knew she was on the other side.

Still, it took him a moment to work up the nerve to knock on the door when he got there. And the silence that followed made it worse.

Finally he heard through the door, "Who is it?"

He'd never expected the effect just hearing her voice would have on him. An odd combination of heat and chill.

"I… It's Ty."

"Oh."

*Oh.* That was it? Okay, that made it a little chillier. "Ashley?"

He thought he heard something else, another voice, he thought male but couldn't be sure through the thick door. The possibility that another man was with her, in her bedroom, hit him hard. Had she started seeing somebody else already, in a week? Had the prof maybe seen his mistake and come to try to get her back? Had she—

"I don't need the car after all, Ty," she said as if talking to the family chauffeur, and without opening the door. "But will you please feed my pet snake for me?"

Every instinct he had kicked to life. That chill he'd felt hadn't been his reaction to her, it had been to the undertone in her voice.

Fear.

He'd been so focused on what on earth he was going to say to her that it hadn't made it through to his conscious mind, but his instinct had picked up on it instantly.

*Feed my pet snake.* Like there was a single chance this side of hell that Ashley, his Ashley, would have a pet snake.

He'd been right about one thing. She wasn't alone in

there. But he'd been completely wrong about the rest. There was a man in there all right. And he wasn't there by invitation.

Ashley was in trouble.

# Chapter 34

She'd been such a fool.

Ashley knew she'd brought this on herself. First, and most importantly, by getting so mad at Ty. Now that she was calmer, now that she'd had a chance to think about it rationally, she should have understood. He was a man with a personal code, one he lived by as few did these days. And falling for a client violated it. Maybe he hadn't been exactly tactful about it, but in retrospect she found she preferred his bluntness to Simon's dodging the issue, letting their relationship simply fade away because he was too much of a coward to face her and tell her he was leaving and it was over. Ty would never do that.

Not that she would ever let him slip away.

Secondly, she should never have left him. It had torn at her so fiercely to leave him lying there, helpless in a hospital bed. She should have known that no matter what he'd said on the proverbial morning after, her feelings for him hadn't really changed.

Not that her parents had given her much choice about leaving. They'd sent a team of their own security who had practically carried her to the airfield where the private jet sat waiting. Only when they'd threatened to fly her to Europe did she capitulate and agree to join her parents in Colorado.

Her most recent mistake had been today, insisting her parents' security leave her alone. Nothing had happened for days now, she'd told them, and there was no indication anyone knew she was even here. She'd promised she'd be staying in her room, catching up online and not leaving the premises. And in fact she'd done exactly that.

But after chivying her reluctant parents off to their previously scheduled meeting, she'd spent a few minutes with her afternoon latte out on the balcony, taking in the clean wonderful smell of the mountains. When she'd come back in, she hadn't locked the doors, intending to take breaks out there periodically. It was a private balcony after all, and in her mind, it was part of her room, so it never even occurred to her.

And then this lunatic with a handgun had landed on it, and found she'd practically welcomed him in with that unlocked door.

She'd wasted a few moments wondering how on earth he'd done it, gotten onto the balcony. A few more wondering how he'd found her in the first place. None of that mattered. He was here, had a gun pointed at her, and she had to figure out what to do.

She'd known why he was here the moment he told her to go to her laptop and make a post. She resisted, but he'd grabbed her and forced her into the chair at her desk. He quoted what she was to write, saying she'd been wrong about everything and was calling off the rally she'd set up.

All her self-defense training was useless in the face of that weapon. Her crazy, quirky mind called up an old saying, that God made man, but Sam Colt made them equal. That mind then leaped from Colt to Colton, and she thought that if the worst happened and she died here, without ever seeing Ty again, it would break her heart. Which was stupid, because she'd be dead.

She reeled in her careening thoughts. *Think!* she silently ordered.

She tried talking, telling the man that Sanderson was making a huge mistake, that coercion would get him nowhere but in trouble. But this guy didn't even know what it was all about—she suspected he wouldn't know a wetland from a bathtub—or care. He didn't even react to the name, and Ashley wondered if he even knew it. No, the man was just the hired gun, and couldn't care less what this was all about. All he cared about was getting paid.

It had occurred to her that if the man could be hired for something like this, perhaps he could be unhired with the same incentive: money. She certainly had access to enough of that.

She had been about to open her mouth again to try the bribe when there had come a knock on the door.

The man's order had come fast. "Don't open it, and get rid of whoever it is. Fast."

She'd gone, hoping against hope it was one of the security guys coming to check on her.

When she'd heard Ty's voice, she'd nearly gasped aloud.

She quickly made up something about the car, hoping he'd get that she wasn't going anywhere because she couldn't. But she doubted that was enough for anyone to make the jump to what was really happening. She tried desperately to think. She didn't think her vaunted mind had ever worked faster in her life. There had to be some way, some words she could say that would warn him. He was smart and quick and he knew her, he knew her so well, even after only ten days…

He knew her.

It had hit her, then. And the words about her nonexistent pet snake had come out easily.

There was barely a moment's pause before he answered. "Sure. I'll do that right now. That rat'll be dinner momentarily."

His words told her "message received" so clearly she felt joy surge within her. And crazily, it was as much because he'd understood as because she knew she now had help. Very real and very, very proficient help.

"Thank you," she said through the door.

She heard—as did her captor—his footsteps going back down the hall. She thought she even heard him starting down the stairs. She didn't know what he was going to do, but she knew he'd do something. All she had to do was stay alive long enough for him to do it.

"Now get back to it. Get this done, so I don't have to shoot you right here."

"And then try to escape past our security? Good luck with that." The man's eyes narrowed, and she realized belatedly that she was so buoyed by Ty's presence that she'd let it show.

"Your security won't be a problem," the man said, and a chill seized her. Had he killed them? She didn't know the two men they'd brought here, but that didn't mean she wanted them to be hurt—or worse—trying to protect her. As Ty had been.

Her optimism wobbled a little as what she should have thought of first hit her. Ty was just out of the hospital, and it was less than a week after he'd been shot and nearly bled to death. She should have been worried about him, not overjoyed that he was here to save her. God, she really was a spoiled child.

*Use that brain you're so proud of and think!* What could she do to help when Ty did whatever he was going to do?

The only thing she could think of was to keep the man occupied, try to give Ty the advantage of total surprise. But how?

She went back to her desk, slowly, making him hurry her along. "You'll have to tell me again what to say, I've forgotten."

The man gave a derisive snort. "Figures. Just say it's called off, tell them not to show up."

"And you think they'll do that?" she asked, trying to keep him focused on her.

"They'd better," he said, and she wondered if the snarl was supposed to be scarier than the pistol pointed at her head.

"And what about the other platforms?"

He looked startled. "What?"

*That's it.* She could tell by his reaction she'd found the key, that he didn't get the complexities of the various social media outlets. "I've organized this on multiple platforms. I have the most followers here—" she gestured at the screen "—but I have well over a hundred thousand or more on two or three others. Oh, and I can't post to the major one without a photo." He looked utterly blank.

"That's what it's for, sharing pictures," she explained as if to a child. "They all have a different focus, and on this one it's photographs. That's why it was established. You can't really make a post without one."

"Then find one."

He was starting to sound even more impatient. This was going to be a fine line to walk. She put on her best dumb socialite demeanor. "But all I have are pictures for the protest, and that would only encourage them to come." She tried to sound worried, when in fact her pulse had kicked up fiercely as, in the middle of her social media explanation, she'd heard the faintest of sounds from the balcony. Her captor's back was to it and he hadn't reacted at all, so she didn't think he'd heard at all, or else he had and had dismissed it.

She saw movement on the balcony, glimpsed a shape past the man's left arm, knew, just knew it was Ty. Her mind was racing full speed now, searching for a way to distract the gunman even more. Just posting wouldn't do it she needed something else, something to keep his attention focused on her, so he wouldn't look behind him.

She suddenly remembered how furious Ty had been with her about that post from McPherson, betraying exactly where she was. An idea struck. She called up the thumbnail of an old picture of the mountains she'd taken from the overlook not far from here. She kept it in the thumbnail size and gestured to it.

"How about this, to show them I'm not even there, so there's no point in showing up?"

As she'd hoped, he had to lean in to see the tiny image. She suppressed a shudder as the cold metal of the handgun brushed her forehead.

"Yeah," he said. "Yeah, do that."

She tried not to wrinkle her nose at his breath that smelled like an old gym bag. "Now what should I say again?" she asked.

"God, you're stupid, woman!"

"I'm sorry," she said, in a meek tone she had never used in her life.

But she was able to do it because while he was utterly focused on her, Ty had made it into the room. He was coming toward her, but so slowly... Why didn't he just pull his own gun? Why didn't he—finally, stupidly, it hit her. Ty wouldn't shoot if there was a chance she'd be hit, and the man was so close to her that if Ty drew his own weapon, it would be a standoff. She could just hear that crude voice saying something like out of a bad gangster movie, telling Ty to drop it or he'll blow her brains out. So for her sake, Ty—just-out-of-the-hospital Ty—was going to try to take the guy down physically.

This all raced through her mind in an instant, and she quickly went back to keeping the gunman focused on her.

"I'm sorry," she said again. "I'm just so scared."

"You should be, honey." The man practically caressed her with the barrel of the pistol, and it made her skin crawl. As she was sure he'd intended.

"Please, don't," she said, and now the tremor in her voice was real. But she reached out in a pleading manner toward him, as if begging. He started to smile, and her stomach turned nauseatingly.

On the edge of her vision, she saw Ty launch himself. The instant he moved she did, too. She slapped as hard as she could at the hand that held the handgun, pushing it sideways. In practically the same motion, she dove off her chair in the opposite direction. She heard the man start to swear but it changed to a startled shout as Ty hit him, low and hard.

They both crashed into the desk. Her laptop went spinning onto the floor. She didn't care. The man was grabbing for something. In the surprise attack, he'd dropped the gun. She scrambled around the grappling men, eyes searching the floor. She saw the barrel, just visible beneath the bottom drawer of her desk. She didn't want to risk getting down on her knees, so she merely kicked it out of reach.

And then it didn't matter because Ty was kneeling on the man's back, holding his arm—the one that had been reaching for the weapon—tight behind his back, wrenching it so hard the man yelped.

It was over.

"Hey, lighten up, I didn't hurt her."

"Shut up," Ty said shortly. "Nobody threatens my woman and gets away with it."

As male bluster went, Ashley supposed it was fairly mild.

As a declaration of his feelings, it was the most wonderful thing she'd ever heard.

She didn't even mind the possessiveness of it. Probably because she was so happy to hear it. Much better than declaring what had leaped to life between them a mistake. A sin she supposed she would have to forgive him for.

Well, after he'd atoned in a suitable manner, anyway.

# Chapter 35

Things had happened fast, once the threat was neutralized.

Ty had disarmed the man—with the wry knowledge that he'd have been better off if this had been the shooter at the cabin, since he was carrying a 9mm rather than Dex's more lethal .45—quickly. He'd called Elite the moment he had the guy contained and he was sure Ashley was all right, and told them what he had and to keep Sanderson from scarpering.

Her parents had been badly shaken, and Ty had been almost amused by the acquiescent way Ashley had endured her father's anger once he found out she'd not only left her balcony doors unlocked but had disabled the alarm on them so she could step in and out as she wanted.

"I was wrong, and stupid, Dad," she had said quietly. "Nothing had happened in so long I thought it would be okay now."

Ty wouldn't consider less than a week "so long" but he didn't say it, mainly because he didn't want to pile on. Her parents were having a sufficient effect on her. Besides, considering how he'd come to feel about her in about ten days, he didn't feel he had much room to talk about time spans. And he had already been feeling self-conscious because of her parents' outpouring of thanks yet again, her mother's delivered as she clung to her daughter with tears unashamedly spilling down her cheeks.

They had learned the two security men—suitably embarrassed and angry—had been dealing with a man they'd caught climbing over the outer wall, a man hired by the gunman to divert them while he came in from the opposite direction. Judging by the look in her father's eyes, Ty didn't envy them. But once all that was dealt with, her father had ushered them into his study, where he made a phone call of his own. Ty could only imagine what power Andrew Hart was bringing to bear.

Ashley gave her mother a final hug before stepping back. Then she turned to Ty, and her smile was the most warming thing he'd seen since he'd set foot in these chilly mountains.

"The minute I knew you were here, I wasn't afraid anymore. I mean, I never thought he'd really kill me, not when he needed something from me, but he made me so mad, thinking he could just coerce me like that."

"And you," Ty said dryly, "are too optimistic for your own good."

She simply grinned at him. Gestured at them both, standing upright. "Obviously not. Besides, I knew you'd get it when I said that about the snake, I just knew it!"

Then she threw her arms around him, and Ty finally

started to breathe normally again. He hugged her back, but the fear-induced adrenaline that had flooded him was slow to ebb.

"What the hell were you thinking, taking that swing at him?" He knew he would never forget that moment when she'd moved, when she'd shoved the guy's gun arm.

She drew back, although she still hung on. "What?"

"If you hadn't made that dive to the right, the guy could have shot you right there."

"That's why I made the dive to the right, honey," she said, in that too-sweet tone he'd learned was a warning. He opened his mouth to retort when, belatedly, the last word registered.

*Honey?* Did that mean she wasn't still furious with him?

"I… If you'd been hurt, I…" It was all he could manage to say.

"Then you'd know exactly how I felt when I realized you were shot protecting me. When you nearly died protecting me. And," she added in a rather fierce tone, "if you tell me that you were only doing your job, I won't be responsible for my reaction."

Since he'd been about to say just that, he appreciated the warning. Just as he appreciated her nerve and her quick thinking.

And the feel of her in his arms again.

On second thought, appreciation was much too weak a word for what he was feeling. He looked down into her eyes and knew he loved everything about them. Especially when they were warm and loving, but also when they were sparking fire. This was not a woman who would make for a comfortable, easy life. A life he wanted more than anything else. That realization didn't even shake him. No, a life with Ashley wouldn't be typical.

But he would never be bored.

"It wasn't only a job from the first moment I saw you," he said. And he would have kissed her if they hadn't been standing in her father's study, with him on the phone and her mother just a few feet away. A mother who was already watching their embrace with a pointed interest that made Ty even more aware of what he had yet to face.

Ty's phone chimed an incoming text, and he was thankful for the momentary reprieve from a set of, at the moment, hovering parents watching him carefully.

"That's Mitch," he said to Ashley. Reluctantly, he released her to pull out the phone. She didn't protest, but stayed close. He glanced at the text and let out a long breath. He looked back at Ashley. "Elite found Sanderson. Called the police in and turned him over. And he's talking."

He heard a small sound from Ashley's mother, and a low heartfelt oath from her father. But all he could see was Ashley looking at him with those eyes...

"Dear?" It was her mother, and Ty looked up in time to see she was gesturing to Mr. Hart. "I think these two need a little time alone. And frankly, unusual though it is, I find I need a drink."

"I hear that," the man answered fervently, and came out from behind his desk. He stopped beside them and gave Ty an assessing look. "You'll be staying for dinner."

Ty swallowed, felt Ashley's gaze upon him. But he steeled himself and faced the freaking richest man in the hemisphere. The man whose daughter he'd fallen for like the proverbial ton of bricks, no matter how unprofessional it was.

"Yes, sir," he said respectfully.

"Thank you," Ashley said after they'd gone. "For not arguing with him. As you can imagine, my father is not used to it."

"Except maybe from you?"

She grinned at him. "Maybe."

He smiled back. "This wasn't the time, not after what nearly happened here." One corner of his mouth quirked. "Besides, the respect was for your father, not Andrew Hart."

She tightened her arms around him again, and he knew he'd somehow found the right words. They stood there for what seemed to him a long time, but he didn't care. He didn't want to move. It felt delicious, and he wanted to savor it. He was feeling a steady, rather fierce throb from his side, but he didn't care about that, either. In fact, it felt right, very, very right, to be standing here with the woman who had kept that from being a fatal wound.

"I won't stop my work," she said, almost in a warning tone.

"I wouldn't expect you to." He grimaced. "And now that my sister's convinced there's a connection between Dad's company and the cancer cases, I see your point. Things like that need to be investigated."

She looked more pleased than he would have expected. "And I need to be more aware of the unintended harm—like that poor man's suicide—that can be done."

He gave her a crooked smile, the best he could manage at the moment. "Compromise?"

"Deal," she agreed, smiling back.

He was only vaguely aware that he was feeling a bit fuzzy around the edges, as if the world around him was

blurring. No, as if the world outside them was blurring.
And that didn't seem wrong at all. As long as she was
here and bright and alive with all her Ashley-like sharp-
ness and wit, the rest of the world could just blur away
and he wouldn't mind.

But he needed—desperately—to kiss her. It had been
too long, and they were alone now, so there was no reason not to, was there? He leaned in, already anticipating
the sweet feel and taste of her. But the blurring suddenly
expanded, engulfing him.

"Whoa!" Her sudden yelp startled him. He felt her
move, quickly, felt her hands on him as if propping him
up. "Don't pass out on me again."

"I'm fine," he said, but even he didn't believe it. She
was urging him to move, although he didn't know to
where. Didn't care where. This was Ashley and he'd go
wherever she wanted him to.

"Sit down before you fall down," she said. They were
next to a long leather couch. When he didn't immediately
move—his processing seemed to have slowed down—
she urged him with some gentle pressure on his shoulder. "You'd better rest up, Mr. Bodyguard. I have detailed
plans for that body of yours later."

"Oh, I hope so," he said, giving her a crooked grin.

Then he sat, rather lopsidedly as his side jabbed him
with pain again.

"On second thought, lie down," Ashley urged, and he
didn't feel like arguing with her. It was belatedly starting to register that his wound coupled with an adrenaline
crash was not something that he was going to be able to
slough off as nothing.

Ashley moved away. He frowned. He didn't like that.
He heard her quick footsteps, then, over what sounded

like a weird sort of soft static in his ears, he heard her yell from the doorway.

"Mom! Mom, we need you in here!"

He liked that *we*.

It was all he had time to think before he went under.

# Chapter 36

Ashley hadn't expected to be spending Thanksgiving this way, but now that she was, she was delighted. After Ty had rested up for a day, he was talking about heading home. But then her mother had stepped in, at first simply offering the invitation to stay and join them on the holiday, but following up with her best nurse's orders that he needed to rest longer, anyway. Ty had clearly felt a little awkward about accepting, but when he'd found out it would only be the four of them, he'd given in.

"What did you expect, a formal dinner for a small glitzy group of fifty?" she'd asked him. And at his sheepish, guilty grimace, she'd teased him unmercifully about those assumptions again.

They spent the intervening days mostly together, although Ty had a lot of reports to file, which she was happy to loan him a computer for. "You'll notice," she said with an arched brow, "we have an excellent WiFi signal, even here in the mountains."

He'd merely grinned at her. "I noticed you're not living with your phone in your hand anymore."

"I had it surgically removed," she joked right back. And silently looked forward to endless days of this.

Not at all to her surprise, even over Thanksgiving dinner, her mother and Ty got along famously. Mom had said Ty had told her his mother was also a nurse, and she expressed a rather pointed desire that they meet soon. All Ashley could say to that, rather dryly, was that if her mother didn't mind, she'd like to meet Mrs. Colton first.

Her father had apparently done a little nosing around, as she should have expected. He had a couple of cogent questions about the information he'd gathered about both the discovery of the two bodies in the wall of a Colton building—which Ty had tactfully said he couldn't discuss—and the shutdown of Colton Construction due to the link to several cases of lung and esophageal cancer.

"My sister Bridgette works for the state in public health. She was the one on that case," Ty said flatly. "She's certain there's a connection to the renovations in the historic district. She had to recuse herself because of our father, and now she's as ticked off at him as I am about it. And he's upset because her investigation resulted in Colton Construction being shut down until it's resolved."

She was a little surprised at how honestly and openly he answered, but she smiled inwardly. It was just another level of that respect for her father he'd mentioned.

Ty had told her about the man Bridgette had fallen in love with—the man's father was one of those who had contracted cancer. His concern for his sister had warmed her, and she found herself eager to see his family. Except, perhaps, his father. She didn't care much for how he'd made his oldest son feel.

If Ty understood he was getting a subtle third degree from both her parents, he didn't let on. He simply continued answering honestly, as if he found nothing amiss in being practically interrogated over the traditional turkey and cranberry sauce. This, too, was an expression of that respect.

She couldn't deny that she took a secret pleasure in how openly he declared his long-term intentions, the plan of a life together, which they had discussed in the late-night hours when she'd slipped down to the guest room her mother had lodged him in. Ashley hadn't missed the glint in her mother's eyes. She knew her mother fully expected there would be some hall traffic between that room and Ashley's own. Ashley had agreed to be that traffic when Ty had, half-seriously, said he didn't want to be the one to make her father mad. Since she wasn't certain she was ready to try to sleep in the room that had been—albeit via her own slacking off—invaded by that lunatic, she'd been more than happy to snuggle up to him in the guest room.

When the meal was done, down to the pumpkin pie, Ty leaned back in his chair, thanked them for the meal—much of which she and her mother had prepared together, leaving only the turkey itself to the cook—and casually asked her father if he'd passed.

Ashley almost laughed aloud at her father's startled, then rueful look. "Lost a little subtlety, did I?"

"She's your daughter, sir. I'd expect nothing less."

Her father nodded approval at that. But they'd still

been cautious. Her father had been, anyway. "Then you won't take offense if I ask Ashley—" he turned his gaze on her "—you're certain? This happened fairly quickly, under stressful circumstances."

She was ready for that. "I did the math. We spent ten days together, round the clock. That's two hundred and forty hours. An average beginner date might last a couple of hours, a serious one four hours, so compromising on three hours, and assuming dates on both Friday and Saturday, plus an extra during the week, that works out in the end to nearly six months of normal dating. And we—"

She stopped herself before the next words came tumbling out. Out of the corner of her eye, she saw Ty gaping at her. She seized on that to escape what she'd nearly said, and turned to look at him. "Problem?"

"I just never thought of it quite that way. How very… Ashley of you."

He was grinning at her now. Somehow she sensed he knew exactly what she'd almost said. And she grinned back, wondering what her parents' reaction would have been had she gone ahead and finished with, *And we didn't have sex until the last day, so that's really waiting a long time.*

When she looked back at her parents again, they were both smiling. Ty looked at them, too, and told them yet again he didn't want their thanks. "I only want your acceptance. Because I am crazy in love with your daughter."

He said it easily, but her pulse kicked up anyway, as it always did when those words came from him. And she believed them, because the man hadn't just told her repeatedly, he'd proven it by risking his life yet again. So that was three times, she'd told him teasingly. Once at the cabin, and twice here in the mountains, first when he'd come over that balcony and then again when he'd faced her parents, the power couple who intimidated world leaders.

"And I'm crazy in love with him," Ashley echoed.

Her parents simply smiled more widely. "We noticed," her mother said. "You look at each other the same way we did at your age."

"Got news for you," Ty said fearlessly, "you still do."

And in that moment, at the look on their faces, Ashley knew he'd won them over completely.

"This is your place?" Ashley asked as the headlights lit up the big modern house with the three-car garage to one side.

Ty gave her a sideways look as he pulled into the driveway and the garage door closest to the house began to rise. "You were expecting a farmhouse, perhaps?"

She laughed, and he smiled as the sound washed over him. "Have I told you I love it when you're a smartass?"

"Do you, now…" he drawled, giving her a suggestive slow smile.

The smile she gave him back was full of promise, and had him trying to remember how big a mess he'd left his bedroom. "It's half the reason I fell in love with you," she said. "You never cut me any slack because of who I am."

"You," he said pointedly, "do not need slack from anyone." The look she gave him then told him he'd found the right thing to say. He told himself he'd best remember that about her. Then he added, "And that's half the reason I fell in love with you."

"What's the other half?"

"Let's get inside, and I'll make you a list."

She grinned at him in that happy, silly way he was coming to treasure. He'd seen it often on the drive, and that alone made it worth it. Her parents had offered their plane for the trip to Wichita, but that would have left Ty's car there. And he thought it might be as well that they had the long drive together to talk. They had things to settle. Maybe it was the chaos that had struck his family lately, but he'd about had it with uncertainty.

He had asked her, when they were beside the car but before they'd gotten in, if she was sure about what she wanted. She'd kissed him so fiercely it left him wanting to go back inside and head for the nearest bed.

And when he'd found out she often drove herself around when she was here at the lodge, he had no qualms about turning the wheel over to her when she suggested she drive. That earned him another kiss; he wasn't exactly sure why. She clearly had more experience with these mountain roads than he did.

He'd taken over once they were back in Kansas. It had felt good to be back.

It had felt better to be heading home with Ashley.

*Are you sure you want to live in Kansas?*

*You know what I find amazing about Kansas? How kind and generous the people are. I'd always heard about the heartland, but never realized how accurate the name is.*

That had made him smile. His Ashley was ever and always willing to learn and change. *Can I take that as a yes?*

*I want to live with you. The rest is just details.*

He'd asked it as they crossed the state line, and her answer had come quickly and decisively, easing his nerves about the idea of Ashley Hart of the Harts of Westport settling down in Middle America. He was still working on the idea of he himself being connected to them, although the warm welcome of her parents had done a lot to alleviate his concerns on that score.

She insisted on carrying her own bag inside, teasing him that when he was fully healed, she'd expect him to do it, along with a few other more athletic things, words that sent his mind racing all over again.

When they were inside, she looked around with great interest, while he watched her a little nervously. He'd called in his mother for help with the furnishings, while he focused on all the electronics and connected devices that made the house state of the art. Thankfully, his mother knew him well enough to know what he didn't like, and so he'd ended up with things he found comfortable and thought looked good.

"I love it!" Ashley exclaimed, standing in the middle of the great room. "It's not ornate, not starkly modern. It's just homey and welcoming."

"Thank my mom for that," he said. "She picked most of it out. I just told her what I needed function-wise and approved her choices."

"I want to thank her for more than that," Ashley said, coming over to him. "She raised a wonderful son. When do I get to see her?"

"I…" He stopped, suddenly uncertain, as he understood he was on the cusp of changing his entire life. What had happened in Colorado had been sort of connected to his job of protecting her, but this…this was just them. He saw something change in her expression, realized he was giving her agile mind too much time to think. "I hadn't thought about when, yet. I just wanted to get you here, then...organize everything."

"At least you said when, not if."

Her tone was a little dry, enough that it bothered him. Hastily he said, "Let me show you the rest of the place."

She was impressed by the media room and his well-equipped office. Glanced at the guest room, which he explained was purely his mother's taste since this is where his parents stayed when they came to the city.

"She has good taste," Ashley said.

He felt a little awkward when they reached the double doors leading to the master bedroom. It was plainer than the rest of the house, a little too uber-masculine his mother had said, but he'd wanted it that way. Then.

And he had left it in a bit of a mess. "Sorry," he muttered. "I was in a hurry."

She smiled at that and looked around. But said nothing.

"Uh...there's plenty of room in the closet," he began, then remembered who he was dealing with, and that she probably had a wardrobe that could fill the entire sizable walk-in closet that he himself only used about a third of.

She walked over and looked, but only nodded, still saying nothing. He was starting to get nervous.

"The bathroom's pretty nice," he said, sounding lame even to himself. "And there's a sitting room over there." He gestured toward the glass French doors that led into the space just big enough for the couch and small desk he had there for late-night ideas or contact with the office.

She nodded.

"Look, I know you'll want some changes." He was now thoroughly into uneasy at her lack of reaction. "If you want, we can gut the place and you can make it how you want. Or we can move, if you'd rather."

She turned to face him, then. "I was just…absorbing. This is a special place, the…lair of the man I love, if you will. It has meaning to me."

He blinked. Would she never stop surprising him? He felt a slow smile curve his mouth. No. No, she wouldn't.

"I mean," she added, glancing around, "I'd add a dash of brighter color here and there, but nothing more."

"Anything you want," he said fervently.

She looked back at him and arched a brow in that way that made him brace himself. "And that sitting room, private but easily accessible, would make a perfect nursery someday." Ty's eyes widened, and he swallowed tightly. "Scare you?" she asked.

"A little," he admitted.

"Good," she said, and at last she smiled. "That means you take the idea seriously."

"I want kids, someday. With you," he added pointedly, reassured by her smile. "I was more worried about… figuring out how to be a father. I haven't had the greatest example."

"Feel free to borrow mine," she said airily.

"Deal," he said instantly. It made her laugh, and he grinned back.

"One thing I definitely don't want to change in here is that." She gestured toward his big four-poster bed.

His pulse kicked up. "You sure?"

"Yes. I love the style."

"I don't know," he said, putting as much doubt as he could manage into his voice. Her brow furrowed as she looked at him, clearly puzzled. "I mean, how can you be sure until you've tried it?"

Her expression shifted instantly to that glinting, teasing one he loved. "Was that an invitation, Mr. Colton?"

"Why, I do believe it was, Ms. Hart."

"Accepted," she said, with that delighted laugh he loved even more.

Ty pulled her into his arms. In the moment before he kissed her, he wondered just how long would be reasonable to wait before he asked her to marry him.

Another ten days, maybe.

\* \* \* \* \*

*Be on the lookout for the next story
in The Coltons of Kansas:*

Colton Christmas Conspiracy *by Lisa Childs*

*Available from Harlequin Romantic Suspense*

SPECIAL EXCERPT FROM

# (H) HARLEQUIN
## ROMANTIC SUSPENSE

*When a lead points security agency Rocky Mountain Justice in the direction of a posh resort in the hunt for a serial killer, operative and single dad Liam Alexander and child psychologist Holly Jacobs work together to hunt the huntress, eventually posing as a family to trap their prey. But as their plan backfires, Liam will do anything to save his child—and the woman he loves.*

*Read on for a sneak preview of
the next book in the Wyoming Nights miniseries,*
Agent's Mountain Rescue,
*by Jennifer D. Bokal.*

"Look at us, we're quite the mismatched pair. Still, we make a decent team." Reaching for her hand, Liam stared at their joined fingers. "Plus," he added, "you're pretty easy to talk to and to trust. I don't do either of those things easily, but then I think you've figured that out already. I like that about you, Holly."

She inched closer, her breath caressing his cheek. "You're not so bad yourself."

He smiled a little. "That's better than you turning me down."

She licked her lips. Looking away, Holly stared at something just beyond Liam's shoulder. "I don't want to complicate things."

"I understand," he said, even though he didn't. He wanted her. She wanted him. It all seemed pretty simple and straightforward. "I'm not going to pressure you into anything here."

"Do you really understand?" she asked. "Because I'm not sure that I know what's going on myself."

"You have your life plan. You need money to keep your school open. A relationship is a complication. Besides, you could be leaving town, which means us getting involved could be difficult for Sophie."

Holly touched her fingertips to his lips, silencing him. "If I can't get the money to keep Saplings, then I'll definitely have to have to leave Pleasant Pines," she said. "You said it yourself—I might not be around much longer."

"Now I'm really confused. What are you saying?"

"Kiss me," she whispered.

It was all the invitation he needed.

*Don't miss*
Agent's Mountain Rescue *by Jennifer D. Bokal,*
*available November 2020 wherever*
*Harlequin Romantic Suspense*
*books and ebooks are sold.*

Harlequin.com

HRSEXP1020